Wind-Borne Sister

Wind-Borne Sister

by
Melinda Holland

RESOURCE *Publications* • Eugene, Oregon

WIND-BORNE SISTER

Resource Publications
An Imprint of Wipf and Stock Publishers
199 W. 8th Ave., Suite 3
Eugene, OR 97401

www.wipfandstock.com

ISBN 13: 978-1-4982-0653-2

Manufactured in the U.S.A.   02/13/2015

*This book is dedicated
to beloved friends, teachers, and family members
who have encouraged, improved, and inspired
my writing over the years. . .*

*Dad and Mom
Arlene Wood
Penny Redman
Dwight Coil
Jim Alderdice
Karen Mikolasy
Chris Harris
Clem Starck
Toby Switzer
Natalia Kacianova
Rachelle Romero
Jen Macnab
Mark Campo*

. . .and Stuart, who wisely invited me to "write forward."

*May the wind of God's Holy Spirit bear you
to places of great joy, intimacy, blessing, and grace!*

Soli Deo gloria

Acknowledgments

With special thanks and sincere appreciation, I honor

Ty Sohlman, my equestrian consultant;

David Paulson, my copy editor; and

Matthew Wimer, my editor at Wipf and Stock

*Warm thanks to each of you for your attentiveness
to detail and your care for my story.*

May the Lord bless you on your journey!

*T*he larks skim the sky overhead, arcing, dancing in the morning light. I want to be one of them, free with that breathtaking acrobatic ease. Gravity and grief weigh me down like this old wool cloak, cumbersome, careworn. The road leads down to the sea, a narrow winding way with shadow-patterns and cobblestones and the echo of memory. My footsteps mar the silence. My presence is unwelcome. Children stare at me out of dusty doorways, admiring and yet distrusting my scarlet shawl. Their sleepy eyes speak truth and distance: "You are not one of us."

I smile at them because they are beautiful. They do not know this, so their beauty is worn lightly, not yet cage or tool. They do not smile back. So early the young can be taught to hate. I do not blame them for their fear.

About halfway down the hill a cart takes up most of the roadway, and I must edge past. A corner of my shawl catches and tears against the ragged wood. It is no matter, for long ago my shawl ceased to be lovely. I make sure not to leave threads behind, however; I do not need evidence of my passing beyond the stories of the small.

I had hoped for a gray day to mirror my soul. Yet the sun is bent on playfulness today, running in and out among clouds just as my little sister used to scamper among the haystacks of our fields. I still see her face, with a sense of wonder and joy shining in her eyes as her last ragged breath caught in her throat. No money for medicine, no hope for the young. I buried her myself. I wonder now what she saw with those eyes that looked past this life; I know it was something more lovely than our poor life had ever shown her.

My hand slides of its own accord into my pocket, fingering the small pewter cross. Anna found it at the seashore one day, and we threaded narrow twine through its loop to fashion a necklace for her. It was her one treasure. Perhaps I should have buried it with her. Instead I carry it always, a link to her and to that vision of her last breath. I carry it, or perhaps it carries me.

Suddenly a man reels drunkenly out of a doorway, shouting epithets at the occupants within. He is large and dangerous, anyone can see that; I also see with my spirit that he is dark-souled and intent on harm. I cannot go back the way I have come. I need to get to the sea. If I cower, he will bully. If I speak, he will hurl his dirty speech at me. But the way is narrow. I stop and wait and watch from a deep place within. He was wounded long ago, a whip striking repeatedly across his shoulders and neck. I see it in my mind's eye: a lad of five, punished for stealing apples. His drunken father nearly killed him. A wind makes its way past us, and the hair on the back of his neck lifts; still the deep scars remain. I focus my compassion on the wounds: balm, peace, a little sacred space of hope. He takes a deep breath, rubs his neck in a puzzled way, then stoops to tie his lacings. He does not look my way. Swiftly but not hurriedly I make my way by him and away.

I do not know what to call that which I do. Some call me a healer, but I have no schooling in those ways. Some call me a witch, but I seek only power for good. I know that it started the day Anna died, the day I put the cross in my apron pocket. But it isn't the cross that makes it happen; I know that much. Maybe it's my love for Anna and my love for the Lord, along with the grounding and closeness I feel to each of them when I finger the pewter outline that focuses the strength. I don't know. I do know that it changes things. And it means that I must go away.

Down the hill I go, step by step, a blur of children's watchful glances, closed doors, murmured voices within. Finally, I reach the turning of the way, and before me the sea reaches welcoming arms. We are friends, the sea and I. By the sea road I will journey to find my future.

Perhaps I should have left before sunrise, yet my leaving is not a secret. Most do not wish me ill; they just wish me not here, not muddling their lives with misunderstood moments of light and sight. My one former friend counseled me to turn off the seeing, to let go of this reaching touch of love, of hope. But it has become like breathing. It is woven into the fabric of my self and spirit. And so I journey on.

I prepared the boat last evening, storing provisions and water enough for several days' journey from this town, with dried provisions for longer. I can trust that it still lies undisturbed; people are superstitious here and do not touch what belongs to me. In the same way I know that our little home and its one outbuilding will not be occupied or damaged, even if I am gone long years. No one will go in. Nevertheless, I do hope the nearest neighbor will work the land. Though a small plot, the soil is flat and rich and fertile. It would bless them to have the extra crop.

What little money I have is tucked in a pouch beneath my cloak, and I clutch it to myself as I reach the boat. I stoop to clear away the few leaves that have fallen overnight. As I collect them my eye is caught by a small bit of parchment. It is nearly hidden under the seat, secured by a stone. In a strong, slanting style are the words: "Peace to you. May God guide your way." There is no signature. I do not know the hand.

I glance around, but of course no one is there. I did not imagine that I had even one friend in this village. I blink to clear the tears from my eyes. I finger the fragment, hold it up to my nose to smell the ink: still a bit of its aroma lingers. Then I place it in my pocket, next to the cross. This will be my sending song, the rhythm of my oars: peace to you, peace to you, may God guide your way, peace to you, peace to you . . . I push off with a slight smile, grateful to this gentle spirit who has wished me blessing.

* * * * *

I have been fortunate. The weather has stayed clear and calm. My little boat must hug the shore and keep to the smaller waves. I found a quiet cove in which to tie up and sleep, with my cloak to warm me and with my hand on the cross. Later this day I know I must hide the vessel and continue on foot. The clouds are gathering for a great storm, and I cannot risk the sea. I watch the shore for a good place, with overhanging branches and isolation, knowing one day I may need my boat again. Still nothing offers itself as safe; signs of habitation and activity alternate with rock faces too sheer for landing. Peace to you, peace to you . . . the rhythm of my oars invites me to prayer, and I listen for God's voice to guide my seeing.

As I shut my eyes the vision of a small house on a promontory, green with white shutters, comes to me. I have not seen such a house along the shore. Most are shacks, gray from the weather and wind. Is my fatigue playing tricks on me? Yet God has not led me astray in the past. I thank him for this hint, as well as for the bit of bread and cheese that will be my breakfast, and row on.

After many hours, the angle of the sun has grown low and long, and the wind is picking up. I have perhaps a half-hour before I must tie up, cove or no cove, house or no house. My eyes are worn from straining, troubled from seeing only the severity of cliffs and treacherous rocks for the past half-day. Please, please, let there be something soon: peace to you, peace to you, the oars plash and pray.

And then I see it, just as in my vision: the green house, the white shutters, high above me. Just as I round the point, a tiny shoreline comes in view. I breathe a deep sigh of relief and praise. I will be safe from the storm at least. I row in, drag the boat ashore as far as the beach will allow, and transfer my pack to my back. Near the far reach of the pebbly cove there is a raised wooden platform and some rope. I lash my boat to the platform in two places; only a mighty storm will cause it to break free now.

Then I realize: I have thought as far as this moment, a short journey by water, tie up, set out on foot. But then what? The water offered me protection of a kind, distance from others, a space apart with risk from the elements but not from people. What do I do now? In my mind's eye I see once again the green house, and I notice what I did not see the first time: the front door is open and smoke rises from the chimney. It is time to risk contact with others.

I follow a narrow path up through overgrown weeds and stunted trees. Its lack of use comforts me: no one has come this way in several seasons. At a turning of the path, I jump back, startled by a face ahead. Then I see it more clearly: the statue of a lion, worn from the years, covered with moss. Yet the eyes remain strangely bright from inset stones. I reach out to touch the lion, to finger the tracery of mane. Someone had a great gift for teaching the rock to speak.

I make my way upward, careful of my footing at a section where erosion has made the way treacherous. I am glad for the sturdy boots I wear. I traded for them last week, giving up the last of our linens, fine ones that mother's sister sewed for her in honor of her wedding. So much lost, let go, given away . . . Yet the memories comfort me as no object could. I remember our aunt's last visit. She had come for Easter, and the weather was unseasonably warm. She and mother washed and cleaned and swept and cooked in preparation for the joyous day. I can see them at the clothesline together, pinning up those same linens, laughing over a story, joining in a silly song. I can even see the butterfly that landed on mother's shoulder and how the two delighted in it and in the day. They are gone, both gone, like Anna, like the father I hardly knew. My heart holds too many hard stories to recount. I find it better to hold to the shining memories and let them give me strength.

I press onward, step by step. The way remains steep and overgrown, though the cliff is no longer so sheer. About halfway up the hillside I hear the sound of a brook, not far off the path. I need water for my journey and cannot be sure what will greet me in the green house above. I step off the path, toward the song of splashing water. I push past branches of evergreen and elm, past scraggly bushes that resist my movement. And then the world breaks open into a green room, a grotto by the brook, a space clearly tended and touched with loving hands. I pull back, worried that someone might be there. Yet my scanning eyes find only a second sculpture: this one an eagle in flight, on an outcropping above the creek's passage. Like the lion, its eyes are bright; yet this sculpture bears no moss, not the weather-wear of the king of beasts below. I trace the beak, sharp and sure; then I follow the gaze of the bird to see where it points.

There is a trail on the far side of the grotto, well-marked, clear and uncluttered. I know it must lead to the green house. I stop to gather water for my way, as well as to wash my face and hands. The water is clearer than most I have seen, and I sold our one mirror many months ago. As I lean over, I am startled by my own face: the tangled dark hair, the worry lines on my brow, the mouth set in a determined line without the smile that used to be its constant companion. But my eyes haunt me most: the sadness and the loss are etched in gray-blue depths. It is there that Anna's death shows most starkly. Even many months later, my sister's passing marks me, lingers as a shadow, even as it gives me light to see and to relieve others' pain. I wonder at the irony and the arbitrary nature of loss.

I take a deep breath. It is time to follow the trail to the house. Please, Lord Jesus, protect me. You showed me this house; help it to be a place for the night at least, if not something more. Peace to you, peace to you . . . My oars rest silent in their locks, at the shore, yet I hear that promise repeated, and in its echo I step forward.

* * * * *

The hike to the house is easy after the damaged path below. On the borders are the last of the summer's wildflowers, flashes of color in the shadowed corners. My footsteps sound terribly loud to me, not knowing who might be living and waiting above. Finally the path opens upon a flat, rocky space, with the house on one side. An old woman has taken tentative steps from her porch, a cane in her hand.

"Anna?" she queries, her voice rich, yet tired.

"I am Anna's sister, my lady." I am startled into speech by the name she has chosen. Why Anna?

"Welcome, Anna's sister. Come closer. I am blind, and so I cannot see you. But in your voice I hear youth and grief, hope and need. Come."

I take tentative steps toward her, assessing her strength. She is small and lean, in good health except for her eyes. I do not think she can hurt me, and her voice holds warmth along with invitation. I come within arm's length.

"My name is Susannah," she tells me, and then she reaches out in my direction. "I would like to touch your face, that I might see you with my hands."

I guide her reach, and her touch surprises me with its gentleness, its searching intensity. "Ah, you are young and lovely, just like your voice. But you are very tired. How have you come here?"

"By boat, my lady. I have tied up at your beach below. It was the first safe place I had found in many hours, and the storm is coming soon."

"Aye, that it is. I am glad you found a haven here. Did you find St. Mark's lion on the way up? How is he?"

My heart lets go its tension. St. Mark's lion. I had hardly dared hope. But when I saw both the lion and the eagle, I had wondered . . . I finger the cross and speak quickly, "He is covered in moss, but his eyes are bright, my lady."

"As it should be, as it should be . . . No one has seen him for many a year."

I forge ahead in hope: "And St. John's eagle at the grotto fares even better."

And then she smiles, a broad smile that reaches to her eyes, even in their blindness. Her shoulders lose a bit of their bracing, relaxed into welcome.

"Yes, I care for him each time that I fetch my water. He and St. Luke's ox are still within my reach. But I am forgetting myself. Come inside, sister of Anna, daughter of God, and I will give you rest."

I follow Susannah inside. My first glimpse of the interior of the green house reveals a sense of order and tidiness that surprises me, given her lost sight. The front room holds shelves full of sculptures, smaller than those I had seen outside, but with the same elegant line, the same strength of vision.

"Are you the sculptor, my lady?" I ask, betraying my surprise.

Susannah smiles again. "Yes and no. My hands have worked the stone. But I think of them as God's sculptures. I have the privilege to be the instrument he uses to bring to light. Please, call me Susannah. We are sisters before God. And what may I call you, Anna's sister?"

"My name is Gabriela. Sometimes Anna called me Brie."

"Gabriela, you miss your sister very much, I can tell. Where is she? Did you have to leave her behind for your journey by boat?"

"No, she left me first, Susannah. She died last winter." And the tears I have held back for so long break free as Susannah takes me in her arms and lets me weep.

J don't recall much more of that evening. Against a background of
heavy rain, rolling thunder, and occasional sharp lightning strikes,
I see glimpses of tasty porridge, a small spare bed, a warm fire. Very
soon the soothing balm of sleep enveloped me. That night I dreamed I saw
Anna, riding St. John's eagle, smiling and laughing as they flew above the
storm. She had tiny starflowers in her hair, and she was no longer rail-thin
as she had been in the weeks before she died.

I awoke to a strange sound: an irregular scratching and rasping. I
opened my eyes just as a large black and white tom jumped from the floor
to my chest, somehow managing to glare and to express curiosity at the
same time. "And who are you, puss?" I asked aloud.

Susannah, who came in by a narrow doorway, laughed lightly. "Ah,
has Ebenezer found you? Usually he sleeps on that bed during the day. He'll
warm to you if you scratch him just so between the ears and under his
chin." I did as she indicated, and soon a rich, throaty purr serenaded us.
"You have a new friend, Ebenezer," Susannah remarked. "Treat her well."

After petting the cat a bit longer, I raised myself to sit on the side of the
bed. "How did you sleep, Brie?" Hearing Anna's nickname for me proved
bittersweet, and I felt tears begin to prick behind my eyes.

"Very well, thank you. I dreamed of my sister."

"A good dream, I hope?"

"Yes, it was. The only hard part was awakening, though Ebenezer did
his best to soften the transition."

Susannah moved quietly into the room and reached out to find a stool
not far from the bed. Seating herself, she turned again to me, and her tone

was different. "What are your plans, sister of Anna, child of God? Why did you set out alone by boat at a time of year when storms are frequent? I tried to puzzle out your story as I sat by the fire last night, and I came up empty. Your body bears no marks of beating that I could see with my hands; you are not sickened by disease or poverty. You know the Lord and carry his light with you . . ." A deep sigh escaped her, as though a painful memory had intruded, and then she shook her head.

"But once again I forget myself. Hospitality first, then the explanation." She gestured out the door to the left. "You will find a tub of hot water in the back room, as well as some fresh clothing. It may be slightly loose on you, but it is clean. I've been drying your boots out by my front room fire; I'm afraid I don't have another pair to offer you."

"Thank you, my lady—Susannah. You have been so kind to me. God showed me your house in a vision yesterday morning; when I saw it just before sunset, I was hopeful. But I did not dare hope for such generosity."

"Once I was in great need, and a couple took me in. I promised myself to do the same when the Lord asked it of me. That spare room has been waiting long years, while I wondered who would come. I didn't think Ebenezer would be the only one to snuggle beneath those soft covers."

She left me then, and I cleaned and dressed myself in a small, tidy room. The only ornamentation was a large sculpture of the woman who reached out for the hem of Jesus' garment. He had his back to her but had just begun to turn his head in her direction. One of her hands was yet on the fringe, and the other was upraised in joy, her face overcome with delight at the change she was experiencing. After dressing, I went over to inspect it more closely. Somehow she had captured a gentle, knowing smile on the Lord's face; it was beautiful to behold. Yet it was the face of the woman that fascinated me. The wonder and awe in the features reminded me so keenly of that last look on Anna's face. Perhaps she also had felt the power of God surge through her, had been given the blessed chance to gaze upon him.

I gathered up my travel-tarnished clothes and carried them with me as I returned to Susannah. Her large front room met many purposes: sitting room, dining room, even a small kitchen of sorts near the large fireplace. But I saw then what I had missed the night before: a large alcove on the side of the house that overlooked the sea served as a studio. Several pieces were in process: one in stone, another in wood. I had not noticed any wooden sculptures elsewhere in the house, and so I asked about it: "You also sculpt in wood?"

"Yes, I've just started. Now that my blindness is complete, working with the stone is more difficult and dangerous. The wood is more pliable and forgiving. I don't know if I will ever finish that last stone carving. It seems fitting somehow, though: it was to be the descent of the Spirit at Pentecost." I looked more closely, and I could just make out several figures, each with a dancing, wavy shape above their heads. The faces were vague, but their hands expressed astonishment, eagerness, storytelling. And the flames seemed also to be wings, reaching upward to the heavens. It was beautiful just as it was.

Susannah and I shared a quiet breakfast, as Ebenezer wound around our ankles, wishing for a bite of fish. I had the chance to observe her more closely this morning. She was not so old as I had first thought: perhaps in her late sixties, it was the white-scaled eyes and hair the color of sea foam that made her seem much older.

As I savored the last bite, she resumed the focus she had laid down earlier. "Brie, tell me your story. How have you come to be here?"

I felt afraid. She had shown me such gracious care; I did not want to risk losing that. I was already beginning to feel at home here on the hill above the sea, among her stone-sculptured stories. The silence stretched between us.

"I can tell that you are afraid. I will not hurt you. What is it, Brie?"

I knew that the best way for her to understand was to show her. I reached into the pocket of the apron that she had loaned me and cupped the cross. My fingers also brushed against the scrap of paper I had found in the bow of my boat: peace to you, peace to you . . . I leaned into trust and gazed with love upon her eyes, marred by the cataracts and other disease. I felt her confusion, then her own fear. I saw a little girl running, running fast and frantically down a hillside, chased by a bull who had escaped from the pasture. The bull was caught, but the girl did not know, and in her running, she lost her footing and fell face-first into a bramble full of sharp, cutting thorns. They tore at her face, her clothes, and especially her eyes. I felt the stinging pain in my own eyes, then concentrated on a deep wave of healing, of light, of hope. The way forward seemed a tangled mixture of resistance and longing. Suddenly I heard her gasp.

"I see a bit of light. From both eyes I see a bit of light! What is it that you are doing, child?"

"This is why I had to leave. The people of my village distrusted me, called me witch. I am no witch, Susannah. I did not seek this power.

Sometimes it has come as protection for me, as a distraction. Sometimes it is solely for the other, to soothe a burn, to soften a bruise. Most of the time I see in my mind the source of the pain: I saw you running away from that crazed bull and the way you fell into the brambles . . ."

I heard her sharp intake of breath but kept speaking. "It started the day I buried my sister. We were alone by then. I did not know my father well, killed in the war. He visited once when I was about eight. I remember his kindness, as well as the way he sat staring into the fire with pain in his eyes. Before he left again, he prophesied that God had a long journey ahead for me, but would always go with me. Perhaps this is the journey that he meant.

"Our mother died two years ago, succumbing to a winter influenza. I thought my sister and I would always be together. But then she fell prey to fever after stepping on a rusty nail while playing in the fields, and she never rallied. Amidst her fever, she told me that she saw our mother dancing on the arm of a tall, red-haired man with long sideburns. She had never met our father, but that's who she had described. After she died, the one thing I kept was this pewter cross that Anna always wore around her neck. She found it on the shore the summer she was four and treasured it always."

I handed the pewter cross to Susannah, and saw with surprise that her hands were shaking. She fingered it with care, even with tenderness, and I saw her straining to see out of eyes that were now slightly less thick with fog. "Anna, my Anna. . ." Her voice held a faraway quality of wistfulness and pain. She did not speak for several minutes, and I waited, feeling that something strange and somber had been reawakened for her.

At length she began. "This cross belonged to my daughter, Anna. She was lost at sea many years ago, as she journeyed home after remarkable travels. I still keep her letters; perhaps later I will ask you to read them to me. Some said they saw the ship in the storm, that they were close, so close to home. I did not want to believe that she could die within sight of our land . . . Her body was never recovered. But I know this is her cross."

She handed the pewter pendant back to me. "Look on the back: do you see the tiny initials, ALM? Anna Leigh Mason. My husband worked it for her; he was a gifted metalworker in his day." Her voice shook as she continued, "Anna shared in her letters that she had begun to experience a gift of healing light, a strange ability to bring comfort to others, to know their pain. We wanted to believe her, but it seemed so strange . . . James and I understood art, bringing life out of metal and stone, but to restore life in the place of disease and scarring? Today you have shown me that she spoke truth.

"Gabriela, I want to know more of your story, I do, but this has been overwhelming. I need to rest. Please know that you are welcome in my home; I do not fear you. You may stay as long as God calls you to be here. Please make yourself at ease here, in the house, the grotto, the fields around. Tomorrow I may ask you to help me with chores and tasks. For today, explore, rest, let your soul be blessed that there is none here to fear you or wish you gone."

She rose and walked to a flight of stairs at the side of the house. "I'll be upstairs for much of the day, I think. We'll meet again over supper, perhaps around six?" And then she was out of sight.

A great turmoil of emotions whirled in my heart and spirit. I felt wonder and fear at this strange interweaving of our lives, having lost beloved young women named Anna. I remembered how Susannah had called me Anna when I arrived. Did I remind her of her child?

I thought also of this strange healing gift. Learning that Anna had also been chosen to serve as instrument for its expression comforted me immeasurably. I was not alone; I was not so strange in my gifting. Yet I wondered also about the cross; was it necessary for this gift, or was it only that in holding it, I focused better on God's voice, God's invitation and revelation for the other in need? I did not know.

I missed Susannah's presence. She had a gentle, quiet heart that radiated peace. Yet I understood her need to grieve and reflect alone. She had not shared how long ago the boat had gone down in the storm; she did not tell how her husband had died. Had he also been on board? I knew from my own life that, once awakened, those sorrowful memories needed a bit of space to be held and then laid to rest once more.

Susannah had recommended a day of exploration and rest. I put on my boots, gathered up my water and a generous portion of bread from the table, and left by the door to see what the day held in store.

3

*T*he storm had left in its wake a gentle morning with feathery clouds and scattered sunshine. The autumn chills had not yet settled in, though I pulled the blue cloak Susannah had loaned me tight around my shoulders when the winds blew. I followed a rutted track down from the house, a winding way that led away from the sea and back toward fields and copses. After a few hundred yards, I came to a disused barn, with one cow grazing in a field nearby. She raised her head to regard this unexpected visitor and then resumed her chewing. Inside the barn I found a milking stall and old equipment on one side and what appeared a smithy's forge and tools on the other. A sturdy wall separated the two, keeping the hay well away from the fire and smoke.

And then I saw him, saw as I often did before the healing power came. He stood before the forge, pounding as though for dear life. His face was contorted with pain and sorrow, and the tears and perspiration mingled on his cheeks and chin. The ringing of metal against metal resonated with his grief: Anna, Anna, Anna. Or was it my own? For I realized that I was on my knees, sobbing for my sister, for her sweet spirit, for her wise ways and quicksilver grin. Anna, my Anna. Why did you have to go? The ringing forge pounded in my head, but I reached out a hand to the man, willing his release from this grief. Did he see me? Was he even there? Or was it all a vision in my mind of things as they once were? I did not know. I sat alone, bathed in tears and sound and memory, letting time seep away.

Then the old cow stuck her head in the doorway with a lowing sound of inquiry and confusion. I shook my head to clear it. I no longer saw the smithy nor the light of the forge. I was still tired from my sea journey. I brushed my skirt free of the dust and dirt and gently stroked the head of the old cow: "Good girl; all is well." And I walked on.

＊ ＊ ＊ ＊ ＊

As the day wore on I saw open fields with few outbuildings and no people. The sun warmed my skin and my spirits after my vision and outburst in the barn. Later in the afternoon I sought a shady place beneath a tree to eat my bread. Susannah's wheat loaf was nourishing and flavorful, and I felt glad for fresh bread after my dry fare on the boat.

Then in the distance I began to hear the regular rhythm of a horse's hooves. After a time it became clear that they were coming closer. I hid myself behind the tree out of habit, unsure of myself. Soon a man appeared on horseback: neither old nor young, he smiled to himself as he rode and hummed a quiet tune. I sensed an old, buried pain, but mostly he was a man of peace, of grace.

"You there, come out from behind that tree; I won't hurt you."

I jumped. I had learned not to trust men and their promises. I stayed back.

"This is the road to Lady Susannah's house. If you are a friend of Lady Susannah's then you are a friend of mine." Still I hesitated, though his voice seemed trustworthy and inviting.

"We are distant cousins, though she calls me 'nephew.' I serve as vicar some twenty miles from here. She does not know that I am coming, but I make these visits every now and then when my parish schedule allows." He reined in his horse and dismounted. He walked slowly toward me around the oak tree. As he drew closer, he extended his hand in greeting. "Allan Donaldson. And you are . . . "

I took his hand, and the grip was gentle, yet firm. Searching blue eyes looked into mine. "I'm Gabriela, sir."

"How did you come here, Gabriela? It is a very long walk from the nearest town."

I was not sure that I wished to tell him my story. The vicar of my town had been the first to call me witch, to move the tide toward rejection and fear. I only said, "I came by boat. Your aunt's beach was the first I had seen in many hours, and last night's storm was about ready to break." He did not need to know why I was traveling.

He peered more closely at me. "So you are on a pilgrimage," he stated simply. "I am glad of it. Are you staying with Susannah?"

"For now, sir."

"Very good. Her hospitality is unequalled, despite her blindness. I know no one with a wider heart. Would you accompany me for the last of my journey?"

It seemed safer to say yes, so I nodded. He led his horse beside us as we traveled in silence for many minutes. Every now and then I glanced his way, both wary and curious. His face was creased from sun and wind, and the gray at his temples implied age, but his eyes were young, even merry at times, as he watched a hopping sparrow or caught sight of a rabbit along the roadside. He wore a pewter cross, heavier and more masculine than the one in my pocket, around his neck. I realized with a start that he must have known Anna.

Before I thought, I asked aloud, "Sir, what was Anna like?" He turned abruptly toward me, startling the horse. "What do you know of Anna?"

I reached in my pocket and pulled out the cross. I opened my fingers slowly, watching his face as I did so. The merry eyes disappeared behind a fog of pain and remembrance. "Were you on the boat? Did you know her?"

I looked up, meeting his eyes directly for the first time. Suddenly I saw Allan, dancing near the old barn, a lovely, green-eyed lass in his arms. They were laughing and young. I could not speak for a moment. Anna was so vibrant and beautiful; no wonder so many struggled to accept her death.

I looked away. "My sister found her cross washed up on shore several years ago. She cleaned it, cherished it, and wore it daily. I never met Anna."

"I am amazed that Susannah even spoke of her."

"It was because she also was startled by the cross. I have been out walking much of this morning, as she retreated to her room after our conversation. I understood that she needed time and space to grieve once more."

Allan looked as though he wished to say something more, and then thought better of it. He resumed walking, his step slower and heavier, no longer humming.

We walked on in silence until the barn. He cared for his horse, drawing water from a nearby well I had not noticed earlier. He also took time to milk the cow, who seemed to recognize him and relax in his presence.

It was close to evening by the time we approached the house. I carried one of his saddlebags, while he managed the second along with the milk pail.

Susannah appeared in the doorway as we came within yards of the house. Her earlier turmoil seemed to have passed, and she smiled in greeting to Allan as she held out her arms. He set down his burden and embraced her. I stood aside, glad that the reunion seemed a joy to both. He had told me the truth. It had surprised me in recent months how many people lied when they were afraid—or lied when they wanted power over you. But here were two faithful people, two people who clearly loved one another and who had loved the vibrant, gifted Anna, now gone from their lives.

Susannah turned her head toward my steps. "Gabriela, it would seem you have met Allan. He is a good man; you need not fear him." She seemed to be reading my thoughts, but I let it pass. Together we went inside to see about preparing the evening meal.

I watched Susannah and Allan, their easy movements, their gentle affection, and thought once more of my mother and aunt. Family can be such a complex gift, fraught with conflict and pain, and yet at times it shines with an inner light of understanding, like a moonglade over the water. I missed my sister with a deep ache and said little.

At dinner, Allan offered a thoughtful grace, even including me—and my pilgrimage. After an interval while all of us relished the rich soup, he spoke to me for the first time since our conversation about Anna on the road. "Few women would travel alone in these days. You are fortunate to have found my aunt as a safe haven."

"I know it well, sir. I saw her home in a vision yesterday morning and see her as a direct answer to prayer. God has been very faithful to me, even in my bleakest times."

"Where is your sister, the one who found my cousin's cross? Did she not come with you?"

I shared again the story of Anna's death, leaving out any mention of special sight or healing power. He wore a puzzled expression, seeming to recognize that I was not sharing all I could, but he did not press me. As the evening wore on, we talked of the storm, of the coming autumn, of Susannah's need for extra provisions beyond what she had been able to store so far. She invited me to stay as long as I needed, provided that I would help her in her daily chores and preparations for the long, cold season that would come all too soon. I agreed, grateful for a place apart from village rumors and furtive looks. Allan looked relieved; I saw that he was worried for his aunt but respected her need of independence, of her own place and ways. It would seem that my coming had been provident for more than just myself.

4

My stay at Anna's grew from hours to days, then weeks. I helped with the milking, the food storage, the harvest. Allan came as often as he could be spared, but the bulk of the fall preparations fell to Susannah and me. I wondered who had helped her in years past, what she might have done had I not come. I wanted to ask, but I also imagined that prying questions on my part would lead to more incisive questions on theirs, questions about plans and pilgrimage that I preferred to ignore for the present. Here at Susannah's home I was welcome. I was just Gabriela, not someone with a strange and feared gift. I was kept busy but did not feel used. In the later evenings, Susannah would sometimes tell me stories of Anna as a child, of her playfulness and loving ways. One day, just as the leaves were at their most golden, she asked me to begin reading aloud from Anna's letters. I felt both eager interest and a deeper nervousness: would Anna's experiences lead to further discussions of my own gift? We sat together by the fire and I began to read.

"Mama, it is so beautiful here. I wish that you could also see these places with me. Today we journeyed within sight of the mountains. Mountains, Mama! Tall and craggy, with snow at the peaks. I understand now why others have told me that I should take this trip. 'I will lift up mine eyes unto the hills . . .' The Lord is still the most beautiful One to look upon, but his mountains are fair indeed.

"I met several young women aboard the ship, and we agreed to travel together for a while, pooling our resources and taking safety in numbers. Molly and Lily are twin sisters and love to laugh together. Katherine is more aloof and wise, but I see her read her Scriptures each night and keep waiting for the right time to speak to her of them. And finally there is Isabella. I know it is not good to say, Mama, but I am not sure whether I ought to trust her. She is friendly on the outside, but there is something hard and heavy about her that leads me to feel wary. Pray for her, please.

"The ship came to land three days ago. After some travel on foot, yesterday we came upon a midsummer fair. I have never seen so many people in one place! There was dancing and music and all sorts of vendors and booths. Molly, Lily, and I wandered around together, enjoying the day. We bought tasty bread and refreshing lemon water. Toward the end of the afternoon, shortly before we had promised to meet up with Isabella and Katherine, we came to the tent of a fortuneteller. I didn't want to go in; I know that God asks us to trust only him. But Molly and Lily are so persuasive when they want something—and you see, I was outnumbered! Moreover, they decided that they would pay for their own fortunes to be told, as well as my own.

"The tent was dark and smelled of old canvas and beeswax. The woman reminded me of you in some ways: wise eyes, a gentle presence. But she also had a touch of evil to her; I don't know any other way to say it. Forgive me. She took Molly's hand first, and she smiled. 'You are looking for love, and you will find it, for you give it freely. He will love you well, and you will have two children, a girl and a boy. Look for the sign of the green boar.' Green boar? We laughed. Then it was Lily's turn. The older woman took more time, tracing the lines of Lily's palm. Lily paled in the waiting; perhaps she also sensed the thread of evil that traced its way through the atmosphere. 'You are jealous of your sister's joy. Seek your own way, and you will find freedom there. Do not linger too long in her shadow, but also trust to love: hers, yours, and that of the older man who will see your beauty past your envy and sadness.'

"Lily's face turned red, and she would not look at Molly. The words surprised me, Mama; I had not thought of Lily as jealous: they are always a team, arms linked, making merry. But I have watched more carefully since, and I see now that Molly is the instigator, and Lily joins in. What impresses me is that Molly has never brought up the fortuneteller's words to Lily, except to joke in a good-natured way: 'Let us keep watch for green boars and older men!'

"Then it was my turn. I nearly ran out of the tent, for my spine tingled and my hands shook. 'You need not fear me, child. Your death will come from water, not from human hands—and it will come too soon. Keep away from the sea if you can, though your death will find you all the same.' I began to cry, angry and embarrassed that my fortune seemed all of death instead of love. She cocked her head to one side and then reached for my cross, the one Papa made for me before I left home. She put one finger out to trace it, then jerked back as though the pewter had burned her skin. 'In listening you will find your gift. In others' pain will be your freedom. Your faith will burn you and demand much, and it will hold you when all else fails.' Then she hurried out of the tent, leaving us to stare at one another in confusion.

"I felt so frightened, Mama. Death by water! And yet I tried to remind myself that in our baptisms, we are already drowned—and then brought to new life. But she also said my death would come too soon. Pray for my safety, Mama, even though I know you do not hold to fortunetellers. Perhaps I should not have told you, but I feel better writing it out and remembering that often it is out of a need for income that older women pretend to see the future, when all that they are doing is guessing in the dark. At least her last words were true and good: I know that my faith will hold me when all else fails. Jesus has never let me down.

"Give my best to Papa and to Allan. Tell the cows I will be back by next fall and they should be good to you. I hope that your sight is holding steady; I know how much you love to see the beauty around you—and the art that you create. God is faithful, Mama. We know that well. Blessings be upon you. With much love, Anna."

I looked up. Susannah's eyes were full of tears. "You read well, Gabriela. Thank you." It was clear that one letter would be enough for now. She closed her eyes and leaned back in her chair, quietly stroking a purring Ebenezer, and I knew she would soon be napping. I ran my hands over the pages of Anna's letter, imagining her up late by candlelight, writing in the bedroom of an inn. I saw again in my mind's eyes the beautiful dancing girl by the barn. Why had her fortune been so dark? Could she have come home safely by the roads if she had spurned the sea? Foolish questions. She was long gone, though she felt real and vital to me through her letters, through the strong, even strokes of her pen. I longed to meet her companions, to learn what had become of them. Had Molly found her green boar—and Lily the wise older man who saw beyond her faults? Did Katherine find peace in her faith? I went to bed with my mind full of questions and a deep interest to read further.

That night I had a strange dream. I stood at a distance from the for-tuneteller's booth at the midsummer fair. I watched the three girls go in, giggling. And then I saw the teller hurry out the back. In a wide arc around the tent, she came straight to me. She grabbed my hand and pulled it to her, opening the fingers only to find that I held Anna's cross. She grimaced, shook her head. "Why won't he let me be?" she asked as though to herself. Then she took my other hand and peered through tired eyes at my palm. "Many losses in youth, a long journey, welcome at the sign of a green lion. Do not doubt your gift; do not hide your strength. You will see things you wish not to see, but they will guide your way. Another who cannot see will lead you. Still Another who sees all will scald your heart and yet give you joy." She dropped my hand and turned. Suddenly all around me was fog. Out of the fog I heard the clang of a ship's bell, the calling of seafarers in distress. Through the fog I glimpsed three men and two women aboard a small dinghy. Waves threatened to overturn the vessel, but the men seemed assured as they plied their oars slowly, as calmly as possible in the midst of a treacherous sea. "Death by water," came the voice of the teller, who came up behind me and laughed bitterly in my ear. "Death by water for one so young and fair."

One of the women turned my way, and I saw Anna's face, pale yet peaceful. She had both hands wrapped tightly around the pewter cross at her neck, and she was praying, her lips moving and her eyes shut tight. Suddenly the woman next to her tore at Anna's hands so violently that the delicate chain at her neck snapped. She reached for Anna's cross, took it from her startled companion, and tossed it as far into the sea as she could. Anna just stared at her, bereft and frightened.

"You bring bad luck wherever you go. Your cross was cursed!"

"Oh, Isabella . . ." Anna bent her head, weeping and praying, weeping and praying, as the boat sought a shore that could not be seen.

* * * * *

I awoke with a gasp, troubled and heavy-hearted. The images of the dream stayed with me through the morning as I went about the chores and daily routine. Had I seen the past, as my sight sometimes permitted me by day, or was it only a flight of imagining, brought on by the troubling pas-sages of Anna's letter?

It seemed to me that Susannah watched me carefully throughout the day. Yet how could that be, with her blind eyes? She held herself attentive and alert in other ways, as though taking in all the clues that my movements and sighs and pace of work could give her. At day's end, instead of asking me to read another of Anna's letters, she spoke the question that had been reflected all day in her behavior. "Gabriela, I can tell that something is troubling you. What is it?" And so I recounted my dream to her, with as much detail as I had courage to share. For a while she sat in a quiet peace, as though settling something within herself. Then she turned back to me.

"Brie, Anna has been gone from us for eight years now. We have missed her and grieved her, but we have peace about her passing. It seems that in carrying that pewter cross, you have been given a connection to her story, perhaps even to her memories. Do not let them weigh you down.

"After long years of living, it seems to me that we spend so much time trying to sort things out inside ourselves, hiding them or fighting them or even avoiding them. The key is to quiet the competing voices and listen deeply for God. Have you asked him lately what he is asking of you? Have you inquired why this connection with Anna exists? Do not run from this gift; run toward it and see what might grow out of its turmoil.

"You have been such a help to me of late, as the colder weather draws near. I know that I have thanked you, but you also haven't taken much Sabbath rest in your desire to serve and assist me. Take a day tomorrow, Gabriela. It looks to be a fair one. Take a day to yourself for listening, for opening yourself to the Lord's voice."

I felt surprised at her suggestion. I wondered if perhaps she wanted a day to herself and this gave her an excuse. But as I watched her face, she smiled, and I felt her growing love for me. She held it out as gift. Why should I look further?

5

The day dawned clear and mild, one of those unexpectedly lovely autumn days that shine with a clear and bracing internal light. I packed a small lunch and made ready. As I approached the door, Susannah called my name. "Gabriela, blessings on your journey."

"I'll be back by sunset," I clarified.

"I know that. It's just that some short days lead us on longer journeys than a year ever reveals when we are not paying attention."

I headed off down the track, past the barn, then much later past the tree where I had unsuccessfully hidden myself from Allan. A few hundred yards onward, the way broadened, and I saw that it divided, leading away in two directions. Which way should I take? I paused, listening to see if God would offer any guidance. Suddenly, a sound off to my right made me jump. It was only an irritable squirrel, chiding me for surprising him, but somehow I saw it as invitation: take the right-hand path.

Bedraggled weeds congested both the edges and the center of the worn pathway. It seemed this was not the main thoroughfare. The track wound down, with dappled shadow, and I was glad of my cloak and the unseasonably warm day. I had walked perhaps a mile and a half when the way opened out onto a promontory, with a few twisted trees and shrubs but mostly a bleak terrain. I gazed out over a wild ocean and jagged stacks that loomed and threatened for miles. This is what I would have come upon in my fragile boat had I not stopped at Susannah's cove. Is this what took Anna's life, I wondered? The view was stunning and arresting, yet also disturbing. Oddly I knew that it was here I was to take my lunch, to sit a while and listen for God.

I found a somewhat sheltered spot underneath and behind the largest tree, now bare of its leaves, and spread out my cloak as a blanket. From here, I could see only glimpses of the ocean; mostly I saw the shaded road I had taken and a more secluded pathway leading further on. For the first quarter-hour or so, I simply delighted in the day, the sweetness of the jam, the crispness of Susannah's bread, the quiet call of a bird not far away. I assumed that it would be a scavenger, looking for crumbs, one of the raucous gulls so familiar to coastal dwellers. I turned and looked, and my face lit up in wonder.

Not fifty feet away, settled on an isolated outcropping, my eyes took in the majesty and grace of an albatross. Twice while growing up, I had heard tales of these birds of good fortune, these long-journeying travelers who spend their lives riding the wind. But only sailors had ever caught a glimpse. Albatross almost never come in to land, except on distant, craggy islands where they mate for life and raise their young. Why was this one here? I watched in wonder, trying to see if it was injured. Fortunately, it gave the impression of peaceful resting, without pain or trouble. Then it turned its head and looked right at me, fixing me with a direct and clear stare.

And suddenly I saw things from his perspective, the memory of a long sea-journey, broken only by feeding and the brief riding of waves when the wind was too still to carry him further. The memories held a mesmerizing quality: sea and wind and sky, sea and wind and sky, sea and wind and sky . . . And then, unexpectedly, a boat, a small dinghy with five figures, bedraggled, careworn, thin, and shivering. They look up as he passes, and one of the men finds the strength to smile: "An albatross means good luck, you know." And once again, sea and wind and sky, sea and wind and sky.

The albatross blinks, and I am back on the promontory. I am struck by his self-contained beauty, by a grace of solitude and peace with himself. I expect him to be troubled by my presence, yet somehow his gaze feels like benediction, an extending of his own peace to encircle and embrace me. "Consider the birds of the air . . ." I think, and then discard it. This is so clearly a bird of the sea, with a deeper, more resonant way about him than his tree-dwelling cousins. He is not hurried or troubled. Time means little; his ways are tidal, decided by air currents and temperatures. And journeying is his lifework. I want to reach out, to stroke the feathers of this wise and gentle creature. I realize that my hand has already extended, slowly, carefully.

The albatross cocks his head, puzzled for a moment, though not threatened. I have nothing to offer, only my fascination. As though on cue, his wings suddenly extend, broad and bold and beautiful. Ah! I expect him to launch on the wind and head seaward once more, but instead he takes a short, rather awkward flight and comes to rest just inches in front of me. Grace: grace of movement, grace of presence, the grace of a creature so fully in tune with himself, with his surroundings. He fixes two brilliant eyes on me once more and settles his wings back in, tucking them with a flourish. I almost expect him to speak.

I smile, a radiant smile of a kind I have not known since my sister's death. It is as though he calls it forth from me, this joy, this sense of being fully here, now, in this place, in the right place. We are born of different worlds, and yet somehow there is communion, a meeting in this sun-blessed moment of autumn light. I notice that he has a distinctive marking just past the crown of his head: several dark feathers among the shining white, shaped somewhat like a shell.

Without thinking, I begin to sing, an old hymn my mother taught me one day long ago that speaks of the sea and long journeys, of the God who never forsakes even in storm. I do not know if I am singing to the bird or to God or to myself, but the words themselves lift me in spirit like wings on my heart, words of praise, of truth, of the certainty of sea and of storm and yet of faith within and through it all. I sense that the bird rests in the sound of the song, watching, receiving, loving. How can it be loving? And yet there is a deep, abiding sense of being connected to this giant-winged beauty for this moment, this space, ours alone.

I sing all the verses I know, wishing there were more. I repeat the first verse, coming full circle, a tidal turn, a coming home. And then silence: a long, rich silence that is both a listening and a speaking. I do not know his language and he does not speak mine, but we find kinship in this place apart.

I extend my other arm, as though I too were a bird, reaching for the sky. I realize as he extends his wings that his reach outdistances mine by several feet. What majesty! Then he nods his head in my direction and re-leases a plaintive, heart-rending sound: a hymn to sea and storm, to wind and journeys home.

And then he is running, running away down the promontory, leaping to catch the wind as it rises to receive him, bearing him onward and away. I stand to watch, to gaze in wonder at this grace-filled flight, this mystery of wind and feather and the artistry of God. After the first flapping movements, he settles in, riding, gliding, soaring; it seems so easy and yet it is the work of great strength, of muscles and sinews shaped just so to receive the wind-swells and vagaries of thermals.

I walk closer to the cliff's edge, mindful of my own risk and yet needing to see him for as long as I may. It takes my breath away, this windborne dance, this wistful ride, this lonely wanderer who is not alone. Can't I come with you?

I watch until the albatross is a faint speck in the distance, a whisper of wings over wave. I blink to clear the tears and realize I can no longer see him.

I sit back down under the tree, lost in wonder and a surprising grief. The encounter replays itself on my mind's eye, and I smile. I have been blessed by beauty, by something far beyond my careworn, circumscribed world. I feel the fatigue of days and stretch out for a nap. In my brief dreams I also skim the sea on strong, silent wings, ever journeying.

I awake with a start and realize that I need to make my way homeward. Susannah will be worried. I pack up my things and then look toward the spot where I first saw the albatross. Among the rocky outcroppings, something shines. Carefully, picking my way over sharp stones, I make my way to the spot. And there, alongside bits of shell and seaweed, is a pearl. I pick it up and balance it in my palm; it reminds me of the bright eye of the albatross, gazing at me with intensity and interest. It seems he has left me a gift, something by which to remember this meeting. I place the pearl in my pocket and find my way back home.

6

*A*llan came for a visit in mid-autumn, wanting to check on our provisions and preparations for winter. He was pleased at how my presence and work had allowed Susannah to be ready sooner, and he showed his gratitude with an offer. "Would you like to come with me to town, Brie? Perhaps there are some things you would like to see or do or buy." I remembered my own village, the stares and distrust, the whispers and doubt. But then I realized that no one would know me in this new place. Surely a short visit need not have any incident. I agreed, and at the end of Allan's visit, I left with him for Lanford.

We talked little on the day's journey on horseback, lost each in our own thoughts, I suppose. I wondered whether Allan were recalling rides with Anna; his gaze held a bittersweet look that was full of reminiscence. By sunset we were on the edge of town, hearing the shouts of children playing, the rumble of cart wheels in rutted roads.

I was to stay with a pair of unwed sisters not far from Allan's parsonage. Their sweet hospitality encircled me, and I slept easily that night. No dreams, not even the rush of wings. In the morning light I smiled to myself. Perhaps the struggles of my early life need not characterize the days to come.

Rachel and Bronwyn invited me to walk with them to market after our modest morning meal. The wind was chilly and dark clouds scudded above, but the mood of the townspeople was lively; market day afforded a break in the routine, abundant color and energy, and sometimes, welcome treasures. I felt impressed by the scope of the market: bigger and brighter and more varied than anything I had known at home. No one really noticed me, intent on their own search for provisions and for deals as the dark sky boded winter's approach.

I chose some orange-scented tea for Susannah, a corded bookmark for Allan; surely they deserved some small tokens for these long weeks of care and comfort and safety. For myself I chose a few skeins of bright yarn, hoping to knit a warm scarf over the long season ahead. Rachel, Bronwyn, and I shared a small lunch of fresh bread and cheese in a clearing near the main road. I felt happy and relaxed in a way that I had forgotten, glad of my new friends, of the grace of anonymity.

And then it happened, all in a flurry of neighing and crashing, of confusion and cursing on the road just beyond. A horse had been startled, and it reared, tipping over the heavy cart behind. At first it seemed a minor incident: the driver had managed to escape much injury and was busy trying to unharness horse from cart and calm the poor animal. But then someone called out for help, sharp and clear in the autumn air. A small boy had been struck by a corner of the cart as it overturned and was bleeding profusely from the crown of his head.

Before I even knew what I was doing, I was up and running into the street, hurrying toward the boy, gripping the cross in my pocket. I knelt down at his side, heedless that my skirts would be dirtied by mud and blood. He looked about nine years of age, his face contorted in pain and fear. I didn't take time to ask questions, only put out my hand to his head where the wound was deepest and began to pray. I felt the old grace returning, the warmth of light in my fingers, the deep peace of healing. In my mind I pictured the little boy running, dancing, delighted, as the watchful, loving eyes of Christ looked on. Though there was shouting and muddle all around me, I only saw his little face, first pain-filled, then puzzled, then peaceful. I shut my eyes and kept praying, letting the healing grace do its work, relinquishing my need to hide in this greater need to serve.

Unexpectedly, Allan's face came into view. "Brie! What has happened?" Beside him stood a weeping woman I took to be the child's mother. She knelt down beside me and gently lifted him from my touch. His eyes opened and he murmured, "Mama." And then I must have fainted, for I saw no more.

I awoke in the spare room at Rachel and Bronwyn's. Someone had lent me other garments, for my own could be seen hanging on the line beyond the window. It was nearly dusk, and with disquiet I remembered my headlong rush to the boy's side, in full view of my new friends and a dozen or more townspeople. Was he all right? I wondered. It wasn't always certain what could be healed and what not. I rinsed my face in the nearby basin and went out to the sitting room.

Five faces looked intently at me as I appeared: Rachel and Bronwyn, Allan, and the little boy and his mother. The child seemed well, looked alert and coherent. Yet alongside my great joy at his recovery, my stomach dropped in anticipation of the conversation to come.

Allan broke the silence, "Have you trained in medicine, Brie? This child had quite an injury, and yet he seems now right as rain. You mentioned nothing of that to Susannah and me."

I shook my head, wordless. Bronwyn spoke up gently, "I told you, pastor. She was not applying poultices or giving him herbs; she was just placing her hands to the wound and praying."

"But you said he was bleeding profusely. There is still a stain on the street. And yet now all we see is a tiny scar on his head. This cannot be."

Rachel looked at me with a hesitant glance, deep kindness mixed with fear. She held out my cross to me. "I found this in your pocket as I washed your garments. I did not want it to be lost." I took it from her and was surprised at the warmth that rushed up my arm.

But Allan was still questioning. "Brie, what did you do? How did you do it? The first townspeople to come upon Michael were not even sure that he would survive his injury."

I could not hide. "I prayed," I answered simply. He looked disbelieving, so I continued. "Sometimes when I pray, a warmth comes to my hands; sometimes healing is worked somewhere between the prayers and my hands and the person who is hurt. I do not understand it any better than you. It is why I ran away from my old village. The people feared and mistrusted this power that God sometimes wields through me. I do not know how it works; I only know that it is."

For the first time, little Michael spoke up. "I heard the horse, and then the cart fell, and I felt a sharp, tearing pain in my head. I fell on the ground hard, and I heard people call out as they knelt beside me. They turned me over, and all I could see were the clouds above and a cloudy kind of darkness in front of my eyes, too. Then this lady came. She was whispering—it did sound kind of like church talk—and she put her hand on my head where it hurt so bad. And then it was like sunshine. Does that make sense? It was like sunshine breaking through this awful pain, pushing it back, like a man who is winning a fistfight. And the lady just kept touching me and saying those gentle words. Finally there was more sunshine than pain, and Mama came."

All five faces turned to me, uncertain, wondering, ill at ease. It was hardest to see the look on Allan's face. I could not read it, but I knew that he no longer felt at peace with me. I did not wish my work undone; little Michael was going to be fine, and that counted for much. But I did wish that the accident had never taken place to draw me out into the open, to make me a spectacle once more.

Then Allan seemed to make up his mind. "Brie will return to Susannah's tomorrow. When asked, you will tell others that Brie had received some training as a midwife, that by good fortune she had some strong herbs with her that helped to staunch the bleeding. Michael, do you understand?"

"Pastor, why do you want me to lie? I know it was the sunshine in her hands, not the herbs at all."

Allan smiled. "You are an honest lad, Michael. I am glad that you are well and will live to remember this day. But Brie's sunshine, as you call it, could put her in danger, if other people know about it. What I am asking you to do is to help protect her. Can you do that?"

Michael nodded solemnly, and his mother held him tight. She had said nothing throughout the whole conversation. But now she turned directly toward me, with a look of fierce gratitude and yet also a shielded suspicion. I had seen that face before on other mothers, other fathers. *You gave me back my child; I must thank you. But I don't trust what you have done or who you are, and so I must push you away.* I both understood and dreaded that look. Above all it was isolating.

Allan and I left early the next morning, before the sun was fully up. He did not want questions from passersby or strange looks and whispering. To their credit, both Bronwyn and Rachel rose to see me off. Bronwyn clasped my hand, and Rachel reached for a quick hug. I felt so surprised and blessed by those little gestures of care, for in the past I had met with only distance, even ostracism.

The journey back to Susannah's was even quieter than the journey out, weighted with heaviness and my own sorrow. Allan seemed distracted, and I did not press him. I worried what conversation would greet me in Susannah's home. I tried to enjoy the beauty of the morning; despite the clouds, rays of sunlight danced on golden leaves in the early hours. But by midday, the rain had begun, and we were soaked and chilled by the time we reached the small dwelling on the cliff. What lay in store for me?

7

hen we reached Susannah's house, Allan asked me to give them time alone. I was glad for the opportunity to wash and warm myself in the bath that Susannah had drawn as she heard the horse's hooves in the distance. However, I worried what the outcome of their conversation would be. Allan's eyes remained shadowed and troubled when he looked upon me. How would Susannah respond to his account of Michael's healing? As I toweled my hair dry near the door, I thought I heard his voice raised in anxiety, even fear, as her calmer voice prevailed, seemed to steady him. As I dressed, I prayed. *Gracious God, you brought me here to this sheltering place, and I praise you for that gift. If it is time to go, I know that you will go with me, yet I would wish to stay.* I looked again upon the sculpture of the woman just touching the hem of Jesus' garment, needing to be encouraged by her look of wonder. Then, taking a deep sigh that said even more than my prayer, I opened the door and stepped into the next room.

Three heads turned my way: Susannah's, Allan's, and even Ebenezer's, who ran to me and butted my ankles with his sleek head. At least I was assured affection from that quarter. Susannah spoke first, inviting me to sit close to the fire. Allan opened his mouth as if to launch into a long explanation, but Susannah stopped him: "Go wash, Allan. Take some fresh water and care for your tired body. You are too worn to make such an important decision this way." Grudgingly, he took the two filled kettles and moved away.

Susannah reached out a hand and found my own. She smiled and then said softly, "Little Michael is very blessed that you came to market yesterday." She nodded to herself. "He will treasure life in a different way now, as will his mother." I said nothing, afraid that my words would be my undoing. "Brie, I can sense that you are very afraid. Your fear in the long run will only harm you. Can you lay it down?" I did not know what she meant; fear had been such an intrinsic part of my life, ever since the cross came to me. With the outward expressions of my gift came suspicion, even hatred, in the eyes and hearts of others. I did not know a way to change that.

Susannah continued, "Allan feels that you are a danger to me. I know better. You are a gifted child of God, and you have the heart of a friend. You did not need to run to Michael's side. Yet Rachel reported that you threw down your packages and ran to his aid the minute you heard his cry. For you, to offer healing took precedence over hiding; that was a self-forgetful choice, and an honorable one. You are very aware of others' needs and hurts—and responsive even when it is to your detriment.

"But Gabriela, what do you seek for yourself? What do you long for? Only when you quiet yourself enough to hear your own heart's cry will you discover where your journey leads.

"Please know that, despite Allan's misgivings, you are welcome here with me. Yet somehow I feel certain that you will not stay, once the last snowfall has come and gone. You have a long and rich road ahead, not without danger, yet also shining with grace and even joy."

Still I said nothing. Her hand remained linked with my own, and I caressed the aged skin with my thumb, gently, thoughtfully. I did not know what I sought for myself. I was afraid of my own longings, so deeply had they been buried under grief and loss and others' rejection. Midst my quiet musings, Ebenezer decided it was time to offer his own form of comfort. He jumped up in my lap, circled once, and made himself at home. His purring, resonant and peaceful, soothed my ragged spirit.

The three of us sat in silence until Allan emerged from his bath. His eyes were not quite so guarded or angry as they had been on our long day's journey. I even fancied I saw some compassion alongside the uncertainty. He settled himself on the floor by the fire, drawing his long legs up to his chest. I expected him to speak, as he had tried to do earlier, but he joined us in our silence, as though waiting.

Unexpectedly, Susannah began to sing. It was a tune I did not know, but Allan did. His rich baritone gradually joined her clear, quiet alto. They sang a haunting tale of a young woman on the run from her destiny, chased by those who misunderstood or wished to use her for their own ends. The music held rich harmonies and unexpected turns that stitched the song through with strength. I held my breath, wondering how it would end, but the song looped round to the refrain, which left the outcome in doubt:

So she runs, her feet fleet, and wind-winged by grace,
So she runs, with the Lord's light abright on her face,
So she runs, but in running one must have a goal . . .
Does she see that while running, she cannot be whole?
Come home, gifted sister, come home.
Come home, grieving sister, come home.
Come home to your Father's grace; come home, find your rightful place.
Come home, wind-borne sister, come home.

I did not realize that I was crying until Ebenezer shook out his dampened whiskers. So there had been others on the run before me? And people sang of them? It seemed incredible. Susannah had asked what I longed for: what I longed for was to know and to find my home. But with Anna's death, my old home had closed up behind me, and I did not know where my new home lay. Would I always be running? And where is home for those who breed distrust in others simply by being who they are? I was too tired to make sense of anything but the questions, and after offering the others my small gifts from the market, I nodded off before the fire, Ebenezer's soft head at rest on my palm.

Dozing by the fire, I dreamed. Once again, I saw the wind-lashed boat, the stricken faces. Far in the distance, I saw the tail feathers of the albatross, journeying on. One sailor seemed determined to row in the direction the bird had taken, and the others seemed too tired and discouraged to resist his intentions, though one muttered, "They journey for thousands of miles over sea. He will not lead us to land, mate." One girl cried quietly, but the other watched the bird with bright eyes, still hoping. The storm was abating around them, but their world was only water, water everywhere.

I awoke briefly to discover that Susannah and Allan had both retired, leaving me with Ebenezer by a dying fire. They had covered us both with heavy quilts to ward off the cold, and I felt too bone-tired and heart-heavy to move. I stroked Ebenezer's head gently before falling to sleep once more. For much of the night I journeyed dreamless through dark and discouragement, hearing in the distance the lapping of waves and a soft sobbing. But just before dawn a light broke over the dreamscape of sea: in the far distance, a patch of sand; and farther still, a trail up a steep-sided hill that led to twisted trees and snow-capped mountains beyond. Now all the sailors were rowing in earnest, rowing with joy. Land! Land! The albatross was perched on a towering crag, just to the east of the beach. His eyes gleamed like pearls in the early light as he watched their approach and surveyed their safe landing. Five figures straggled to shore and collapsed, just beyond the high water mark. Only Anna knelt and spread her hands in a brief prayer of thanksgiving before also falling faint to the sand.

I awoke to the smell of baking bread and to the sounds of Susannah's breakfast preparations. I could not shake the memory of Anna's upraised, grateful hands, nor the vision of the steep hill with mountains beyond. In those first moments of hazy consciousness, a conviction grew within me: Anna was alive, far from home, but alive!

Despite the dire fortune she had been told and the lost cross, she and her four companions had come safely to land somewhere far distant. Should I tell Susannah and Allan? Yet what purpose could it serve? Who would believe the tangled dreams of this wind-borne sister? I held my peace.

8

ll through that winter, I raised my hands in prayers of thanksgiving, much as Anna had done. I was warm and safe, beloved and encouraged. Susannah taught me a few of her carving tricks, and I coaxed the rough-hewn form of an albatross from a bit of driftwood over the long dark nights of midwinter. She taught me new recipes, simple preparations, ways of combining just a few ingredients for nourishment and delight. I knew in my heart she was seeking to prepare me for a long journey ahead, one with few provisions and unpredictable circumstances.

Sometimes in the evenings I would read aloud to Susannah from Anna's letters, coming to love and understand this vibrant, faithful young woman through her own words. I looked for clues in her letters as to where she had been: town names, plans, descriptions of vistas, and landmarks. They were few and far between. Besides, her point of embarkation would not necessarily have been anywhere near the deserted beach to which I imagined the party had come after storm and despair, guided by a wise old bird. Who was I to think that I could find her? To travel alone as a young woman, even one well-trained in cooking, wise in boating, versed in healing, was a foolish plan altogether. But it was only midwinter. Perhaps the coming months would reveal God's deeper plan.

Soon snow insulated us in our cottage world, with only brief forays out to tend the cow. Then came ice and wind, and it became clear that spring would be late in coming this year. At intervals, in the quiet evening, I would sometimes feel compelled to extend my hands toward Susannah, inviting the light to return to her shaded eyes. Over time she could see vague forms and outlines as she had not for two years or more. It helped her to navigate her home more confidently, to take up her old craft with less anxiety. I watched in wonder as she coaxed the figures of two dancers from a glossy, rich piece of wood; by the end, I recognized them as Allan and Anna, just as I had seen them in my vision in the fall. Her artistry revealed both their joy and Anna's radiant spirit.

When the refreshing rains came at last, I knew that it would soon be time to journey forth. Allan had not come often over the winter, and his brief visits had clearly been for Susannah's sake, with little time for me. On his most recent trip, he had at least begrudgingly thanked me for the bit of sight Susannah had regained. I rushed to assure him that was the Lord's work, not mine. He neither agreed nor disagreed, only looked at me thoughtfully. I knew he nonetheless wanted me gone.

One evening Susannah brought out another of Anna's letters, longer and more rumpled than any I had read over the intervening weeks. "This is her last letter. When I could still see, I read it over and over again, once word reached us of the ship lost in the storm. I wasn't ready to share it with you before. But I sense that you will be leaving soon. You need to know the fullness of her story."

And so I took up the letter, its words slightly blurred from old tears.

"Dearest Mama, how I miss Lily and Molly! I am glad they found their sweethearts during our travels together. I could tell from the faces and voices of their menfolk that their marriages are fortunate ones, that they will be well-loved. But journeying with Katherine and Isabella has been strained and difficult. And I can't quite seem to shake the fortuneteller's words.

"The other night, Katherine and I shared a difficult talk. Her faith is deep, yet also judgmental. Because she had praised how Jesus has gifted his people in surprising and beautiful ways, I dared to speak of how he sometimes works his healing touch through my own. Her face changed dramatically, and she turned away. 'Healing powers are witchcraft, not the ways of the Lord,' she intoned, as though reciting from Scripture. But I know no such words are in the Good Book. I spoke more timidly but persisted, 'When the power comes, I feel his peace and presence. It is not my work, but his desire for others' healing, as well as their openness to receive.' Her look became even more severe. 'Turn from this "gift," Anna; it will be your demise.'

"Oh, Mama, I felt so heavy with disappointment. It is clear that Katherine's faith is strong, but her rejection of what I shared was intense. The next morning, she walked far ahead of Isabella and me on the road, as though she wished to separate herself from us both.

"It is so hard to write what came next. I still don't know quite how it happened. Isabella and I had stopped to gaze at some lovely roadside flowers. We were distracted and lost sight of Katherine. Suddenly I heard her scream. We lifted our skirts and went running as fast as we could, though with travel packs, running is awkward at best. It was a full minute before we came upon her.

"I think that she must also have been stopping by the roadside to admire some of the springtime color. But she did so beside a steep ravine, lost her footing and fell some thirty feet downhill. Even from a distance, I could see that at least one arm and one leg were broken, and her head had come to rest against a heavy tree trunk. Isabella and I quickly hid our packs behind a tree and searched for a safe way down to her. It was very rough going, with much slipping. Isabella fell a few feet, but she caught herself on a young sapling, thank the Lord. When we finally arrived where Katherine lay, her face was ashen, and she was shuddering with fear and pain. I put out my hands to her, believing that God would want to bring her some measure of comfort, perhaps even healing. Oh, Mama, she spit on my hands, and then spit on my face! 'I want none of witchcraft's touch, even in my pain!' she cried. I felt my heart break within me, and I felt something else, most strange: the warmth that had surged to my hands vanished like mist in the wind. You see, Mama, she had rejected it outright. It shocked me, and I began to shiver a bit myself.

"Isabella and I prayed for help to come, as we knew no way to get Katherine back up to the roadside ourselves. After about twenty horrifying minutes, during which time Katherine fell unconscious, we heard hoofbeats and the crunch of carriage wheels on the track above. We screamed ourselves hoarse, praying to be heard over the road sounds. Presently, the wheels stopped. A young man peered down into the ravine and saw our frantically waving hands. There was a second man with him, older but clear-thinking, who worked together with the first to rig up a sort of sling with which to carry her. Very carefully they made their way down the slope and managed between them to get Katherine to the top. Isabella and I slipped and slid but somehow found our way up as well.

"We were very fortunate that the men were kind and generous—and their carriage accommodating. They placed Katherine gently on one seat and invited Isabella and me to accompany them to the next town, where they would seek a physician. Mama, I prayed and prayed and extended my hands all through that lurching, frightening trip, but nothing happened. Katherine's condition worsened, and by the time we found the gentle doctor in Kenton, his face was grave and creased with worry.

"He spent a long time in the room with Katherine, ministering to her. I knew that he would set the bones in her limbs; they could heal over time. It was the blow to her head that troubled me deeply. If only she had welcomed the healing right away! It always seems to be most powerful just after a wound has been received. I sat outside with Isabella, and we tried to keep one another's spirits up, yet our hearts were heavy.

"When the doctor finally emerged through the door, I knew before he spoke. She would not live. For a man who has seen much of the world, of illness and of death, I expected a more detached telling. But his eyes had tears shining in them as he told us, 'Young friends, I am very sorry to tell you that Katherine will likely not last the night. The wound to her head is severe, and her spirit has already turned to embrace death.' I intuitively knew what he meant by this, but Isabella cried out, 'Embrace death! Doctor, what are you saying?' He sat down next to her and gently laid his hand on her arm. 'Those of us in the healing profession see many strange things. One of the things they don't teach you in school but that you come to see early is that a person's spirit often has far more to do with their healing than any medicine or care. Some people survive in the worst of situations, fighting and fighting for life to the surprise of everyone. Others die when they might have lived. I cannot say whether Katherine might have lived; injuries to the head are unique to each person. I can see, however, that she does not wish to fight, and I feel sorry for that.'

"Isabella began to cry quietly, and the doctor laid a tender arm around her shoulders. Later, after Isabella had spent some time with our dying friend, I also took my turn. As I entered the room, I recognized the labored breathing of one who is close to death, and I stopped short several feet from the narrow bed. 'Katherine?' I began. I took a few steps closer, and she raised her head just an inch or two from the pillow. Her eyes were clouded, yet no longer angry. She looked right at me as though trying to memorize my face. 'Anna,' she whispered. 'The Lord holds you close now,' I began, 'very close.' 'Yes.' 'I will stay with you by your side if you wish.' 'Yes.' There was a long pause, a deep quiet broken only by her ragged breath. 'My Bible,' she said at last, with a weak wave of her hand. I had not noticed earlier, but the kind men who came to our aid must have carried Katherine's pack up the hillside with her. I rummaged in her rucksack and found her dog-eared, much-loved copy of the Word. I turned to the Psalms and began.

"It was a very long, sad night, Mama. Isabella brought me some soup that the doctor's wife had prepared, and he came in every few hours to take Katherine's hand and to offer her some light medicine to ease the pain. Mostly I just read aloud in a halting voice, trying to keep my eyes on the Lord in that room full of pain and my own deep conviction of unnecessary loss. I did not read all of the Psalms aloud, Mama; perhaps it was wrong of me, but Psalm 73 speaks of feet slipping and slippery ground, and somehow I could not; it seemed too cruel.

"I believe that Katherine gave up her spirit to the Lord somewhere in the midst of the promises of Psalm 86; surely he has shown her mercy, as he promises in those passages. I love that psalm, and I did not look up until I finished it, to see her face. Though ashen, it was peaceful, Mama, very peaceful.

"I did not call out to the doctor or Isabella right away; I felt that some quiet space alone would be all right. I smoothed back her hair and straightened the coverlet. I even stroked her face. She had a lovely face, Mama; had you met her, you would have longed to sculpt her, I know. It was still before dawn, and the candlelight played on her hands and face with gentle, subtle shadows. I turned to I Corinthians 15 and read aloud to her peaceful form—or perhaps more truthfully to my own grieving heart—the promises of the resurrection: 'The trumpet shall sound, and the dead shall be raised.' They shall be raised. She shall be raised. And you and I, Mama, when the time comes.

"As I turned to close the Bible at last, something fell out on the floor. It was a letter. I felt a sort of stirring inside, as though that letter was important, so I tucked it into my pocket to look at later. Then I went to share the sad tidings with the others.

"Katherine had not had much money, and though the doctor was most generous, Isabella and I pooled most of the rest of what we had to pay for her burial in the village churchyard down the way. We knew she would have done the same for us, but it left us with a difficult decision; was it time to return home? I miss you deeply, Mama, but I did not find a certainty in my heart that I had accomplished all that was meant for this journey. However, Isabella was adamant: we should take the shortest route to a port city and make our way back north. I would be too frightened to travel alone. I thought about trying to find Molly and Lily, but knew that their lives were going forward in other ways, and I could not press on their generosity. I agreed to make the short journey back to port and home.

"So perhaps you will see me before you see this letter, Mama. I do not know the route the courier will take. It will be lovely to see your face, to wake early and milk the cow, to dance with Allan again. And yet in my heart I am puzzled; I can only see those things as through a dreamy mist, not sharply as I imagined. I wonder why?

"Oh, I nearly forgot. I opened the letter from Katherine's Bible late last night. It is from her sister, Betsy. I had not realized that Katherine had come from so far south in our country; she never spoke of home. The letter describes tall mountains and a beautiful valley with 'praying oaks.' I wonder what they are? I hate it when I remember that Betsy does not know that her sister is dead. When I get home I will write to her at her home in Nybron and try to tell her gently. Please pray for Betsy, Mama; it is clear from her letter that she loved her sister and that she, like you, has hands that shape beauty where none has been. She had little sketches throughout the three pages; I think one must be of her and Katherine together when they were a little younger. I can see the family resemblance! There was also a small design of a kitten; it made me think of our little tyke, Ebenezer. Such a grandiose name for a wee bit of fur! Though I imagine he is grown big and self-satisfied now. It will be good to sit with him when I return.

"I love you, Mama. Give my love also to Papa and to Allan. Pray for travel mercies and safe passage, and I should be home before long. As always, rest in the arms of Jesus; he loves us so! Your Anna."

Susannah and I sat for a long time in silence, with the rumbling purr of Ebenezer as counterpoint to our thoughts. I imagine that Susannah was remembering her daughter with both deep grief and aching love. I was struck by a different sense: that somehow the letter from Betsy and my dream of weary stragglers washing up on a beach, tall mountains beyond, were part of one mystery, with Anna at its center. I turned the last page of the letter over in my hand. Very delicately lined on the back, as though they had been traced, I found both a landscape of mountains, with a valley and trees in the foreground, and the depiction of two young women's heads, foreheads touching as though they laughed in a moment of shared joy. Which was Katherine and which Betsy? Had Anna found the latter? I did not know, and yet I felt certain that my journey led south to find out.

9

We saw the last of the frost before long, and soon I was packed and ready to begin my journey. Ebenezer did not wish to stir from my side as I rose earlier than normal, and he greeted me with a grumpy meow of complaint. I would miss him and yet was glad he would remain as furry companion for Susannah in my absence. Susannah also was preoccupied, wondering if she and I had packed and prepared properly for all that lay ahead. A woman alone carried risks with her that male travelers did not. I would not be going by boat this time, and one never knew who might be met on the road. I thought of my meeting with Allan, of Michael and his description of my "sunshine," of the surly man on the first day of my journey many months before. Would I be as fortunate in future as I had been with Susannah? As I packed a last few things, I spied on a small shelf of treasures the pearl "given" to me by the albatross. Anna had been on the brink of death, but she and her companions had come to land. I put the pearl in my pocket, remembering. The good Lord would go ahead of me, as the albatross had led Anna, and take me to places of hope. On my journeys of change, perhaps yet threaded through with grief, I would ever be held up on his sustaining wings.

Susannah was older and more practical, it seemed. A few moments later, she turned to me with a different tone to her voice than I had heard over our many months together. In her hand she held a short, sharp dagger, with a hilt inlaid with amethyst. "This belonged to my husband," she told me. "I have never used it and pray that you will have no call to wield it in self-defense. But it may be useful for other reasons; it may help you in tight situations. I awoke this morning certain I was to give it to you." She sheathed it carefully in a leather case and held it out for me to take. "Gabriela, go with God. You have been a blessing to me these many months. You helped me to navigate a hard winter. You let me hear Anna's letters again. And to be able to see light and form again! What a marvelous grace to an old woman who aches to work with her hands. I know that the Lord brought you here; I pray that he will bring you back again one day." She paused and then held out an envelope to me. "Allan gave me this when he was last here. He said that I was to give it to you as you left on your journey. You are not to open it until the seventh day. Allan is not usually given to such strange directions; I imagine he wants to be sure that you will be well beyond his village before you read what he has written. But Brie, know that he is not an unkind man. He just carries so much pain that he cannot always walk in welcome."

She embraced me then and waited patiently as I packed the last of my provisions. My heart felt divided between a longing to stay in this place of safety, known and loved well, with Susannah and Ebenezer and the song of the sea to lull me to sleep each night, and a longing to risk what lay ahead, to follow the promptings of my heart that called me forward and away. Susannah interrupted my thoughts with a final word, "For I know the plans I have for you, says the Lord, plans to prosper you and not to harm you, plans to give you hope and a future." I took a deep breath. "It will be all right, Gabriela. Know that it will be all right." Ebenezer rubbed up against my leg one last time, and I rubbed him just under the chin, where he loves it best.

Then I knew it was time. I looked around the cottage, at the grace of Susannah's sculptures, the warmth of her home, at her lined and love-filled face. "God be with you, Susannah. You have blessed me more than you know." And my new journey began.

* * * * *

The weather smiled on me as I followed the trails and byways southward. The spring rains were lighter than usual, and the first few nights I happened upon abandoned outbuildings or heavy tree-cover to shelter me. I met few travelers, which was as I had hoped. The few herdsmen or mounted travelers I passed simply nodded in my direction and kept going on their way. I tried to walk with heavy stride, with my long hair hidden in my hood; it would be better if they didn't see right away that I was a woman alone.

Those first days, my provisions were abundant: Susannah's tasty breads, dried fruit we had stored up over the winter, and a small store of dried meats as well. Wells and clear-flowing streams along the way kept me safely supplied with enough water, and I carefully portioned out the cheese that Susannah had insisted I take for my journey. After a week, however, I began to worry that I did not have enough. My pack was lighter and less cumbersome, it was true; and I had been wise to eat just enough each day to give me strength for that day's travel. I knew I would have water enough in this land full of fresh waterways, especially in the springtime, but my food supplies were dwindling. Berries would come in a month or so, other fruits later, and yet my stores did not look as though they would hold out until then. At dusk on the seventh day, I found shelter in what appeared a long-unused shed, far back from the byway.

To my delight, I found matches and two candles within and spent several minutes exploring the site by candlelight. A bed, a table, and a broken chair proved the only furnishings, but as I looked up into the rafters, I spied several odd-shaped containers that intrigued me. Setting the candle on the bed, I moved the table and stood upon its surface to reach down the items. The first object, a modest-sized jar, I set on the table without ascertaining its contents. The second, a long wooden box, rattled as I lifted it down. The third item remained obscured in a burlap sack but felt solid under my hand.

I pulled the table back over beside the bed, set the candle on the table-top, and tried to decide what to do. The layer of dust in the shed indicated that no one had lived here for many months, perhaps years, yet these objects still were not mine. What could it hurt to see what they were, I told myself. I opened the jar. Inside it, I found dried meat, still in good condition after its long storage in the rafters. I recognized how much this could help me, both light to carry and nutritious.

Then I took up the long box; it had been beautifully worked, with a pattern of wildflowers on the top surface that emerged as I wiped away the dust with the hem of my cloak. I found the clasp and lifted the lid. Within lay the pieces of a chess set, each hand-worked. The faces of the horses on the knights particularly drew my attention; the craftsman had clearly known and loved horses and understood their distinctive personalities.

And suddenly I was no longer seeing the shed. In my mind's eye, I was standing at a rail fence overlooking a field not far back along the road I had come. An elderly man, stooped and careworn, offered a meager store of feed to two horses younger and healthier than he. As they ate, he smoothed their manes and called them by pet names, lulling, loving. And then he fell, the seed spilling, the horses whickering nervously, butting him gently with their noses. He did not rise again.

The owner of these items would not return. Likely thieves had come upon his body, lying among the whinnying mares, and taken them for their own. I wondered if they had given him a decent burial? Then I chastised myself; why could not family or friends have found him? But I looked at the chess set in my hands; family or friends would have known of this work of art and taken it home in memory of him. Thieves would have snatched the horses and run.

The burlap sack remained unexplored. I felt hesitant, feeling as though I pilfered this older man's treasures. But curiosity won; I wanted to know what had formed that solid weight as I lifted down the sack. Gently I shook it free of the burlap, and I gasped. On the table sat a beautiful silver cross, larger and more intricate than the one I carried. Yet the similarities were unmistakable: the clean lines, the delicate tracery in the details, the beveled edges. I turned it over in my hands. Far down on the stem of the cross, I saw the touch mark: JM . . . James Mason. Susannah's husband had worked this cross, and it had come to the elderly horse-lover, also gifted in his own right as a worker of wood. I marveled at having found it, and my sense of guilt became a sense of peace. This item would come with me on my journey, to be given to Susannah upon my return.

With gratitude I ate a small portion of the meat and a few of my own provisions as a modest supper. During the meal, my eyes kept returning to the chess set, to its figures and lines. As I finished, I reached for one of the black knights and turned it upright to view the base; carved in the wood in tiny letters I beheld the words: faithful Midnight, age 27. The second black knight bore a similar inscription: irascible Tempest, age 29. So he had outlived these horses. My hands stretched out for the other two knights, for the horses that nuzzled him in my vision had been white: sweet Meadowgrace and wise, beloved Dancer. Yes, he had cherished his horses. Did the other pieces hold inscriptions as well? I upturned them eagerly.

Seven of the sixteen pawns bore whimsical names, and I wondered if perhaps these had been childhood pets, cats or dogs long gone but still remembered. Looking more closely at those figures, compared to those without names, I laughed aloud in the shadowy shed: discreetly wrapped around the base of the figures I saw tails: fluffy and long for Mischief; thin but upright for Hero. I felt light tears on my face. The woodworker had taken his grief and love and fashioned it into beauty that delighted even in his absence.

I reached for the rooks: three of the names were unknown to me, though they seemed to be place names. The fourth jolted me: Nybron. Nybron, Katherine and Betsy's home! Could this man have known them? It seemed too amazing. I lifted the bishops next: Matthew, Mark, Luke, and John. I smiled. Indeed, he had worked detail into each piece: echoes of a man, a lion, an ox, an eagle. I loved the wings on the white bishop, the ox-tail on the black. Susannah would love these, such an intriguing counterpoint to her own sculptures representing the Gospel writers!

Only the kings and queens were left. I hesitated once again. Clearly this man had carved into this set those places and living things most deeply beloved. I chose the black set first: Mama and Papa. Of course. The black queen held a tiny emblem on the back, as though tucked into flowing garments: knitting needles. And the king's robe bore the figure of a chisel; so he had learned his craft from his father. I smiled.

The white king and queen sat side by side on the table, lovely yet sad. Why sad? I didn't know exactly; no visions came as I gazed upon the last two figures. I lifted the king first: Andrew Shelton, his work and love. He had struggled to fit the words on such a tiny surface, but it was clearly the artist's signature. The white queen remained. I held her in my hand a moment, willing a vision; only deep sadness came over me in waves, crashing heavily and then subsiding. I looked at the inscription: my Betsy. Somehow I had known. And then my brain did the math: the man in my vision was perhaps eighty. Even if Betsy were Katherine's older sister, even if Katherine were older than Anna, even though Anna had been gone for many years . . . it couldn't be the same person. I puzzled, wondering if perhaps Betsy had been named for her mother, for an aunt, for a beloved older friend from Nybron. Clearly my destination had been reconfirmed.

I slept well in that tiny shed, having hidden away the treasures in the bottom of my travel sack. The added weight seemed small price to pay for the beauty and the unexpected links to my own journey. I did not dream, except for a brief moment when I watched two black stallions chasing one another on a golden afternoon. I had no doubt that I beheld Midnight and Tempest.

Just before dawn, I awoke with a start: Allan's letter! It was now day eight, and in my excitement over the shed and all it contained, I had forgotten. Should I take the time to read it, or wait until my noonday meal? I smiled, remembering the dried meat that would help to vary my choices for a time. And that made me remember Andrew and all I had learned of that gentle, gifted soul. I recalled my commitment to find the place I had seen in my vision, to verify if his body still lay where it fell. Allan's letter would have to wait.

I gathered my items and whispered a quick prayer of thanksgiving for having been brought to this spot. Stepping toward a tumble-down fence, I tripped over an old hoe and nearly fell. My heart felt heavy; I imagined that I would need it. I made my way across the barren fields in the first rays of light, looking for the fence line and the tree of my vision. There. Stepping more carefully now, my heart heavy, I found Andrew. Clearly it had been several years, and the weather and the scavengers had done their work well. I willed my hoe to be a shovel, but it would have to do. Thankfully, spring rains had worked the ground loose in places, and my task, though sobering, was not impossible. Tears fell as I saw bits of burlap sunk into the ground nearby: some of the seed bag had remained.

As I covered over the last of Andrew's remains, the now-brighter morning sun glinted off an item half-buried in the ground. I knelt to investigate. My hands unearthed a pearl. Had mine tumbled from my pocket as I worked? How fortunate I had not lost it! But no, the pearl that reminded me of my unexpected and shining encounter with the albatross remained in my pocket. I took it out and compared the two beads: the one from Andrew's field had a pink cast and larger dimensions. After removing the last of the dirt, I placed it also in my pocket.

I traced a cross in the dirt over Andrew's grave, then traced the outline of a horse's head. Part of me wanted to leave his silver cross there, in memory, in testament. Or perhaps one of the tailed pawns? Yet weather would destroy both before long, and they were beautiful things yet to be enjoyed by the living. "I know you already rest in peace, Andrew," I murmured, "But now at last your earthly remains are also laid to rest. I will seek out your Betsy. I'm sorry about Meadowgrace and Dancer; let us hope that those who took them have loved them well, even if they did not do right by you. Thank you for your legacy of beauty in wood. Thank you for a night's stay in your home. God's peace, friend."

And my journey went on.

10

*L*ater that day a period of heavy rains began, soaking the ground, soaking me to the bone through my cloak. Day after day, I did not stop for lunch, simply munching on handfuls of dried meat and fruit along the way, as there was no dry place to sit and rest. The track that I was following became muddy and treacherous, and I was glad for my sturdy boots. At least bad weather meant fewer travelers.

On the fourth night, it was nearly nightfall and I still had seen no place I might rest for the night. I came to a fork in the road. The right-hand turn boded more of the same: long stretches of muddy road through deserted countryside. A lettered sign pointing left indicated that a village would greet me if I proceeded in that direction. Did I dare risk it? As I considered, the rain seemed to increase, heavy drops streaming down my face. I had a little money set aside, which I had promised myself not to use unless in dire straits. Yet I could not sleep outside in this. I turned left and hoped all would be well.

The outskirts of the village included tidy farms and cottages, mostly built of stone. The weather was so foul that no one was out and about; I caught sight of a stray cat streaking from the protection of one overhang to another, but that was all.

In the murky twilight, I drew closer to the center of town, looking for an inn that might cater to someone like me whose coins were few. I passed one with a grand entrance and another with a fine placard, listing famous folks who had slept there. Discouraged and bedraggled, I turned the last corner, praying for a haven. And then I saw it: a hand-carved sign, faded yet still green in the half-light, advertising "The Inn of the Green Boar." I could hardly believe it. Was this Molly's home? Whether or no, I knew this was my place of solace from the rain, and I stepped in at the door.

A man with a warm smile and a look of concern greeted me at the desk. He took in my state—mud up to my ankles, everything dripping—and called out, "Lily Mae, come quickly with a cup of hot tea!" A girl of seven appeared very shortly thereafter and curtsied in my direction before handing me a lovely cup with a welcome fragrance steaming out. She curtsied again and looked to her father. He advised her, "Go make up the garret room. Add extra blankets, bring in the tin tub from the hall closet, and heat more water for a bath. This traveler is chilled through." I worried how much it would cost but was grateful for his courtesies.

"Welcome," he told me, as Lily Mae scurried away up the staircase to my right. "How far have you come in this foul weather?" "Far, sir." I did not want to appear standoffish, yet I knew not how to answer his question in any useful way. To soften my vague answer, I smiled. He raised an eyebrow but did not press. He slid the register toward me and explained, "The price of the garret room is half that of our other accommodations, as you can see on the list. It is drafty but has no leaks, and we keep all our rooms equally tidy. If you want something larger, with a fireplace, we have two other rooms available . . ." His voice faded and he looked at me questioningly. "No, sir, the garret room will be best for me. Thank you so much." I signed in and handed him the coins, paying in full.

"We've already had dinner with our other guests," he continued. "I'll have Lily Mae bring up some hot soup for you after you've had your bath, and for a little extra, I imagine my wife would be willing to wash your clothes and dry them for your travels on the morrow." He did not assume that I would be staying long, and I knew I had not the budget for a second night.

The bath was scalding hot but a welcome comfort after many days of trudging through mud and rain. Lily Mae had even set out some rough but comfortable nightclothes, perhaps in anticipation that I would ask her mom to launder my garments.

My garret room was spare, just a bed and chair and enough floor space for the tub. Two of the four angled walls were clearly the bricks of chimney flues, which offered some heat, though not the comfort of a fire. I climbed into the bed, heaped high with half a dozen wool blankets, and discovered a heated brick at the foot. These proprietors were generous, despite the more modest appearance of their inn. I was reaching for my bag to find Allan's letter when a polite knock came on the door. "Come in." Lily Mae appeared with a shy smile and a bowl of delicious-smelling soup. "This is Mama's best recipe," she bragged proudly, "And she's teaching me how to make it." I smiled. "I bet that you're a good cook, Lily Mae." She beamed. I offered an earnest prayer of thanksgiving for this place of warmth and food and safety and took a first taste of the broth. Ah! It proved well-seasoned, thick, and full of sustaining chunks of vegetables, potatoes, even some meat. As I ate, Lily Mae was dragging the large tub back into the hall. Then I heard her taking out my dirty wash water, one bucket at a time, and hauling it downstairs. Such hard work for a little girl! And yet she clearly enjoyed contributing to her parents' business.

The soup gave me renewed strength. I set the bowl gently on the floor and reached again for Allan's letter. I had not dared to read it during the days of dousing rains. Thankfully it was close enough to the middle of my bag that it was not soaked through. Other items I spread on the floor, in hope that they might dry even a little by morning. Then I opened the envelope. Inside were a close-written letter and a smaller envelope. In an elegant though cramped hand, Allan had written, "Brie, it is true that I have not known what to make of your gifts or your presence in our midst. Yet I know your faith is genuine, and you have been such a blessing to Susannah with your presence and service over the winter. I gather that your journey ahead may be long and your needs great. I have no doubt that Susannah has spared all the provisions she can, but I fear it will not be enough. The enclosed is offered in thanksgiving for your work and for your care for my dear 'aunt.' Use it sparingly as the good Lord guides you so to do. May he watch over your every step, Allan." I opened the smaller envelope and was astonished at the financial gift he had made. Where did such money come from on a preacher's salary? Had he made economies for months, thinking of me? It made no sense, given how he had treated me. Yet those bills would have allowed me to stay at the Green Boar a whole fortnight—and not only in the garret room!

When Lily Mae came back for her fourth water-fetching, I called her into the room. I told her that I would indeed like to have my cloak and clothing washed and dried. Was there also provision for my boots and pack to be cleaned as well? Lily Mae nodded reassuringly; they would be glad to clean everything! Then she dutifully listed the fees for each, out of my reach just minutes ago, and yet now a welcome possibility.

She continued, "Please double-check all your pockets and things. Sometimes we find loose change in the bottom of the wash pot, and since we do several travelers' clothes at once, we cannot know to whom to return it. Mama lets me keep some of those coins," she confided, "Though they do not come often." She explained that she had two more trips to make before the tub would be empty, and she would take my items then.

I felt grateful for her reminder about "pockets and things." I kept back one semi-dry handkerchief in which to wrap the pearls and my cross. I lined up the other precious items under my bed, drying off the damp with my underskirt: Andrew's cross and the chess set, my few remaining provisions, the albatross I had carved at Susannah's, the dagger, Allan's letter, and the ragged remnant from the bottom of my boat, "Peace to you." Indeed, I felt a sense of deep peace in this attic room I had not felt since leaving Susannah's home. With a smile, I tucked a small coin back in the pocket of my apron, hoping it would end up in Lily Mae's hand later.

When Lily Mae came back, I invited her to sit on the foot of the bed for a minute and rest. She had been running up and down the stairs, often with full buckets of dirty water, for nearly ten minutes. She thanked me and began chattily, "Aunt Lily calls me the busy bee! I'm named for her, you see, Mama's twin sister. And Aunt Lily's daughter, Molly Anna, is named for my mama and an old friend of theirs, Anna. Isn't that funny?" I stared. When I had heard Lily's name, I had hoped, but this was such clear confirmation. What should I say? However, Lily Mae kept on, unaware of my pleasure at what she had shared. "Mom and Aunt Lily are very much alike in some ways; they told me that when they were my age they used to be in-sep-ar-a-ble." She enunciated this last word carefully and looked to me: "Did I say that right, miss?" "Yes, indeed." Another of Lily Mae's smiles bloomed.

"When they were about your age, they took a long journey together one summer and had their fortunes told. Mama was told to watch for 'the sign of the green boar.' Isn't that amazing? Less than a month later, they came through this town. Daddy had just opened the inn that spring, barely making ends meet on a little money left him by an old uncle. People see the other inns in town, and because they are grander, they think they are better. And I suppose they were then, because they didn't have Mama's cooking— or my help!"

"You are a good helper, Lily Mae."

She nodded and continued, "Mama and her friends all stayed here, sharing two rooms among the five friends. Daddy is a handsome man, and one of the other girls—was it Isadora? . . . that doesn't sound right—wanted him for herself. But Aunt Lily believed in the fortuneteller and knew that Mama was the one meant for him. She played a trick that made the other girl look bad, and sure enough, Daddy asked Mama to marry him within a week! Later he told Mama he had no interest in that other girl, only her, but Aunt Lily didn't know that. Daddy allowed the other girls to stay on for a fortnight, in exchange for their help with cooking and cleaning, until he and Mama could be wed. I love that story!"

She paused finally, with glowing eyes, loving that her parents had their own fairy tale story. Without thinking, I corrected her, "The other girl's name was Isabella." She jumped off the bed, "That's exactly right. I knew Isadora didn't sound right . . ." Then she looked at me with startled eyes. "But how could you know that? Are you a fortuneteller too?" "I know Anna's mother," I said simply. "I would like to talk with your mother about her after breakfast in the morning. Would you please ask her if that would be all right? If I take her away from chores, I would be glad to help in re-turn." Lily Mae looked at me appraisingly. "I like you," she said simply, "And I bet Mama will too. I'll ask her, and you'll meet her at breakfast tomorrow morning. I'll take your empty bowl also," she offered, stooping to pick it up as she gathered all my wet things in a bundle in her arms. "Oh, I forgot . . . if you need another blanket, there are two more in the closet in the hall; just don't trip over the tub down front. I can't prop it up like Papa does. And breakfast begins at eight in the dining room. I'll have your clothes back to you by a quarter till, so that you can appear in sar-tor-i-al splendor!" She whispered, "Daddy has wonderful word books, and when I get breaks, I find new words to try. Do you like that one?" I assured her I did and watched her go, still full of energy despite her heavy load of soaking gar-ments. No wonder Anna had missed Lily and Molly at the end of summer, if they were anything like this vibrant, confiding, sweet little girl!

My sleep was restful under the generously piled blankets, with vivid dreams that lingered with me as I dozed in the early morning light. I saw a younger Andrew riding Midnight, a wide and joy-filled smile transforming his face. In a second dream I watched Susannah coaxing the figure of a young woman out of red-hued wood. But in the last moments of the night I dreamed of the beach again, saw the abandoned boat, the figures collapsed in exhaustion on shore. I wanted to feel joy, knowing that they were free of "death by water." Instead I felt a gnawing dread; they had no provisions, and the way up the cliffs looked treacherous at best. Perhaps reaching land had only been the beginning. I tried to shake off the heaviness with thoughts of Allan's unexpected generosity, with imaginings of the conversation that I might share with Molly. Anna had always been in God's hands after all. Yet somehow her journey and mine had grown intertwined over these last weeks, and I ached to know what had become of her.

11

*L*ily Mae appeared as promised with my dry clothes, clearly warmed by the fireside, as they still carried the scent of pine and burning wood. Lily Mae looked full to bursting with news. "I told Mama that you knew Anna's mama, that you remembered the girl's name was Isabella, and she nearly fell off the stool she had been standing on to reach down something from the high cupboards! She looks forward to talking with you after the breakfast things are cleared. We would also welcome your help so that the work will go faster."

Breakfast was warm and tasty, complete with flaky bread and rich jam. The other boarders talked in pairs or stared into space, not interested in me, for which I was glad. I never liked to call attention to myself in a circle of men. I ate eagerly, for Molly's cooking was excellent and the portions generous.

When she saw that my plate was empty, Lily Mae tugged gently on my sleeve and nodded her head in the direction of the kitchen. I rose, taking my place setting with me, and followed her into a spacious and light-filled room that still smelled of the morning meal. An older, red-haired version of Lily Mae stepped toward me with a smile and embrace. "You are a friend of Anna's mother? How did you know about Isabella? I can hardly believe it!"

I smiled back and answered, "My name is Brie. I look forward to telling you all that I know, but first I want to honor my promise and help with the breakfast dishes." Molly laughed. Lily Mae had already headed back into the dining area, ready to fetch and carry. The three of us quickly found a rhythm for washing and drying and storing items away. At one point I heard Molly humming under her breath and thought I recognized the haunting tune of homecoming that Susannah and Allan had sung for me many months ago. I felt goose bumps rise on my arms but said nothing.

The dishes done, Molly glanced out the window at the bright spring sunshine that had followed on last night's storm. "Lily Mae, bring out two of the older chairs to the courtyard, please." "Just two, Mama?" I saw the hope of story and of inclusion in the little girl's face. "You know that the second-floor guests have already checked out. Those rooms' linens need to be changed and readied."

"I know, Mama. I'll get the chairs."

Molly and I sat in the sunlight, welcoming the unseasonable warmth of the day. I told her of my visit to Susannah's and shared as much of the content of Anna's letters as I could recall. I left out how I came to be at Susannah's and any mention of my own struggles; I also did not mention my vivid dreams of what I imagined to be Anna's journey from shipwreck to land. Molly listened attentively, laughing at my retelling of her and Lily's exploits, impressed by Anna's faithful, loving correspondence with her mother. When I told of Katherine's fall, however, she sobered and later wept. "Why did Anna and Isabella not come back here? We could have helped them! We would have welcomed them!"

"I do not know how far they had traveled from your inn when the incident happened. It may be that it was too far with what resources remained to them."

"Yes, they may not have realized how the roads curve and the land lies. Kenton is a scant three-day's journey from here, but knowing the road they had been following, they may have assumed it was as many as ten." She sighed. "I would have expected Katherine to live to be an old, critical, but productive woman, one of those examples whom all admire but none like. I wonder if she had a deep disappointment about which none of us knows, which made her lose heart?"

She stared off into the middle distance for a while, remembering, and then turned to me abruptly, fear in her eyes. "You have not mentioned Anna, only Anna's mother and cousin. Did she move far away when she married? Does she no longer write so faithfully to her mother?" I heard in her tone and saw in her face that she knew that those speculations were unfounded.

"There was a shipwreck," I told her as gently as I could. "Susannah has never heard from Anna since then." I fingered the cross in my pocket and decided to bring it out. "My little sister, also called Anna, found this on the shore near our home a number of years ago. When Susannah held it in her hands, I believe that she was convinced that it was proof that her daughter had died at sea."

Molly's head snapped up suddenly. "Death from water, just as the old fortuneteller predicted . . ." In my mind's eye I replayed the dream in which Isabella had torn the cross from Anna's neck and thrown it far into the raging waves. Was it real, all that I had seen, visions to summon me toward reunion, or just my own too-hopeful heart rewriting the truth? I did not know.

Molly looked straight at me then. "It's strange," she began. "When you told me that Katherine had died in a fall, I felt a deep conviction that it was true, much as I had not expected to hear that. But when I hear that both Isabella and Anna perished at sea, it does not feel real to me, despite those words of the old woman in the tent. She was wonderfully right about me and very insightful about Lily, embarrassingly so. But it is hard for me to believe that Anna is dead. Of all the young women I have known, she most clearly possessed a sense of mission, even of call. May I see the cross?"

I passed it over to her, and she fingered it gently, lovingly, much as Susannah had done. "Anna wore this around her neck always. Her father had made it for her, and she cherished it. Unlike Katherine, who touted her faith and pushed it on Lily and me like an angry old woman hawking wares at a dingy booth, Anna carried it like a steady, radiant light inside her. When she talked of God, I had the sense that she knew him as well or better than she knew me, that she sat and talked with him about all she saw and felt and dreamed." She paused, gazing on me with a certain intensity of speculation, as though assessing. She nodded and continued, "Anna had healing powers, you know. I could tell she thought that they were tied somehow to this cross, but I knew it was something deep within her, born of love and other-seeing and that deep bond she had with God. I am convinced that she saved Lily's life one day."

I gazed on her, startled. Anna had not written anything of this in her letters. Molly spoke again, her eyes on another time and place, "It was shortly after Tom and I were married. Lily and the other girls knew that it was beginning to be the high season for travelers, and their presence meant two rooms for which we received no income. So they set out again, well stocked with provisions. Isabella and Lily had always had some measure of animosity between them, with barbed banter and occasional forays into something darker. I always looked out for Lily and acted as a sort of buffer in the group. Two things contributed to what transpired: I was no longer in the traveling party, and Lily had played a nasty trick on Isabella when we first came to the inn, seeking to assure that Tom's eyes would be all for me. Isabella was awaiting a chance for revenge. At the next inn they visited, Isabella snuck into the kitchen just before dinner. She hunted through the slop bucket until she found what she sought: a piece of particularly rancid meat. She wrapped it in a napkin and managed to slip it into Lily's stew when she was turned the other way, chatting with Katherine.

"Lily always ate everything that she was served; we were raised that way, and often the innkeepers along our journeys charged us less than we ought to have paid in exchange for chores or other assistance, so she wanted to honor their cooking. At one point, Lily made such a face that one of the other lodgers whom she did not know gazed at her in alarm. But the rest of the stew had been so tasty, so Lily bolstered her courage and swallowed. That night she was horribly sick, writhing in pain in the bedroom that she shared with Anna. Her moans awoke Anna before long, and through her tears of pain, Lily remembers seeing Anna take her cross in her right hand, praying and speaking odd words, while she laid her left hand over Lily's abdomen. Lily described a vivid sensation of peace flooding through her whole body, starting with her belly. Within a short span of time, she called out for Anna to hand her the bedside basin, and she vomited severely. Even among the other remnants of her dinner and the bile, that piece of rancid meat was clearly visible. You might speculate that Lily would have vomited anyway—and perhaps that is so—but my sister tells me that she was terribly frightened that night, with a sense of imminent death. More than anything, the peace that Anna's touch brought her allowed her to see past her pain to hope."

"But how do you know for sure that Isabella caused that, that it wasn't just a terrible mistake in the kitchen?"

"She confessed the next day, laughing at the pain that Lily had experienced, claiming it was a fair return for her own emotional humiliation with Tom. The other girls were horrified, and the teasing stopped altogether after that. Isabella could be very funny at times—what wonderful stories she told—but she also had a mean streak a mile wide. I never trusted her, and though I forgive her for her hurtfulness, I would not have her in my inn, even now."

Molly continued to finger the cross. "We loved Anna, you know. It is because of her that Tom and I began to attend the old church in the village.

I cannot claim to have the strength of faith of my old friend, but because of her gentle witness, I am a believer today."

Silence settled over us, each of us thinking our own thoughts: of Anna, of God, of the journeys we had known. Ought I to tell her my suspicions that Anna was not dead? Should I share my own experiences with the cross? I sensed her to be trustworthy, someone with whom I would wish to be a friend, were I to dwell in this town. But my old fears stopped me; to tell of my visions and experiences was to make myself too vulnerable, to show myself too different. I held my tongue.

As we sat companionably in the sunlight, I recognized how strongly my fatigue still held me, even after such rich hospitality. I decided to linger one more night and asked Molly if I might stay in the garret room again. She smiled, "Yes, I would be glad for you to stay. You seem so weary through the eyes, as though something weighs upon you. Take your rest with us. And late tonight, after dinner chores, perhaps you will pass a little time with Tom and me, with Lily Mae and Jimmy, our three-year-old handful and joy."

I felt deep surprise. "You have a son? I haven't heard a thing from him during my time here."

"He is beautiful and healthy, and yet he is deaf. He does not shout and yell like other boys his age unless he is in great pain."

"But who cares for him, when you and Tom and Lily Mae are so busy with the inn?"

"We have a special nanny, who has worked with other deaf children. In the mornings and afternoons, when there is so much to be done, she cares for him."

That afternoon, I walked through town, admiring items in the fancy shop windows and treating myself to tea in a modest shop not far from the Green Boar. I felt a lovely freedom having money for this luxury, knowing that I had a warm place to sleep that night, and anticipating fellowship with Molly and her family. Thank you, Lord, I prayed, as I sipped my tea and looked out on a golden afternoon.

That evening, after all the supper items had been cleared away, Molly and Tom invited me to their private chambers. Modest and comfortable, warm and welcoming, the furnishings reminded me of Molly herself. Tom was fairly quiet at first, letting Molly and Lily Mae entertain me. Jimmy sat on Molly's lap, his head nodding with fatigue. Before long, Molly said that she needed to put Jimmy to bed, and Lily Mae jumped up to help.

"Remember his horse, Mama. He never sleeps without his horse." And she hurried to a toy basket in the corner to pull out a beautiful carving of a stallion. As she moved past me, she held up the sculpture for me to see. "Tempest!" I cried aloud without thinking, and Lily Mae nearly dropped the beautiful toy in her surprise. "Do you know everything?" she asked with wide eyes.

Tom also had turned astonished eyes my way. "Did you know my friend, Andrew?" he inquired. I did not answer; instead I asked if they would excuse me for some minutes. Returning to the garret room, I fetched the chess set and returned to my hosts' apartments. I handed the beautiful box to Tom, who gasped in amazement. "Where did you get this?" Again I did not answer. I watched him open the box, knowing that he had seen it before, that he knew what treasures lay within.

Lily Mae returned from the side room where Molly was putting Jimmy to bed. "What is it, Papa?" She sensed the charged atmosphere in the room, the heightened energy of expectation. One by one, with what I read as gentleness and tenderness, Tom placed the chess pieces on the table in their traditional configuration. At once in my mind's eye I saw back in time to a night like this one, in which Andrew and Tom had drawn the table up before the fire and competed long into the night with the marvelous, sculptured figures. An easy grace and camaraderie flowed between the two men, a warmth of deep respect.

"Andrew was special to you," I observed, not betraying what I had seen.

"Yes," he replied, fingering one of the knights. "And yet I knew so little of his story. Every now and then, he would stop by the inn for a night in the garret room, and we would play chess late into the night with his work in progress. This is the first time I have seen it finished. Many of the pawns were very rough for a while, and only three had tails when last we played. Sometimes many months would pass before I saw him again, and though I would press for information, even ask if I might visit him now and again, he never revealed where he lived. I sensed that his needs were great, yet he was a proud and quiet man. It was not for me to push too hard.

"I did know that he loved animals, especially horses. He carved the horse that is now Jimmy's treasure many winters ago. I sensed that in truth he did not wish to part with it, yet he presented it to our family with love and gratitude, brooking no refusal. That was the last time we saw him. I've always wondered what became of him."

Once again I was torn. Dare I tell Tom that his lost friend had lived only a few days' journey away? What good would that do? I did not want to describe what I had found in the field nor share what my visions had shown. I feared that this welcoming family would turn on me, as so many other kind people had done when they learned of my gifts. What should I say? How could I explain my possession of Andrew's chess set, my knowledge of his horses?

Tom continued to look at me with an intense, questioning gaze. I remembered James Mason's cross and sought refuge in a stretching of the truth. "Andrew and I had a mutual friend, a man named James Mason. Did you know him?" Tom shook his head. "I spent the winter with James' widow, Susannah. She presented me with gifts before I left." I thought of the dagger upstairs, safely hidden away in a fold of cloth. I let Tom draw his own conclusions from my statements. I did not say that Susannah had given me the chess set nor that James had possessed it before her, but I also knew that Tom would likely think so. He nodded and spoke again.

"So he is dead then. I know he would not have parted with his chess set in life; he loved the game, but more importantly, he had chiseled into these pieces all the people and places, animals and truths he loved most. I had hoped that perhaps in his later days he had returned to Nybron and stayed there with a relative or friend."

"Nybron?" I tried to keep the stark curiosity out of my voice, but the word quivered on the air all the same. Just then Molly returned to the room, and the distraction kept Tom from noticing my tone.

"Nybron is a lengthy journey southward from here. One of the other innkeeper's wives grew up there, but she never talks about it. Sometimes Andrew would hold the white queen in the embers of an evening, share a fragment of a memory before he remembered himself, and then grow quiet and sad before he made his way up to the garret room."

"Do you remember anything he said about Nybron or about Betsy?" I queried.

Molly looked up from her mending. "Katherine was also from Nybron, I think," she murmured, but let us go on with our conversation.

"It has been so long ago . . . I am sure that Andrew was born in Nybron. He went back once just after I met him, for the funeral of his parents; both died of the same illness only days apart, and it devastated him. Come to think of it, I suppose he began work on the chess set just shortly after that.

"One night, after beating me soundly twice at the game, Andrew was more garrulous than usual. He described the area around Nybron, its beachside cliffs, its praying oaks, its beautiful valley. He painted such a stunning picture, I asked him why he had not stayed. He looked me right in the eye and answered, 'When Betsy died, part of me died also. I couldn't stay where everything reminded me of what I had lost.' It took the joy right out of him, and I was sorry that I had asked."

"Did he ever explain about the praying oaks?"

"Oh, you don't know about the praying oaks! I thought everyone around here knew of them." He smiled and turned to his wife. "Tell Brie about the praying oaks. I have one more chore to do before bed." He rose and then looked down at the chess pieces, still in stately rows on the table. "Thank you for showing these to me. It brings back so many memories of a man I greatly respected." His voice broke a bit as he went on. "I am a better man because of him, though it would be hard to explain just how that is so." And he left us.

Molly turned to me with a soft smile. "Tom loved Andrew like a second father. They didn't talk much, but their camaraderie was rich. I always wished that Andrew would stay longer, that he would let us extend hospitality to him, but each time he insisted on paying and could not tell us when he would next visit. I think he had experienced such painful loss early in life, he only risked closeness with animals, not people, after that.

"But you asked about the praying oaks. The town of Nybron is nestled in a beautiful valley, protected from the sea by cliffs and from the severity of winter by the nearby mountains that draw off the snow and rain. Yet once in a long while a storm will come through the valley and linger; the locals are superstitious about it, and say it is a curse of a long-dead stranger who sought shelter in Nybron and was refused. They believe the storms only return when an act of significant inhospitality or cruelty transpires in the town, so they are renowned for their welcome and grace to strangers."

"What does this have to do with the trees?" I pressed.

"Two particularly severe storms have come through in the last century. Each time, the massive and beautiful oaks that decorate the valley suffered the most. In the first storm, three oaks all in a row lost their main trunks. Yet the villagers nursed the trees, hoping that with loving care and protection they would not die. Their husbandry paid off, though the trees maintain an odd shape, like praying hands lifted around an empty central space—where the trunk would have been. Those are the praying oaks.

The second storm ravaged a different stand of oak trees, pulling up all but two by their roots. Those two grew very near to one another, with intertwining branches, and somehow their combined strength resisted the storm, though now they lean even more markedly one into the other. Those oaks are known as the Old Lovers. I'd like to see them one day."

Lily Mae had been silent through the whole long exchange about Andrew, Nybron, and the trees. But now she spoke up, trying hard to hide her yawn. "I'm going to see those trees, Mama. I'm going to meet my husband there!" Molly laughed. "I don't know how the legend started," she mused aloud, "But many young women think that a visit to the Old Lovers will reveal to you your future spouse. I can't really mock them; I followed the words of an old fortuneteller to the sign of the Green Boar, and the rest is history!" I nodded, and she looked on me with surprise. "You knew of that, too?"

"Anna recorded a good deal in her letters to her mother."

At that, Molly rose and began herding Lily Mae toward the bedroom. "It's been lovely to spend time with you. May you sleep well."

I gathered Andrew's chess pieces back into the wooden box and then carefully set it on the mantelpiece next to Tom's glasses. It belonged here.

12

That night, toward dawn, the distinctive trees of Nybron found their way into my dreams. A young woman raced through wet grass, her eyes wild and her breathing labored, as though her life depended upon it. Overhead arched the praying trees, as though supplicating the Lord on her behalf for protection. I could not see what pursued her, nor could I distinguish the woman's face. Was it Anna? She ran on, blindly rushing, carrying nothing, not even taking time to look back over her shoulder. Suddenly a strange yet graceful shape rose ahead of her: the two trees entwined, reaching heavenward together. As she passed the tree, a man who had remained hidden behind the Old Lovers reached out and grabbed her. Was he friend or foe? Was he saving her or sealing her fate? But then the dream shifted, and I saw only fog, with the sound of lapping water beneath. I strained my eyes to see through the mist and thought I saw a pearl shining not far from me. The fog parted for just a moment, and I realized it was the eye of my albatross, who winked at me before flying on.

In the morning, though refreshed by two days of rest and hospitality at the Green Boar, I awoke, troubled by my dream. Upon reflection, I felt certain the woman had been Anna, and that she had been in grave danger. More than ever, I was convinced that my journey led to Nybron, toward Katherine's sister and the praying oaks and perhaps even Anna.

After breakfast I told Molly that I planned to journey to Nybron and would welcome any suggestions for the best route. She smiled and replied, "Tom and I were hopeful that might be your plan, and we have a proposal for you. Lily Mae has been eager to visit her aunt, uncle, and cousin, and though we can spare her for a time, neither of us can leave the inn at this season. Lily Mae is a bright child, and she has been to her aunt's home many times. It lies a four-day's journey south of here, along the road to Nybron. It would be easier for her to show you than for us to explain it to you. How would you feel about taking her with you?"

I felt conflicting emotions. Lily Mae was a vibrant, light-filled spirit, and I would welcome her company in that sense. Yet as I imagined the dangers of the road, I quailed; I knew that my own life could sometimes be at risk as I journeyed, but did I also want to be responsible for a child? I spoke my fears aloud to Molly.

Her eyes gentled as she heard my concern. "I am glad that you care enough about Lily Mae to think of that. The stretch of road from here to Sitton remains one of the best maintained and safest in the region. The towns are interspersed at good distances to allow for overnight lodging—and we would give you money for those three nights—and the people along this route look out for one another. I would not have suggested that Lily Mae accompany you if I thought the risk were great."

And so it was agreed. Lily Mae was called down from the upper stories, where she had been industriously changing bed linens, and told the good news. The joy that filled her face shone like the sun's rays on water, dancing and pure. She and Molly went off to pack travel clothes, supplies, and a few items for her Aunt Lily and her cousin Molly Anna while I received some pointers about the route from Tom. He also reassured me that the way to Sitton, though busier than the roads I had taken to reach the Green Boar, would offer a welcome change from the dark curves and lonely stretches through which I had passed previously.

Lily Mae and I planned to leave after a small lunch of bread and cheese. Her parents embraced her warmly and hugged me as well, thanking me for my assistance and pressing a bag of coins into my hand. They knew the innkeepers along the way and were familiar with their fees; what little was left over would be for midday meals. Aware of the money from Allan hidden deep in my pack, I felt as rich as I had ever been with this additional boon. I asked if we might say a prayer to bless the journey ahead, and Lily Mae chirruped, "Circle prayer!" She could tell from my puzzled expression that I did not understand, so she explained, "That means that we hold hands in a circle and each person prays. Jimmy prays in his heart." And so we stood as she had described, with Jimmy standing between his mother and me. Molly prayed for joyous reunion for her sister and daughter. Tom's prayer for safety was short, yet behind it I discerned his deep love for Lily Mae.

Lily Mae offered energetic thanks for this break from her chores, bouncing up and down on her toes as she told Jesus how glad she was to go with me.

As my turn came, I prayed blessings and peace upon all those who lived and who lodged at the Green Boar, that it might be as restful and welcoming for them as it had been for me. I thanked the Lord for Andrew, for the friend he had been to Tom. And I invited Jesus and his angels to accompany us on the journey ahead. No matter how much reassurance her parents had given me, I felt a different weight on my shoulders with Lily Mae as companion. And then, before I had a chance to reconsider, I prayed for healing for Jimmy, aware of my hand in his mother's, resting just behind his head. Immediately after shouting a happy "Amen!" Lily Mae turned to me with a kind of wonder. "When you prayed for Jimmy, your hand in mine became very hot! It was good of you to pray for him." She smiled and went to say goodbye to her little brother. She approached him from behind, with his head still turned away, and called out, "Goodbye, Jimmy!" He turned his head abruptly in her direction. Both Molly and Tom looked on in shock. "He's never done that before!" "Did he hear her?" Lily Mae was oblivious, hugging her brother close and laughing. As she pulled away, we looked closely at Jimmy's face; his eyes, as big as saucers, looked first from the still-laughing Lily Mae to each of his parents. I knew that he had begun to hear, though how much I did not know.

Molly held Jimmy tight to her. Both parents gazed at me with a combination of wonder and uncertainty. After several false starts in speech, Molly managed, "Have you prayed for healing for others and seen results?"

"Yes."

"Perhaps that cross has power after all. I always thought it was Anna herself."

I replied, "I don't think the healing comes from the cross or Anna or me. All healing comes from God. And where two or more believers agree on something, the power of the prayer is strengthened. This healing is more likely to have come from the longing you and Tom share, definitely not from anything I have done." I could see in Tom's eyes a glimmer of distrust, a shade of worry that he had entrusted his daughter to me for the next four days. But still he smiled and took my hand. "Whatever has been the cause, you have been the catalyst. May God protect this gift in you and you who bear it." He enfolded his daughter in one last bear hug, and we made our way out to the road.

Lily Mae's cloak was green and a bit too long for her, but I was grateful it would keep her warm on chilly mornings and evenings. Her pack was stuffed full, yet it was clear she welcomed what it represented, for she slung it on her back without complaint. Molly had invited me to carry a few items meant for Lily and her family, which I was glad to do. Lily Mae waved to her family as we walked away down the road, tiring her hand out until we reached the turning of the road. Then she blew a kiss to her mom, who still stood with Jimmy at her side, and turned to reach for my hand.

With her family out of view, her voice shook a little. "This is my first time away from my whole family. Mom and I traveled alone once, and Dad and I once. Aunt Lily brought me back one time from Sitton. This feels different. I'm glad that I'm with you." And she blessed me with one of her sunshine-bright smiles.

"I'm glad that you're with me too, Lily Mae. I need a good guide." I saw a look of pride behind her eyes, and we walked on in companionable silence for a good long time.

Toward evening, we came upon a snug little town, with homes and businesses nestled together just beyond the curve of a river. Lily Mae pointed out the inn without difficulty, and the innkeeper's greeting confirmed that he knew and enjoyed little Lily Mae. He offered her a sweet treat to tide her over until dinner and assigned us a comfortable room, charging less than he might have for a second-floor corner with a view of the river. It was as though my way had been charmed since my time at Andrew's home. Yes, I had slogged through rain in those early days, but now I felt a deep sense of peace and protection. "Thank you, Lord," I whispered quietly, as Lily Mae and I settled our packs. "Lead me each step."

That night after dinner, a number of guests gathered by the fireside downstairs, bringing their homemade instruments and joyful voices. They sang a number of songs I did not know, but then a shiver went through me as I heard again the haunting strains of the song I first encountered at Susannah's home:

> *So she runs, her feet fleet, and wind-winged by grace,*
> *So she runs, with the Lord's light abright on her face,*
> *So she runs, but in running one must have a goal . . .*
> *Does she see that while running, she cannot be whole?*
> *Come home, gifted sister, come home.*
> *Come home, grieving sister, come home.*
> *Come home to your Father's grace; come home, find your rightful place.*
> *Come home, wind-borne sister, come home.*

The tears ran in streams down my face. Lily Mae, sitting at my side, had known some of the words and sung along. As she looked my way, her eyebrows lifted in surprise and concern. "Are you hurt, Brie?"

"I'm all right, Lily Mae. Sometimes a song sings to your heart and calls it to speak. My heart speaks through tears."

With the ready acceptance so common in children, she nodded and smiled. "My mama sings me a song that makes my heart speak sometimes." And she laid her head on my shoulder, her face a sweet combination of winsomeness and trust. In my mind's eye I saw my own sister, Anna, who had leaned against me so many times, both in health and in illness. By moments Lily Mae's eagerness and her joy would recall my lost sister to mind. Despite my awareness of responsibility, I knew it would be hard to leave Lily Mae behind with her aunt. It was best not to think of that now. I let myself be lost in the voices, the crackling of the fire, and the warmth of the young head burrowed against me. The song called me to come home. For a moment, this fireside circle whispered of home; in my spirit I crawled into my Abba's lap in thanksgiving, surrender, and deep rest. Home. How I have longed for home.

13

The next few days mirrored our first: a lengthy but uneventful day of journeying, followed by a gracious welcome and safe haven at day's end. Lily Mae kept me entertained with stories of her little brother and funny guests who had stayed in the inn. Mostly I focused on her face, its animation and delight, its intelligence and warmth. But then a new story caught my attention and held it.

"One night I came and sat by the fire with a man who said he had been in a shipwreck! His name was Paul; I remember because Daddy teased him over dinner about the man in the Bible who was in a shipwreck too. But this Paul didn't laugh; he was very somber, and his face had lots of lines and pain in it. He told us that he had thought that they would die out in the ocean, he and two of his shipmates and two women who had been on the ship. They had rowed and rowed, not seeing land; the storm had made them lose their way. And then an al-ba-tross (that's a big, beautiful bird, Paul said) flew overhead, and Paul decided that he would follow it. The other men mocked him; they said that those birds hardly ever come to land but spend their days journeying on and on over water. They must be lonely creatures, don't you think, Brie? Anyway, Paul decided that he would row after the bird, and the other men were too tired to fight him. And you know what?! The bird saved them! He led them to land within just a few hours. I'd like to see an al-ba-tross one day."

Lily Mae was silent then, looking up at the sky, as though training her eyes to watch for the albatross who would one day cross her path. My heart was beating fast, wondering if Lily Mae might also hold a clue to this strange journey of mine.

"Did Paul say what happened after they reached land, Lily Mae?"

She shifted her gaze to my face. "He got quiet for a while after he talked about coming to shore. But later he said something else strange. Maybe he didn't think I was listening, since I had my eyes closed, but he half-said to himself, 'Who would have thought that getting to land would be only half the battle?' 'Where did you land?' Daddy asked him. 'The cliffs of Nybron. Trying to get up and over those cliffs after several days with little water and only stale bread proved equally daunting as the open sea.' He told how his two shipmates left him and the two women, stealing the last of their provisions in the night. I couldn't imagine it, Brie: no food, no shelter, no map, out beyond the cliffs! I had a nightmare that night, but Mommy held me after I cried out in fear."

"Did Paul share any more about it? Did he say if all three of them made it to Nybron?"

Lily Mae shook her head. "About that time, one of the other guests got up to go to bed, and Paul left too. He only stayed the one night, and in the morning, he was very quiet at breakfast. I do remember that right before he left, he looked at me and said, 'May all your journeys lead you home, little one. Trust the birds; they know the way. Humans may betray you, but not the birds of the air or the birds of the sea. Follow the path of wings.' I thought that was so pretty, like a poem." Lily Mae grew very quiet. "Most of the time, I don't think much about our guests after they leave, but I worried about Paul. Isn't that funny?"

"It sounds like Paul gave you a kind gift with his words; it makes sense that you thought of him afterward. You said his face held pain; is that why you worried?"

"I'm not sure. When he said that to me, I remember thinking that Paul did not have a home or else could not find it. He reminded me of a stray dog that came through our town once, wandering and heavy with sadness. I was so glad when our neighbor took him in, and yet . . . his eyes never showed peace like other dogs' eyes. Paul's eyes were like that, Brie."

Lily Mae's insight nearly took my breath away. I doubted that she had received any formal schooling, and yet her speech and her observations occasionally showed a maturity and wisdom that few adults possessed. We walked on in the spring sunshine, in silence and remembrance.

Late that afternoon we came to the outskirts of Sitton. Lily Mae pointed out landmarks, the home of the wealthiest man in town (also the grumpiest!, reported Lily Mae) and the church where she attended worship when she stayed with her aunt. Soon I could hardly keep up with her as she hurried down the narrow but pleasant streets, rushing toward her aunt's home. Her energy after four days' walk astonished me, and I envied her strength.

She stopped in front of a tall building, with an office on the first floor and two stories above. "Uncle Henry has been a lawyer a long time. He was in his office the day that my aunt came through town. He admits that he saw her though the window and decided then and there to make her his wife. He actually left one of his clients sitting in front of his desk and ran out the door to meet her! Aunt Lily remembers how he ran up to her, took off his hat, bowed, and smiled. So gentlemanly! The other girls giggled, because they could all see that he was older than Lily. She held out her hand, and he kissed it!"

I was curious to hear the rest of the story, but at that moment, the door opened, and I had the pleasure of meeting Henry himself. He had the kindest eyes I had ever seen, green with a bit of dancing mischief tucked behind the steady gaze. His whole face filled with joy when he saw Lily Mae, and he picked her up and swung her around in the road just beyond the threshold. She laughed and teased him, "Uncle, you should have let me put down my pack first!" For surely enough, a few items had escaped and were lying in a circle around the two. His laugh in response was hearty and glad.

"I couldn't wait, Lily Mae. You always do my heart good!"

At that moment, Lily herself came to the door. She had the same grace of movement as Molly, though her hair was dark, not red. Her eyes were both playful and peaceful, a combination I rarely saw. I wondered if Henry had brought that gift to her.

She hurried to embrace her namesake in a bear hug and then turned to me with open curiosity and interest as Lily Mae stated proudly, "This is Brie!"

"Thank you for bringing Lily Mae to us. Are you a friend of Molly's?"

"Yes, a new friend. But I am also an old friend of Susannah, Anna's mother."

"Anna? What do you know of Anna?" Lily's face grew focused and eager at the mention of her friend's name. However, I didn't have time to reply, for Molly Anna came rushing out to greet her cousin. She was younger and slimmer than Lily Mae, yet with a quiet beauty that drew on the most striking features of each parent. Clearly the cousins were fast friends.

Henry, more practical in nature, smiled at his wife and daughter. "If they have come from the Green Boar, they have walked a long way in recent days. Let's give them the chance for a wash and a meal; perhaps then they will regain strength for the sharing of story." I smiled at him, thankful for his courtesy, and yet also eager to talk with Lily as I had with her sister.

Their home over the legal offices proved very comfortable and spacious. I could hardly conceal my wonder at the guest room they offered me; each furnishing held a rich beauty and grace that spoke of the workmanship and quality of its manufacture. Over dinner, Lily Mae caught them up on family news, though I noticed she did not mention what had happened with Jimmy during our prayer time. Lily did not have the culinary gifts of her sister, but her simple offerings were nourishing and welcome.

After Molly Anna cleared the plates away, Henry rose and explained that he had more work yet to do downstairs. He kissed his wife and left us to talk. Lily Mae and Molly Anna quickly disappeared up to the top floor for their own time of sharing.

Lily told me frankly, "I've been watching you all through dinner. Like others before you, I see that you have fallen in love with my niece. Lily Mae is a joy! Yet you also showed kindness to my quieter daughter and to my earnest husband; thank you. It's strange; you remind me of Anna in some ways. Your spirit is attentive and open; your eyes are watching for ways to offer grace. And yet, like her, I have the sense that you have not yet found where you belong."

I felt goose bumps on my arms. A snatch of "Wind-Borne Sister" whispered through my mind, and I did not reply.

"Forgive me. My sister says that one of my gifts *and* one of my faults is my blunt speaking. I like you. I want to know you, and I can tell that you have stories for me. Let's go sit in a more comfortable spot, and then I'll let you talk." She giggled, "I always used to hide a bit in my sister's shadow. But after these years with Henry, I've grown to be quite the chatty one!" Smiling warmly, she rose and led me into a lovely parlor, also furnished well, with graceful lines and gentle colors. I sank into a remarkably comfortable chair and began.

For some reason, my words flowed more freely and readily with Lily than they had with Molly. Perhaps it was the sense of privacy in this space; perhaps more comfort came in the second telling. Yet I sensed that a deeper reason came from an affinity I felt with this warm-hearted, gracious woman who had welcomed me so eagerly, though she hardly knew my name. I shared with her about my winter with Susannah, the contents of Anna's letters, my recent stay at the Green Boar, and all the rich connections that had come to me during those days. I even risked telling Lily my dreams and visions as well, of my sense of being led to Nybron, my hope that Anna might yet live.

At one point I excused myself and came back with my treasures: the pearl from the albatross, the pearl from Andrew's field, Andrew's cross, and finally Anna's. Lily gazed on them in wonder. With her husband's wealth, she possessed the privilege to assess and own beautiful things, yet she handled these objects with deep appreciation, even delight. After touching each item lovingly, one by one, she sat with Anna's cross in her hands, much as Molly had done. Her eyes traveled to my face, and her intensity startled me. "I am convinced that these items have come to you for a reason. You have the same gift of healing, don't you?"

I wanted to look down, but found that her directness prevented any dissembling on my own part. I nodded.

"And it has set you apart and brought you challenges, as it did for her." Again I nodded in silence.

"If she is still alive, I am confident that you will find her. I hope along the way you will also find your peace."

My tears in response startled me. Suddenly I felt a kinship with the sailor Paul, with the stray dog that Lily Mae had described. I could not say that I had been unhappy during my journey; I felt deep gratitude for the friends I had encountered and for the unexpected bounty of resources. But I was not at peace. I felt driven toward Nybron; yet I also felt driven forward in a different and deeper way by my own nameless longings, by my sense of being an outsider who sought a lasting haven.

Lily looked at me searchingly, waiting with eyes that spoke grace and trustworthiness. Without stopping to consider any further, I told her about the incident in Lanford with Michael on market day, how that sweet little boy had described the "sunshine" of my touch on his wound. Feeling a strong sense of relief as I shared my story, I also described his mother's eyes, that look of deep gratitude threaded through with fear and distrust. After I finished, we sat companionably together in silence, each focused inward.

Finally Lily spoke, "I felt that sunshine from Anna's hands once. What a blessing! I am convinced that she saved my life. Did Molly tell you?" I nodded. "I also saw on a few occasions the look that you are describing: people fear what they do not understand, even if it has brought them bounty or unlooked-for hope. I am sorry that your journey will necessarily be a lonely one at times."

Then Lily took my hand. "Please know that you will always be welcome in our home, Brie. We are blessed with resources, and we love to have guests. I recognize that you are seeking for something different than a guest room. However, I hope that you and I may be friends for long years." Her smile lit up her face, and a flood of warmth passed over me. Susannah and Lily Mae had both extended trusting hands to me, and Rachel, Bronwyn, and Molly had shown kindness. But Lily was the first one near my age to seek to call me friend. The smile I returned in kind spread so wide and lasted so long that my face muscles ached when we parted.

I stayed with the Bartons for nearly a week. I lingered both for the gift of friendship shown to me by all the members of that family and because of a lingering sense of a missing piece that needed to fall into place before I would be ready to make the longer trek to Nybron. One evening mid-week, Henry set aside his habit of late work hours and invited all of us into his study. On a wide, low table, he had spread a beautiful and detailed map, richly decorated in calligraphy and colorful markings. I had only seen a map one other time, and it had been frayed and grubby in the hands of a traveler who stopped by our farm years ago. This map offered both welcome pleasure for the eyes and a wealth of information for which I hungered.

Henry pointed to Sitton, smiling at the girls as he explained, "This blue dot represents all of us here in town." His slender finger slid gracefully back along the path that Lily Mae and I had journeyed: "And here is Canton, the green dot." "Green for the Green Boar!" Lily Mae exclaimed. My eyes searched and searched for Nybron, and my heart sank to see how far south it lay from Sitton, with few towns along the way to offer safe haven for the night.

Henry had learned of my desire to journey to Nybron, and though he understood my sense of urgency and saw it mirrored in his wife's eyes, he had tried on several occasions to discourage me. Like Lily, he had assured me of a welcome in their home, even if I were to choose to stay for many months. He worried that the road south would be too dangerous, too long, even in the more gentle summer months. I suspected that he had brought out the map not as a guide for my plans but as a deterrent to my hopes.

Glancing at my face, he intoned, "And these are the cliffs of Nybron." All along the southern reaches of the map, I saw the jagged coastline, the contour lines revealing stark geography and rugged journeying for those who came by that path. "Though the road south to Nybron is a worrisome one, to go by sea is far more treacherous, both for the currents and the cliffs, once one lands. I met a man once who had been shipwrecked in the southern waters; he claimed an albatross had led him and his few compatriots to land and initial safety."

"Paul!" Lily Mae shouted. "Did you know Paul, too, Uncle Henry?" He turned toward her in surprise. "Yes, I believe that was his name. I had been taking a walk in town to clear my head after a particularly difficult client, and I came upon him sitting on one of the park benches, staring into space. For some reason, he took a shine to me, and he told me his story. It felt so fanciful in places that my logical brain wanted to dismiss him as a spinner of yarns, but something about his eyes told me that he had indeed lived through such misadventures."

"What happened after the other two sailors left them, Uncle Henry? What happened to Paul and Anna and Isabella??" At Lily Mae's words, Henry looked in shock and surprise at his wife. "Were your friends the women with whom Paul traveled?" His face paled. "The old sailor had not mentioned any names; I had no idea that you had known them. Paul related that after the first rush of relief to find themselves on shore and a number of hours of prostrated sleep on the beach, the five felt fortunate to find a spring of water nearby. The sailors had canteens with them; after washing and slaking their tremendous thirst, they filled their containers and set off along the one narrow trail. It proved dreadfully steep, and all the journeyers had cuts and bruises by the time they came to a flat area after nightfall that seemed the best place to rest.

"The next morning, Paul awoke just after dawn with a deep sense of foreboding. He found his sailing buddies had left him with the women, stealing their water and the last of the moldy hardtack that had sustained them thus far. He admitted to me that he wept in shock and anger, as well as honest fear that he could not provide alone for these two women whom he hardly knew. He felt briefly tempted to rush after the men, but his sense of honor kept him rooted to the spot. He let the women sleep a bit longer and spent that time searching his brain for a plan, always coming up empty.

"When the women awoke, he told them in plain terms what had happened. I do remember that he related that one woman burst into tears, as he had done, yet the other carried a deep calmness and asked if the others would like to join her in prayer. Paul told me he never had much to do with the church, but that something in the woman's demeanor and peace of spirit led him to agree. He described that the three of them held hands as they prayed, and that at one point, he felt a rush of warmth come through the hand of the praying woman. Suddenly he experienced a sense of peace; he didn't know why, but he felt a bit cheered, even encouraged.

"After the prayer, the three explored the clearing nearby. It was mostly flat, stark rock, with no water source. But off to one side, partially hidden by boulders, they found two bushes covered with edible berries, as well as a small burlap sack that had fallen down and behind some brush. They ate their fill and then stuffed the sack with all that they could pick. In their eagerness to gather all the food they could—not knowing if they would come upon any other resource for days—they pushed around to the back of the bushes and discovered to their surprise that stone steps had been carved out of the face of the rock in that place. After his first cowardly instinct to join them, Paul had felt worried about taking the path after the deserters, not knowing if at some point they would set upon them with ill intent toward the women. These steps seemed to offer a welcome alternative, both a gentler ascent than the steep path and, hopefully, a route away from danger.

"And so the three climbed and climbed and climbed. The steps wound behind and among sheer rock faces and tumbled boulders. They saw no wildlife and found no water. Thankfully, the berries were moist and fresh still, and they ate as they had need. Paul recalls turning his head downward only once and experiencing a dreadful vertigo that nearly knocked him off the steps. He gently advised the women to keep looking ahead, only ahead, and that is what they did. By nightfall no place to rest or sleep had materialized, and the three decided to keep climbing, afraid that in their sleep they might tumble back down the steps through the darkness to severe injury or death. Their pace slowed, yet they kept journeying. Paul shared with me that sometimes his dreams are yet haunted by those steps, by a sense of endless repetition in the black of night. It was the woman who prayed who began to sing when their spirits had sagged most deeply. Sitting there on the park bench, the old sailor shared it with me in a strong yet burred baritone:

"Father mine, my way winds long,
Father mine, the risk grows grave;
Father mine, my fear flows strong,
Yet you shall shield and save.
Jesus mine, I stumble, fall,
Jesus mine, my heart's aghast;
Jesus mine, I praise, I call—

For you will hold me fast.
Spirit mine, you promise peace,
Joy amidst our pain-laced view;
Spirit mine, your grace increase.
You triumph, Triune, true!"

Henry's voice filled the room, lovely and haunting. I had not expected such a gift in an introverted, serious lawyer. About halfway through, Lily began to join him, adding a warm alto harmony to the lay. He raised his eyebrows but kept singing. I closed my eyes and saw vividly the night-clad climb of Paul, Isabella, and Anna: the stark rock, the aching muscles, the fearful hearts—and yet rising out of it, Anna's faith, Anna's song.

When Henry and Lily reached the end, they circled back to the beginning, and the girls and I joined in, a chorus of hope in this secure home, so different from the treacherous climb the others had known. As the last strain faded away, Henry turned to Lily, "Had you heard me sing that before?" "Never, love; Anna taught it to us one night at the fireside, sharing that it had been her father's favorite hymn. I hadn't thought of it for years. Now I am certain that Anna was indeed one of those women with Paul. Did he share any more with you?"

"It was growing late in the afternoon, and I had work to do. Yet I felt I could not leave without learning more. After singing, the old sailor had lapsed into silence, so I prompted him, 'Did that song keep you going until you found safety?' He grimaced and grunted, 'Of a sort . . . there is no safety in Nybron, as I know it. We began to sing the song together, climbing in a weary rhythm. Just as the first rays of dawn began to light our way, the path opened upon a grassy meadow and a small brook. All three of us laughed and cried in relief. We fell down beside the river and drank and drank. The women wanted to sleep then, but I felt this gnawing in my gut. Something wasn't right. We had no receptacles within which to carry any water, but the women ripped strips off their already ragged skirt hems and soaked them liberally. The singer offered me one as well, and we journeyed on along a northeastern trail.

"'I don't know to this day what made me nervous about that place. The one woman was angry, complaining that we might have had a wonderful sleep and refreshing afternoon in the glade. The other was quiet, watchful; she confided in me later in the day that she also had had a premonition that, aside from the water, only evil would come to us in that space. A winding path up from the cliffs had approached the glade from the south as well, and I have sometimes wondered if my shipmates lingered there and came to their doom—for they were never found.

"'We walked until our feet were full of blisters and bruises. Our berry supply was waning, with mostly crushed fruit clinging to the sides of the sack. Every time I see a berry, even now, I give thanks. Without them, I do not know that we could have climbed those steps without falling. The northeastern trail proved solid, even soothing in its way; small trees began to appear, and when we saw our first bird, the singer clapped her hands. I know why she did it; somehow the presence of other life seemed a promise of hope, of food, of safety. Near dusk, we found a tumble-down shack of sorts, leaning precariously against a cluster of elm trees. We had no energy left to give. Our feet throbbed; our bellies longed for something more than fruit. But sleep won, and we did not awaken till mid-morning the next day, sore but relieved, thinking that we had come through the worst and would soon meet with human kindness. We were wrong.'"

Henry paused and looked down at the children's enrapt faces, assessing, uncertain. His gaze led fear to spring up in me; what had befallen the journeyers? I couldn't tell if I felt more relieved or pained when Henry returned his attention to the map. He gestured toward a particularly steep and wild section of the Nybron cliffs: "I imagine that they were caught in this section of the landscape. Even the mapmakers admit that their illustrations here are estimates, not surveyed, not plotted out. Folks from Nybron know not to journey there, and the few bold young men from other places who enter on a dare do not return."

"But Paul did! Paul made it out, and I bet that Anna and Isabella did too!" Lily Mae's certainty shone like a beacon. "Paul was smart, and Anna had such deep faith, and Isabella was lucky to be with them. What happened next, Uncle Henry?" Lily Mae clearly experienced the tale like a storybook, certain to have a happy ending. Lily and I exchanged glances. If Anna and Isabella had survived along with Paul, why had no one heard from them? And what of the woman I had seen, running for her life under the praying oaks? Had that been Anna? Was Paul the one who had saved her? And what of Isabella?

Henry shook his head. "That's enough for tonight, girls. It's time for bed. I promise that I will tell you more tomorrow night." Lily Mae and Molly Anna sighed, but they did not complain. Their trust held true; they knew he would keep his promise. Yet I wondered if he would take the twenty-four hours to make up a happy ending that Paul had never told.

14

U p until that day, my time with the Bartons had flown by; I felt encircled with love, with welcome. Lily would sometimes take me around town as she did her shopping and introduce me as a friend. My heart glowed whenever she used that word; it felt so beautiful and foreign, like a piece of ivory I had once seen on a rich woman's necklace.

But on that day, time seemed mired in dread for me. I had seen the look on Henry's face, a guarded one of deep concern. Yet I also knew he was intrinsically an honest man, one who would rather tell hard truths, even to his daughter, than gloss over them, knowing that truth would serve her better in the long run.

That night we gathered once more in Henry's study. Instead of the map, he had the family Bible open on the table. Before saying anything about the journeyers in Nybron, he read aloud from Psalm 27:

"The LORD is my light and my salvation—whom shall I fear?
The LORD is the stronghold of my life—of whom shall I be afraid?"

I sensed the stillness in the room, broken only by the crackling fire. The girls also seemed aware that this night was different, not a time for eager questions, such as Lily Mae had brought the evening before. Henry sat down next to his wife and took her hand in his as he stared off into memory.

"Paul grew very quiet once again. I thought perhaps he would say no more, and I hadn't the heart to question him. After that, his narrative style changed to broken, disconnected bits, as though he couldn't bring himself to focus on what had happened. After awakening in the shack, renewed by sleep, yet muscle-weary and intensely hungry, the three continued on down the path. Aside from that one bird of the day before, they saw no animals or winged creatures. I remember clearly how Paul's face grew ashen as he said, 'Even the animals knew that to be a place of death.'

"From his snatches of story, I pieced together that the afternoon grew very difficult: no water, no food, no signs of habitation. The woman who must have been Isabella sat down hard on the road at one point, wishing for death to come. Anna rushed to her side, placing gentle hands upon her, one on her forehead, the other over her heart. Paul recalled seeing a sense of peace replace the defeat on Isabella's face, and she rose once more. Yet he also shared that it seemed the other woman took on the defeat somehow, that her interaction had cost her dearly.

"Dusk came too soon, still with nothing to eat or drink, still without a safe place to stop or sleep. Ahead of them they caught the sound of hoof-beats. Paul and Isabella wanted to hide, but Anna stood firm, emphasizing that without aid, they had nothing and were already in grave danger. They stood to the side of the path, uncertain how well they might be perceived in the half-darkness, and waited.

"The three men who found them proved to be a band of ruffians on the far side of the law. They laughed in Anna's face as she pleaded with them, in the name of God, to give them some water and bread. As they dismounted, Paul felt a deep instinct to run for his life, yet he knew he could not leave the women.

"The ruffians pulled out switchblades. Paul tried in vain to fight, but he was exhausted from all that they had endured. After two swift blows from the strongest of the men, he lay unconscious upon the path. When he awoke in daylight, aching and fearful, no sign remained of Anna or Isabella, the ruffians, or their horses, except for several piles of horse manure and a pool of blood that made his heart constrict with foreboding.

"Clearly he must have found water and food and a way out, because he lived to tell of it. Once he reached that point, he only shook his head over and over, repeating, 'I failed them. I failed them.' I remember setting a hand on his shoulder, wanting to comfort, and he raised sunken, careworn eyes to my own. 'Don't you see? That woman's faith got us up that cliff, but I wasn't strong enough to keep her from those blackguards.'"

Henry stopped. No one spoke for a while, and then Lily rose and re-read the passage from Psalms aloud.

"The LORD is my light and my salvation—whom shall I fear?
The LORD is the stronghold of my life—of whom shall I be afraid?"

I looked at Lily Mae. Tears had traced her face, and she snuggled up next to Molly Anna for comfort. Yet she perceived my eyes upon her and turned to look right at me. Without thinking, I stood up and began to walk toward her. With a broken, earnest voice she asserted, "No matter how bad it looks, I believe that Anna is all right. And Gabriela is going to find her; aren't you, Brie?"

She came to me and put her arms around me in a fervent, needy hug. I stroked her hair and answered, "I don't know, Lily Mae. I only know that I am supposed to go to Nybron. I may find answers there as to what happened to Anna and Isabella, or I may not. I do know that the Lord was with her, and that he will continue to journey with me. After all, he led me to all of you. I have never felt as blessed as I do at this moment, surrounded by this circle of love and trust."

Lily Mae would not be deterred, "I know that you will find her, and you'll bring her back to us."

Lily reached out for her namesake with gentle hands and spoke, "Oh, Lily Mae, you hold such hope in your heart. Cling to that as you go through your life. It will sustain you well. It will also mean disappointment and pain in certain seasons, yet it will sustain and uplift you in ways that bless you and others."

I looked at Henry at that moment. His eyes were shadowed and heavy with care. Somehow the telling of the story had aged him. He took a deep breath and forced a smile at his daughter, "Molly Anna, it's time for bed, sweet pea." After a round of hugs and kisses, the girls made their way out of the room, and Lily followed. I began to move in that direction as well, but Henry stopped me.

"Brie."

"Yes."

"I left part of the story out."

"I was afraid that you had."

"I want my little ones to know that darkness exists, so that they can be prepared. As a lawyer, I know too well the many shapes that darkness takes. Yet I also believe that certain things need not be said to the young before it becomes necessary.

"However, since you seem intent on this journey to Nybron, you need to know the risks more fully. Paul felt certain that both Isabella and Anna were raped that night. Certain articles of clothing, discarded and torn, spoke volumes. He worried that the pool of blood indicated that they had both been killed afterward, their bodies later hidden in some corner of that forsaken wilderness. That is why he did not hunt for them. He believed if the women had been alive, the ruffians would have killed him, so that he could not pursue them."

Henry's green eyes looked upon me with a depth of pain that astonished me. "My younger sister was raped long ago. She survived, but the memory of that violence colored all her days. When she was taken ill by fever two years later, she did not fight for life, but let go quickly. Still to this day, I feel that that man killed her, by taking her spirit of joy from her. I became a lawyer in her memory, determined to see justice done for other women, for her rapist was never found.

"Brie, even if Anna and Isabella live, they have been severely wounded by what took place that night. Are you prepared for that, as well as for the risk in which you place yourself by journeying alone to such a far city?"

At first I could not speak. I felt honored that Henry would trust me with the story of his pain and startled by his frankness. What he had just shared helped to explain both his determination and his tenderness; out of a broken heart, he had found his mission. I also wondered if it was why he had married at a later age, perhaps not trusting his own longings for a woman until they had been tempered by the years. It struck me that before me stood one of the few men whom I had met who was truly good, not without fault, and yet a man who had let pain transform and lead him toward strength and witness and even joy.

I reached to hug him, briefly but warmly. "I am so sorry for what happened to your sister, Henry. I am deeply grateful for your truth-telling and your warnings. But I feel that I must go. I'm not sure of all the reasons why, and when I stop to consider, fears and doubts rush in that would sway me from my course. Yet somehow, in the deepest places of my knowing, I feel called to make this journey. I know that you and your family will hold me in prayer, and that gives me courage for the way ahead."

"Brie, Lily and I are in a position to make your journey easier: maps, provisions, a better pack. Please let us help you."

"You have already helped me so much, and I would be glad of anything you feel would be of assistance for what lies ahead. It is remarkable to me that I have made it so far. Leaving my home many months ago, I had not imagined all that the journey would hold, but God has been merciful and protected me." As I made my way to bed that night, I heard again the sound of my oars against the waves—"Peace to you . . . peace to you . . .

peace to you . . . "—and wondered how much longer I could hope that peace to continue.

* * * * *

The next two days were full of preparations and conversations about the coming journey. Lily and Henry outfitted me generously and astutely for the rigors of the next leg of my journey. As I looked at all the items laid out before me the afternoon before I was to depart, I despaired of carrying it all. But at dinner that evening, they revealed their most generous surprise of all.

Just before mealtime, we heard hoofbeats at the door. Lily Mae and Molly Anna ran to greet the caller, with the rest of us gathering in the foyer moments later. A young man dismounted with the confident grace of one who has spent much of his life on horseback. Henry stepped forward with an outstretched hand, and the man embraced him with a bear hug in return. "Well, Henry, you're looking well."

"And you, Toby. How was your journey?"

"Better than usual. When the weather's good, the roads are dry, and we make good time, Windstar and I."

Lily Mae jumped up and down: "Toby! Windstar!" And she found herself picked up and swung around in a full circle, giggling with delight. Though Molly Anna hung back a bit, she also had her turn at a bit of flight. The girls were eager to care for the stallion, and with Toby's help, led him round back to the small stable. Henry came back inside and took Lily's hand.

"Is Toby joining us for dinner?" I inquired.

"Yes," Lily answered, "And he will also serve as your escort to Nybron." "What?!"

"Did you honestly think that you could carry all that we have gathered for you? Those are provisions for two people and a horse, not for one woman on foot. Toby is a trusted friend of ours from our church; he and his brothers farm together on some property far outside of town. When Henry learned that you were determined to make this journey, he immediately thought of Toby. He's the most skilled horseman we know; his horse is strong enough to carry two without trouble; and he also has a bit of a restless spirit. Giving him a chance to see more of the world may ease that longing."

"Or feed it," Henry muttered.

Lily smiled at him. "You don't understand that part of Toby, because you are a man with roots deep in one place. Toby and his horse are two of a kind, strong and ready for adventure."

I had listened to this exchange with growing apprehension. Traveling with a seven-year-old girl from her parents' home to her aunt's house meant one thing; journeying with an unmarried man for at least a ten-day journey meant another.

"But I . . ." I began.

"We know no one of greater integrity than Tobias Graham. He will treat you like the lady you are, no matter how primitive your surroundings may prove."

"But has he had only brothers?"

"He has a beloved mother and sister, who also work the farm. He will treat you as well or better than he would treat one of them. I'm sure of it."

"I still think . . ."

"Gabriela," Henry cut in. "The road that you are set on taking is not safe for a woman alone, even a woman on horseback. Without Toby with you, the chances of your reaching Nybron unscathed are slim to none. We were not willing to let you run such a risk, even though it is clear that the Lord has watched over you thus far. We invited Toby to spend a meal and an overnight here with us, so that you two could meet and converse a bit before your early-morning departure."

I heard the steel behind Henry's voice; he and Lily were adamant that I not travel alone.

I turned to face Lily and quizzed her, "What does he know?"

"He knows only that you are a friend of ours with business in Nybron. He knows that you walk with God. And Henry told him that you are beautiful and single."

I rolled my eyes and looked at Henry's face. The broad grin confirmed his wife's words.

"You assured me that he is a man of integrity!"

"He is. Even a man of integrity can hope, Brie."

I sighed. I wasn't sure that Toby had seen me as he rode in, preoccupied with his horse and the girls. Feeling sheepish but also museful, I went upstairs to primp before the meal.

As I looked in the mirror, I wondered what Toby would see in me. Did I want him to find me beautiful, as Henry had named me? No man had ever called me so before. Wouldn't it be better if he didn't find me attractive, if he saw me only as a charge and duty? I didn't know. Once he learned of my gifts, it wouldn't matter anyway, I told myself.

"But what do you think of Toby?" my secret heart asked me. I kept seeing in my mind's eye the way his face had lit up when Lily Mae reached for him, the mirrored delight in his posture and features as he swung her up and around. I also remembered the kindness and warmth of his greeting to Henry. Here was a man who cared deeply and openly for others; he was not prickly like Allan, not as formal as Henry. Yes, I liked him. I prayed that he would prove as trustworthy as his friends believed he would be.

Lily Mae came to fetch me for dinner. With a conspiratorial look, she sat down on my bed and invited me to sit beside her.

"What do you think of Toby, Brie?"

"He clearly loves you," I answered with a smile.

"I love him, too! He's one of my favorite people, and Windstar is the best horse. You're lucky that you get to travel with them."

"They won't be as good for company as you were, Lily Mae."

She blushed, though her eyes met mine with warmth and joy. "I was good company because you are good company." She took a deep breath. "I love you, too, and I'm going to miss you terribly." She reached to hug me and burst into tears.

My heart soared and ached at the same time. Somehow Lily Mae had touched the places left vacant and raw when my sister died. Leaving her would be different than leaving Susannah. Yet, if Henry spoke the truth, I would not want her anywhere near the dangers of the Nybron road.

"I love you, too, Lily Mae. I hope we'll always be friends."

"You are more than a friend, Brie. You're like the older sister I always wanted."

Through my tears, I sought to memorize her sweet, wren-like face. Lily Mae, child of my heart, how can I leave you behind?

* * * * *

I realized that I was making excuses for not coming downstairs, tidying my room, fussing with my hair, trying to clear my eyes of their honest tears. I felt grateful that I could attribute it to my grief over leaving Lily Mae, yet I recognized that my stalling grew as much from nervousness over talking with Toby as it did from managing my sadness.

Finally Lily Mae put her hands on her hips. "Brie, we are late for dinner; Uncle Henry hates it when we are late for dinner. Please come." She reached for my hand and led me down the stairs, smiling bravely through her own heartache.

Lily had outdone herself in setting the table, bringing out their best dishes and silver. In the candlelight, the dining room became even more beautiful, and I gazed at the beloved faces of my friends one by one: Henry, Lily, Molly Anna. Then I took a deep breath and glanced at Toby, seated on Henry's left. He smiled at me, a warm, open grin, and stood to pull out the chair beside him. As I came closer, he whispered in my ear, "I know that this must be hard for you. Believe me, I will do my best to earn your trust."

I turned my head to look him in the eye, and his face revealed earnestness of purpose, laced through with deep kindness. I realized in that moment that I could choose to relate to him from a place of assumed trust or a place of wariness and caution. My friends believed that he merited the former, and our journey would likely unfold better if I did not bring distrust along with me. As I sat, I prayed under my breath, *Please, Father, help me to trust this new companion that you have brought to my journey.*

The dinnertime conversation flowed with a vivid energy. Toby proved a gifted storyteller, with dancing hands and a playful spirit that made his tales live. The girls' faces shone with their admiration and enchantment. Lily glanced often between Toby and me, the only one at the table not really focused on the conversation. I sensed that she was weighing her decision thoughtfully, wondering if Toby and I would find a grace-filled camaraderie for the way ahead, worrying that even together tragedy might befall us on the road. I tried not to think about it; I knew that my journey lay southward and I had to continue.

After dinner, we gathered once more in Henry's study. He and Toby pored over maps, several of which he gave to Toby for the journey. I overheard the name Hollow Junction and saw Lily flinch. I raised a questioning eye to her, but she just shook her head and smiled, though the smile did not reach her eyes.

The girls were ushered to bed early, so that they might have energy to see us off for our early-morning departure. Lily went to help them, and Henry followed her out only a minute later, commenting, "You two need a chance to talk alone." Toby and I both followed him with our eyes, not looking at the other right away.

After an awkward silence, he invited me to sit down beside him at the table. Once more he pushed in my chair and then sat and cleared his throat.

"Do you prefer that I call you Brie or Gabriela?"

"Brie is fine, Toby."

"Gabriela is a beautiful name," he mused, almost as though to himself.

"Thank you. I like both my names; I've just come home to Brie somehow."

He smiled then, and a radiance entered his face that astonished me. "I like how you explain things," he answered. "It's like poetry."

I caught my breath. On the one hand, his evident pleasure and warm compliments fed a hunger in me I hadn't known that I held; on the other, keeping distance would be necessary for the journey ahead. I felt my brows furrow and puzzled over what to say.

Toby cocked his head to one side and considered my face. "You're worried that I like you too much," he remarked frankly.

"Yes."

"Wouldn't it be worse if I liked you too little?" he quipped, and we both laughed.

In the midst of the shared laughter, our eyes met, and in that moment I knew at a deep level that somehow it would be all right; it would not be easy, but it would be all right. He continued, "My task is to journey with you on the road to Nybron, to serve as your guide through some rough territory. I've been to Hollow Junction before, which lies about two-thirds of the way to Nybron; it's a vile place, and it will be best if we bypass it all together. Depending on what we encounter along the way, that may not be possible, but we'll see.

"Brie, I want you to know that Lily shared a few things with me. I understand that you feel that God has called you to Nybron and that you are looking for a woman named Anna, or at least for clarity about what happened to her. My brothers thought you were crazy; as for me, I think you possess a courageous heart and a gift for seeing what others do not." I looked at him, startled, thinking that Lily had told him about my gifts after all. But Toby went on, "You see that taking risks is worth it. You see that staying in one place may be faithfulness, but it may also be fear of change. You see that we grow through our journeys." He stopped abruptly, and I recognized that he had spoken out of his own longings, out of what Lily had named his "restless spirit."

"I'm sorry," he stammered, "I think that last bit was more about me." He bit his lip. "My brothers love working the farm; they don't see why I have this deep hankering to see the world, to go places I've never been. They especially don't appreciate why I would want to journey to a destination as dangerous as Nybron." He looked me in the eyes then.

"It is dangerous, Gabriela. Some people talk of Nybron as the City with Two Faces. On the one hand, the Nybronese have a reputation for marvelous hospitality, and rightly so. I've heard descriptions of their inns, their libraries, their city hall. No one throws a party for the newcomer like the folks in Nybron. But there is a sinister underbelly to the city, another personality almost. Too many times people have disappeared without a trace in Nybron and its surrounding lands.

"Henry told me not to tell you. He didn't think that scaring you would serve any purpose. But I see your strength, and I sense that you have a deep listening spirit that will serve you well, no matter what we encounter. Trust your instincts, Brie. If you feel that someone or something is not what it seems, you will be right. Keep attuned to what God might be telling you as we go forward.

"And I need to say one more thing. I didn't want to tell you, but I prayed about it and see now that I must. I had a very vivid dream last night, and I believe that the Lord sent it as a warning. At one point on this journey, you and I will be separated, Brie. No matter what you fear may happen to me, you must focus your attention on saving yourself. If you come to my aid, it will mean your death. If you leave me, we might yet both survive. Do you understand?"

Over the course of the last few sentences, Toby had placed a slightly shaking hand on my shoulder, and his eyes were locked on mine. My heart beat wildly as it took in his message. The journey ahead would be far more dangerous than I ever imagined. By choosing to go, I would place both our lives at risk. But strangely, what struck me most powerfully in that moment was kinship: this man also has the gift of vision. I am not alone. Perhaps he might yet understand me.

As I reflected on this, my eyes softened, and I smiled at him with recognition, with vulnerability and hope. And he kissed me.

It startled both of us, I know. I don't imagine he had planned to do it or meant to do it, but in responding to my open look, he was drawn in. And I was startled by the eagerness with which I met his kiss, with the degree of trust my willing response implied for a man I had met only hours before.

Abruptly, he pulled away, rose, and walked several paces from me. He shoved his hands in his pockets and stood staring into the fire. I looked at his back, astonished at the tenderness that surged into my hands, longing to be expressed, waiting to see what he might do or say.

He spoke softly, keeping his gaze averted. "Brie, I . . . you . . ." He took a deep breath and began again. "I hadn't meant to do that. I didn't mean to do that. I mean, I'm glad I did that, and I shouldn't have done that and . . . Oh, hell!" He walked to the mantel and began fussing with a small figurine of a lion that stood there. "I want so much to be worthy of your trust. Why would you trust me now?

"Henry said you were beautiful," Toby continued. "I thought that he was just saying that to get me to blush and to get me to come here, because he knows how shy I usually am around girls. I didn't even look at you when I got off my horse; I was too nervous. When you came in to dinner, I thought I was going to faint dead away for two reasons. One, you are beautiful . . . not just your face but the energy that comes into the room with you. Does that make sense? But two, I had seen you in my dream the night before—even though I hadn't met you yet—and it scared me so much to know that what I had seen was the future. Knowing that confirmed for me that we are supposed to make this journey together. But seeing that also made me realize that we might not come back . . . or at least I might not." He set the lion down, after one last stroke of its broad back. I saw that his hand was shaking.

"Just now when you looked at me, I had the feeling that you understood all that—without my having to say it, that you could identify. Without thinking, I wanted my touch to show the kinship that came to me in that moment . . . and so I kissed you. Can you forgive me? Could you even begin to trust to leave with me in the morning, or do we need to find you a different guide, one who can show restraint?" He turned then, and his face held a vivid mixture of regret, hope, frankness, and strain. But beneath them all I discerned something richer, the first seeds of love. Or was it just out of my own longing that I imagined something I wanted to see?

I stood and walked over to the fire. Not knowing why, I took his hand. For several moments, I traced the lines of his palm, not saying anything, not looking at him, just letting the tenderness have its way in a quiet path of fingertips on skin.

I let his hand fall and stepped back a bit before raising my eyes to his. "Toby, I trust you. Perhaps even more because of what just happened and what you just shared. I know that you will bring your best self to watch over us for what lies ahead. I also know that we are both vulnerable, deeply vulnerable to feelings for one another. I imagine it is better to know that now, before we find ourselves alone on the trail. I hope you agree that we can't give sway to those feelings on our journey? I worry that if we do, we won't be attuned to the dangers around us, that we won't stay focused on what we need to do."

He nodded, and in his gaze I saw both relief and hope. I continued, "Thank you for trusting me to share your dream. At times God also speaks to me through dreams and visions, and I know how that experience can be both inspiring and deeply disturbing all at once. I feel strongly that you and I will need to use all the gifts we have if we are to return together. I am convinced that you are the one the Lord chose to accompany me. I feel confident that he will journey with us and go before us."

I hugged him then, a short hug because I feared where a long hug might lead. Yet I know that it strengthened us both, that brief full-bodied connection, that circle of grace. As I moved away, he cleared his throat and said, "We have an early start tomorrow. Best to turn in." I smiled up at him, and he winked at me. I headed up to my room then, but the warmth and promise of that wink stayed with me all night long.

15

*T*he first rays of the sun were just finding their way over the treetops as Toby and I prepared to mount Windstar. The whole family had assembled out by the stables, sharing final prayers, good wishes, and hugs goodbye. My heart felt heavy to leave Lily Mae and this couple who had extended such generosity, concern, and friendship. Just before leaving, Lily Mae pulled me aside and whispered in my ear, "I had a strange dream last night, Brie. You were in it. You told me two things, but somehow I think the words were for you and Toby, not me. Does that make sense? 'Watch for the albatross; he will not lead you astray.' That was the first thing. And then you said . . . you said . . ." Her eyes brimmed with tears, and she turned her head away. She gulped and looked back at me, and her eyes reflected both pain and love, "You said that, 'The road of fear would lead to death; only in surrender could there be life.' Do you think that you are going to die, Brie? Are people going to capture you? Oh, I wish you didn't have to go." She reached up and held me tightly, then ran to her uncle for comfort. He held her against his side, stroking her hair.

Lily pulled me to her with a strength and a love that comforted and sustained. "Trust your gifts, Brie. I believe that the Lord will keep you and Toby safe, so long as you trust your gifts. You will be in our thoughts and prayers every day."

Henry and Toby embraced, and then Henry turned to face me. "Gabriela, go with God. It seems you have a call to follow, though you do not understand all that it asks of you. Remember that risk can be the door to healing, yet also to pain. Keep your ears open and your heart attuned. Remember that he will hold you fast." In his words I heard echoes of the tune

Anna had sung on the treacherous steps. Now I too would be making my way to Nybron, a town of secrets, a place of mystery. Was Anna still there somewhere?

Toby helped me onto Windstar's back, then followed suit. We were grateful for the cool, clear morning in which to ride. Henry led the family in a short prayer for safe travel, for God's grace to go with us, and then we were riding southward and away. At one point, I turned back and saw that Lily Mae had run to the edge of the street, straining to see us for as long as possible. She was waving furiously, standing on tiptoe. I waved back until the road turned and she was out of sight. I cried then, quiet tears obscuring my vision, shadowy doubts clouding my heart. What was I doing? How could I bring such threat of harm upon myself and upon this good and gracious man in front of me? I imagined myself tossing my anxieties and doubts upon the roadside, one by one, like so many crumbs lofted for the birds. In my mind's eye, I saw the albatross, swooping in to catch them on his broad wings, rising again to bear them far away. I needed to let him. Lily Mae's words rang in my memory, and I felt convinced that were I to insist on dwelling in my anxiety and fear, all would be lost.

I turned my face forward and grounded myself in the steady beat of Windstar's hooves and of Toby's heart. Peace to you . . . peace to you . . . For now, my lot was to ride and wait and pray.

* * * * *

The first three days of our journey passed without incident: long hours of riding; short stops for food and water and basic needs; and late evenings spent in inexpensive, wayside inns in separate small, spare rooms. Henry had given Toby quite a generous supply of coins and other trade-worthy items for the journey; in this part of the country, not everyone shared the same preference for payment. True to his word, Toby treated me with gentle circumspectness and courtesy, touching me only to help me off and on the tall back of his stallion. I came to realize how much I treasured those brief moments of his touch, especially when he lifted me down. One time I misjudged the angle and nearly fell off into his arms; though flustered, I knew that we both savored the closer contact that resulted. The rest of the time, he stood close, protectively but not intimately; I imagine the innkeepers thought us siblings or cousins if they thought about us at all.

On the afternoon of the fourth day, shortly after a creekside break to water Windstar, I felt Toby tense in front of me. Something inside told me not to peek around him, but instead to keep my head down, my focus inward. I was grateful that my long hair was hidden under hood and cloak. I heard a gruff voice say, "Why would a young man brave this road? Don't you know there are ruffians who mean you harm?" The man laughed, a nasty laugh without light in it, and I felt my spirit shiver. I took a deep breath, and as I did, my inward sight showed me a little boy, frightened and grave, as his father beat him again and again for something he had not done.

I looked up then, wondering if the boy in my vision was this same man. Yes, those were his eyes, brown and beaten, with a painful longing behind. To my astonishment, Toby fumbled in the pack to his right and threw the man a small loaf of bread. The latter caught it neatly and turned a half-bow to us as we sped past. "I see you are a man of character," he shouted, "May it go well with you!" And he turned and slid back among the trees. I hugged Toby more tightly after that and felt immense relief when we were safely settled at a threadbare but tidy inn for the night.

* * * * *

We rode through another day without incident, yet I sensed that both Toby and Windstar, like me, carried greater tension and an intensified focus on our surroundings. That night we were pleased and relieved to discover the cleanliness and warmth of the inn at which we stopped, as well as the hospitality and genuine welcome of the proprietress. I perceived that she also was glad of the company, to find only weary travelers at her door, with no ill intent in their eyes. Only two other guests came to her inn that night, a barefoot, kindly man of orders in a rough tunic, who turned in immediately following the evening meal, and a watchful older man who withdrew quickly to smoke his pipe in the courtyard. We were left alone with Georgina, who smiled and leaned back in her chair after the men had withdrawn.

"You took separate rooms, but are you lovers?" she began, startling us both to blushes and stammered denials.

Georgina's laughter rumbled out to fill the room. "I knew before I asked," she offered, "But I believed that the way you answered would help me to gauge your trustworthiness. Why are you on this forsaken road?"

"Why are *you* here in this forsaken spot, Georgina?" Toby spoke with more vigor than I had heard in him before. I wondered if the energy of his voice was born of a need to recover from his embarrassment.

"Ah, I perceive that you are also careful. That will serve you well in the days to come, Mr. Graham. Do not trust anyone, no matter how welcoming they might seem outwardly. Mine is the last waypoint of any merit on the road to Nybron; you will need to make camp or take risks with the few outliers who occasionally take in travelers. With such a lovely traveling companion, I would opt for the former, if I were you."

"You still haven't answered my question," Toby interjected.

"Persistent, too. That's good, very good. You will need all those gifts, as well as that fine, fast horse of yours if you are to make it to Nybron unscathed. Your reasons must be good ones to have brought you this far. Why am I here? I'm a gambler, I suppose. I like the edginess of life, meeting the riff-raff and the ruffians. To be honest, I don't always know how to treat the likes of you, with your clear eyes and unlined faces. On the one hand, I was relieved at the sight of you; the sound of heavy hoofbeats can often mean an unsettled night ahead . . . but they pay well; yes, they pay well." She chuckled and unconsciously rubbed middle finger to thumb, as though polishing a coin.

"My late husband, God rest his soul, did not always watch his steps, and it killed him in the long run. But he taught me well, how to assess by a glance the tricksters from the trustworthy, how to tell men hardened by pain from those hardened by violence. You two are easy to read: some quiet lines of loss and loneliness but no guile. And you . . ." Georgina turned to me with green-gold eyes that reminded me in that moment of the searching eyes of the fortuneteller. "You have a gift of sight that both drives you forward and allows you to see beyond appearance. It will not fail you, though it also cannot protect you in the most dangerous places of the world. Nybron is one of those, so beware."

She turned again to Toby. "What weapons do you carry?" she asked now, in a voice both blunt and concerned. Toby would not meet her eyes. "Young man, I will not rob you of the very things that may yet save your life. You have paid well, and I would like more of your coin on your return journey. Without weapons, you may not have a return journey."

Not knowing quite why, I drew the dagger from the folds of my skirt and laid it on the table next to the empty plates and waning candle. Both Toby and Georgina turned to me in wide-eyed surprise. I had kept the dagger within reach since leaving the Bartons' home, but I had never shown it to Toby. Georgina spoke first, "Good, very good." And then I heard her sharp intake of breath. Her eyes had come to rest on the amethyst inlay of the handle, and she leaned closer to examine it. "Those are Nybron amethysts! How did you come by this? They say the amethysts bring good fortune to those who carry them. Clearly they have brought you this far . . ."

For a moment her gaze was focused on the middle distance, and then her green-gold eyes sharpened back, illuminating the face of a wise, watchful, and somewhat greedy woman who nonetheless seemed to wish us well. "Good fortune will not save you if your opponent can overpower you. Do you know how to use it?" One glance at my expression told her all she needed to know. She invited me to draw the dagger from its leather casing, and taking a steak knife in her own hand, she demonstrated techniques of self-protection that turned my stomach but nonetheless etched themselves upon my memory. Toby watched wordlessly, though twice I noticed his hand at his waist when he thought that Georgina's instruction came too close to a threatening, dangerous movement toward my person. At last she sat back and replaced her knife upon her plate. "You will know what to do now. May you not need what I have shown you . . . yet I fear you will."

Her gaze settled once again on Toby. "And what kind of knife do you carry at your waist? You were right to reach for it just now, though you would not have been quick enough, you know. If I had wanted to slash her throat, you would have been only halfway across the table before the deed was done." Toby paled, and he stood up, his long knife quickly drawn and extended toward Georgina. "Gently, gently," the older woman replied, raising both her hands in the air. "I said that not to threaten you but to prepare you. You must be two steps ahead at all times or your lives may be forfeit. Have you practiced with the knife with other men who are trustworthy?" she inquired, her voice softer, more measured.

Toby lowered the knife, though he did not sit. "My brothers and I have engaged in hand-to-hand many times for sport; all of them agree that I am the fastest and most nimble."

"Good. But remember these men will not be brothers or allies. If they attack, both your lives will be threatened. Do not trust to nimble; be ruthless in return."

She grew quiet then, as though weighing a decision deep in her spirit. Her eyes returned to our faces, searching, discerning. "Yes." The word once spoken, she turned and hurried from the room. At that moment, the pipe-smoking guest returned and made himself comfortable beside the fire, not far from our table. He asked Toby to join him in a game of cards, and since Georgina did not return, he obliged, thinking that a bit of camaraderie might be a good choice in light of the man's rugged appearance. Minutes passed; Toby lost quickly and handed over a small coin in good humor. I was glad to see that he did not retrieve it from the heavy, full pouch at his chest, but from the smaller stash of lesser coins in his overcoat pocket. The man chuckled, winked in my direction, and withdrew to his room.

Georgina did not come back. Toby stoked the fire, feeling as I did that we were to remain here, to await her return. I imagined that she was doing chores in her private rooms, or perhaps caring for the animals in the stable. For once, Toby and I did not talk; on previous nights, he had shared laughter-filled stories of escapades with his brothers or of family Christmas celebrations, rich in love and faith. On rare occasions, I shared a memory of my sister; his gentleness in listening softened the pain that rose up as I remembered her. But tonight the room felt heavy with waiting, with an expectation that interwove both hope and dread. What had Georgina decided?

Without realizing it, my fingers closed around the cross in my pocket, wishing for answers. As I gazed upon the flames of the fire, I was transported in my mind's eye to this very room, but on a winter evening. I could see snow accumulating on the windowsills, could feel the deep chill. Georgina stood far across the room, stark fear on her face. Two men with hooded capes had just entered through the front door, bearing the lifeless body of a wiry, bearded man. Georgina fell to her knees but came no closer. One of the men snarled, "You are wise to stay back. He was not so wise." They set the body on the rough wooden floor and left as quickly as they had come. Georgina emerged from her grief and stupor long enough to rush to bar the door behind them, and then all I saw was flame, consuming flame, and the ashes of dreams.

I was startled out of my vision by Georgina's reappearance. Something was slung over her shoulder, and she carried a heavy sack also. She sniffed the air. "Am I right that our pipe-toting guest has been inside and upstairs by now?" We nodded. "Good. He is not the kind to come back down with late-night complaints or requests. I'm sure that we will be graced with his snores through the thin walls, but that is no matter. She set the sack in front of the fire and revealed what she carried over her shoulder. It was a fine sword, with silver hilt and a rich engraving. Clearly this object had been fashioned with love of art as much as it had been honed with skill as a blade for protection. Georgina traced the lines of the engraving with a long finger, and suddenly I recognized David and Goliath in the figures on the hilt.

"It strikes me that you two are like David, small, seemingly helpless against the threats that await you, and yet . . . God is with you. I know, you probably imagine that a greedy innkeeper has no time for God . . . and I often don't. Yet every now and then he speaks loudly in my ear, and he did so tonight. These items were my husband's. He lost his life on a winter night when he ventured out without them, thinking he had heard a lost horse in distress, whickering and whinnying off down the road. I don't know to this day if the horse was real or a clever trick, but he came back dead all the same. It comforts me in some small measure to know that his death was due to his compassionate heart, rather than his propensity for gambling and drinking, but he is still dead, and I miss him."

She paused to pass her hands over tired eyes. "You will need this sword, young Graham. I know that now. I've kept it for years, knowing I am not strong enough to swing it but feeling the great risk of selling it. It's too beautiful; the buyer would more likely kill me than pay me to have it in his possession. It's the only time that my husband won big in his gambling, and the loser only left him alive because there was a great crowd gathered who knew and valued my husband. We were so grateful when he saddled his horse and rode off angry, rather than staying another night beneath our roof. Have you carried a sword before?"

Toby nodded. "Two summers ago, I took some lessons from a neighbor who had been to the wars. I no longer have the calloused palms that would help me, but I know the heft and steps to guard myself."

Georgina nodded slowly. "I am glad to hear that. I know the knife, but not the sword. She handed it to Toby with a wry look. "Practice in your room tonight, though please mind the furnishings. This is too public a place, even though I trust our barefoot brother and expect to hear the snorer before long." She reached into the sack and pulled out two objects, a weatherworn map and a five-inch pewter cross. It was my turn to gasp. I knew that workmanship; the cross had been fashioned by James Mason. Looking more closely, I realized that a strange circle graced the center of the crossbeam: someone had affixed a small compass to the cross, a compass in a rich setting of pewter.

"Did your husband know James Mason?" I asked, reaching for the cross. I turned it over and gestured to the softly etched JM of the touchmark.

"No, that was another of his gambling winnings. Thankfully, the man who lost that to him was a friend, not a foe. He felt grateful that Frank had won it, rather than the others in the circle of card-players that day. He had lost so badly that he risked his greatest treasure in hopes of regaining even a little of his money. Frank let him stay with us two extra nights in exchange for chores, knowing the difficulty he had brought upon himself. I'm certain that Frank offered him the cross back and he refused. For all their reckless-ness, gamblers like those two still honor the game."

Georgina spread out the map, her long, careworn fingers smoothing it slowly and with a long sigh. "This map shows trails other maps do not. Most people believe that there is only one road to Nybron; there are three. The one you are on now is the most direct but also the most dangerous. You need to take one of the others; I wish I knew which, but you will have to trust to God's guidance for that. The other two are overgrown, so you must travel with care for your horse's sake. Frank used both of them on different journeys to Nybron and boasted when he had too much ale that he was the only man to visit that city five times without incident. And then he was killed just outside his own door . . ."

She shook her head as though to clear the memory. "On these other roads, you will need that compass. There are side trails and misleading turns that double-back on themselves. One road skirts the steep cliffs for which Nybron is known; the other runs deep through the forest beside caves and crevices. Frank only spoke of them on rare occasions; despite his boast, he only went to Nybron when he felt he had no other choice. Most times, he made longer trips north to refill our provisions that we could not supply for ourselves. As for me, I pay the most trustworthy travelers handsomely to fetch items for me from the northern towns. Most of the time they return, and they receive the second half of a generous reward. Sometimes they don't; either I have been wrong to trust them, or they could not come back. But even with my losses, I prefer it to setting foot on those roads alone."

Toby gazed intently at the map, tracing the slim lines toward Nybron, one beside the sea and one far inland. "The sea road looks easier," he com-mented. "What do you think, Brie?" One hand around my own cross, the other tracing the touchmark on the compass cross, I gazed at the map and prayed. Suddenly, I had a terrible vision of Windstar losing his footing be-side a steep slope, tossing Toby headfirst down a deathly cliff. I cried out in horror. "We need to take the forest road." Both had seen the fear in my eyes, and neither questioned why.

I slept deeply that night, without dream or vision. Perhaps I knew it was the last safe place I would know for many a day. Looking upon Toby's face in the morning, I realized that the opposite had been true for him:

either he had stayed up too late becoming familiar with the heft of the sword, or his worries had haunted him too long. He rubbed a hand over his face and sent a wry grin my way. "Brie, we can still turn back if you wish it." At first I felt a rush of anger—he knew my determination—and then I recognized that his words flowed from his deep concern and care for me. "Thank you, Toby, but no."

We breakfasted in the dawn light, and I slid a few extra coins under my plate for Georgina to find upon clearing them. She had extended great generosity and concern to us, with nothing in return but her own sense of faithfulness to an inner prompting. Yet I also knew that if I offered the coins to her openly, she would not accept them.

The pipe-smoker was still snoring as we readied Windstar in the stable yard; we could hear the grating sound through his open window. The friar had already headed northward, a wooden staff in his hand. Toby was busy securing the provisions that we had purchased in Windstar's saddlebags. To our surprise, Georgina rushed out of the inn just as we were preparing to leave: "I must tell you one thing more!"

In hushed tones, she described the marker for our forest path. Just two bends along the southward road from here, we would see a boulder on the right-hand side. On the boulder's far side, we would see what appeared to be fencing but was instead a cleverly constructed gate. She explained the working of the gate and then sighed deeply. "I awoke in the middle of the night, dreaming that you had missed the marker; my sense of dread would not leave me. The map does not reveal all secrets. That is the only one Frank ever showed me; he knew better than to bring me any further toward Nybron. Brie, you will want to keep your long hair covered at all times; you may even wish to speak in a gruff voice or walk heavily, like a young man. I don't know what else to tell you. I hope one day to hear again the steady, strong gait of your mount and know that you are safely returned. May God go with you."

And then she was hurrying back into the inn, as though she did not trust herself to watch us ride away. I was relieved to hear that the snores continued unbroken and glad of the sword hanging openly at Toby's side. He removed it and affixed it to the saddle, taking care to place it where he could draw it if necessary. I felt tempted to ask if he and his brothers had ever practiced combat on horseback but did not wish to hear the negative answer that seemed likely. Toby glanced up then, catching the doubt in my eyes. He took my hands and said a brief, faithful prayer, asking for the

Lord's protection and for swift, safe passage to Nybron. It occurred to me as I listened that we did not even know what to do upon reaching Nybron; even if we arrived safely, what then? But an unexpected peace settled over me as the prayer continued, and I leaned into trust at a level my life had never before asked of me.

16

*W*e found the marker easily. We dismounted and Toby listened attentively for the sound of hoofbeat or footfall. We knew that gaining access to the forest road unseen would be critical. We heard only birdsong and the wind playing in the branches overhead. Thankfully, the path since Georgina's had been so rocky that we would leave no tracks behind. Toby worked the latch, and the fence sprang back, allowing us to pass through and lead Windstar to the other side. He secured the false fence once again, and we hurried forward down the path, not taking time to remount, wanting only to move quickly out of sight of any who would pass along the main road.

The forest path held an odd stillness, as though it had been waiting for us. Once we had gained a distance of three hundred yards or so from the gate, the trees were much closer together and the trail grew narrower. Windstar balked a bit in protest, and Toby stopped to soothe him, rubbing his nose and offering a sugar cube he had taken from the breakfast table. Uncertain, I spoke, "Toby, should we ride or walk on this path?" He peered ahead down the way, which looked more like a tunnel than a trail. He gauged the height of the lowest branches, then looked back at me. "It would be easier if we walked, I'm sure, but far safer if we ride. We will need to keep our heads low, our backs hunched. They will ache long before we find a place to rest. But I don't trust this place; I would rather have the advantage of horseback, even if my own back must pay the price."

So we mounted and rode in silence for much of the morning and afternoon, with Toby checking both map and compass each time we came upon a strange turning or a meeting of two ways. We stopped only once, beside a welcome stream, giving Windstar time to drink and a moment's respite for ourselves. Even then, Toby urged us on in minutes, as though worried that even the smallest delay increased our risk. I did not argue.

By mid-afternoon my back ached with the bending, yet I knew we had come further because of it. At last the landscape changed, and I wondered whether to feel relieved that my need for a bent back had ended or deeply nervous for what lay ahead. The forest had opened upon a boulder-strewn valley, with steep sides and steam escaping from eerie crevices in the ground. Toby spent several precious minutes poring over the map, confirming with the compass. "We have not gone astray," he stated firmly, "Yet I see no safety in this rockscape and foul steam."

I took a deep breath. "Let us continue to follow the map until we have no more daylight," I answered. "You have been clear before that there is no safety in delay. Let us pray that few know this road, that in Frank's drunken boasting he revealed only the journey, not the means."

Windstar clearly disliked our new surroundings. Toby had to coax him to a faster pace; of his own volition, he would have turned back, or at least stepped only gingerly among the fallen stones and odd smells. We saw no creatures here, whereas along the forest path we had startled the occasional squirrel or other small rodent, who would scurry away as we approached. I wondered if Frank had traveled by horseback or on foot, but recalled that Georgina had praised the strength and speed of our horse for a reason. Though he was ill at ease, we remained far safer with him than without.

Near nightfall, we were grateful to hear the sound of water once more, though we could not distinguish the source. Making our way around a large boulder, the mystery revealed itself: off to the right, partially hidden by other boulders and an obscuring cloud of steam, a cave mouth yawned. The water sound was magnified by the cavern and clearly came from within. Toby drew Windstar back behind the boulder and held out the map for me to consult alongside him. Where the cave stood, the map showed only a small cross, lightly penciled, hardly visible in the fading light. "What do you think, Brie? I do not like caves, and Windstar even less so." My eye traveled further ahead on the map, tracing the route we were to take, discovering two other crosses of the same size, about an equal distance from one another as this cross was from the gate. "I believe the crosses mark places of refuge for the night," I told him. "I see no other place to shield travelers from weather or from sight anywhere else in this otherworldly landscape. Let us trust to Frank's guidance."

Windstar's gait slowed markedly as we approached the cave mouth. It became clear that we would have to dismount and lead him in. As we entered the cave, the sound of water intensified, resounding off the walls with a ghostlike echo. Thankfully, not far from the entrance, yet out of sight of anyone peering in, we found a grotto-like opening with several stakes in the ground, clearly used for tethering horses. Toby secured Windstar, belted on the sword, and told me in whispered tones that he would go in search of the water source. He asked me to stay with Windstar and cautioned me to keep my hand on my knife, to be ready for danger. While he remained in my sight, my hand strayed first to the cross in my pocket, listening for deeper warnings. I saw nothing, neither sign of peace nor of threat. My heart told me that the real risks dwelt a day or two away, but I honored Toby's wish and stood alert, my dagger at the ready.

By now I knew Toby's footfalls and breathed a welcome sigh of relief when he returned a few minutes later, carrying two leather bags full of water. His face still carried tension, though not quite the foreboding I had seen when he first spied the cave. "I don't think anyone has been here for a long time," he commented. "How can you tell?" I queried. "At the water's edge, there are two buckets, as though left as a boon to travelers. They are coated with dust." "You did not use them," I pointed out, gesturing at the bags. "Perhaps others have done as you have." His confidence dimmed a little. "None of the footprints was fresh. Besides my own, I would guess the others were made months ago." I wanted to believe him, wanted to trust my own heart. Yet we both agreed to take turns on watch that night, just in case.

Toby took the first watch while I slept. I remember nothing from the moment I lay down until he touched me lightly on the shoulder to awaken me, though he assured me that four or more hours had passed. I splashed my face with cold water and tried to shake off the heaviness of sleep. Very soon I heard Toby's even breathing and wondered how I would keep alert in the darkness. For the first time in many weeks, I allowed my thoughts to trace back over the journey I had taken: leaving the village, traveling by water, the grace of my long stay with Susannah, the complications that resulted from the healing for Michael, Allan's unexpected generosity and Andrew's bounty, and then the many joys of my time with the sisters and their families, especially Lily Mae. As I thought back to my meeting with Toby, I found myself fingering the cross. Had the Lord brought him to me for other purposes besides this journey? Why, when I had felt so certain that I must go alone, had this gift of friendship come to me? Again and again, he had shown himself trustworthy; traveling together offered greater assurance of anticipating, forestalling, or perhaps combating danger.

Before long, the first rays of sun began to creep in from the cave mouth. I decided to let Toby sleep just a bit longer, for I knew how tense he had been the day before, and we did not know what the day's journey would bring. I thought back to Georgina, and I smiled at her pluck and strength, admiring her capacity to thrive as a woman on her own, still astonished at her generosity and care. Just as I began to reach out in the half-light to touch Toby's shoulder, my vision clouded. I saw before me a desolate stretch of road and two women weeping as men with ill intent converged upon them. One was praying openly, even as the tears streamed down her face, "Father, protect us. Jesus, forgive them. Spirit, guide me now."

She turned to her companion with a strange light in her eyes, "Isabella, don't fight them. They are well-armed. I feel in my spirit that it will go better for us if we do not fight." Her companion stared at her, eyes alight with anger and determination. "You can be foolishly passive if you wish. My brothers taught me how to fight, and I shall." The nearest of the men reached for her, and she struck out like a fury, sending a blow full on his jaw. It caught him by surprise, and the knife he had meant only for threat jabbed full and mean into her side. I heard her scream and knew the blood that Paul had seen was Isabella's. As Windstar stamped a hoof, pulling me back to the present, I wondered if it had also been Anna's.

Before leaving the cave, we replenished all of our water bags and made sure that Windstar had his fill as well. Who knew when we would find the next clean source? Though Toby had slept soundly during my watch, he was once again agitated and alert, wanting to leave the cave and yet reluctant to face the unknown. I could tell that something was troubling him deeply.

"Toby, what is it? What's the matter? I can't remember seeing you like this."

He sighed deeply and avoided my eyes. "Toby, I think it will be better if you tell me."

"You may be right." He looked up, and I was startled to see tears shining at the corners of his eyes. "Do you remember my telling you that I had seen you in a dream the night before me met?"

"Yes."

"Well, in that dream, the landscape was just like the one out there, all boulders and crevices and steam. I've never seen a place like that, except in my dream. I suspect that the threat I have feared will come our way within hours, and I don't know what to do. I also know that if we stay here, you are not being faithful to your call to seek for Anna, nor I to my call to accompany you and provide safe passage."

"Toby, what do you remember of your dream? Do you recall the time of day, a landmark, any detail that might give us warning?"

He paused and reflected deeply, his eyes straying leftward in remembrance. "I was on Windstar, and you were on foot for some reason. I sense that it was the light of mid-afternoon, though I cannot tell you why. All I can remember is that there were far more trees than we saw last night, as though we were coming to the other side of this valley. There will be three men, Brie, all wishing us grave ill. I believe that I kill one. Another is wounded. The third seeks my life. I do not know if he succeeds. I do know that if you try to help me when he attacks, you will die. I am more certain of that than I am of my own name. It may be that they do not realize that you are present, that you are on foot and conceal yourself somehow, though I do not know how. No matter what happens, I feel certain that we will be separated before dark. It is important to me that you have necessary provisions in your backpack, more than you would normally carry. Make sure that you have your dagger to hand all day. Pay attention to any prompts from your instinct or your vision or your heart; you will need them all. I wish that I knew more than that. I wish that I knew you would be all right, that Windstar would be all right. I only know that danger is coming, and it is better for you to flee than to fight for me. Do you understand?"

Toby's eyes bored into me with an intensity I had never seen before. Though I perceived fear and strain, I recognized behind them a tenderness and a cherishing that I knew he would not voice. "Yes, Toby, I understand."

Together we pored over the map one more time. Toby made a few rough sketches on the back of a stray sheet of paper and thrust the map at me, despite my protests. "You need to get to Nybron, Brie. If I have Windstar, we will find our way. You need the map." We then spent a few minutes redistributing supplies. I had grown used to the luxury of letting Windstar bear our loads, so my back groused a bit as I hoisted the pack to my shoulders. Toby wanted me to walk all day, thinking that somehow that would protect me. I pointed out that if I were exhausted from walking, I could not run if an attack should come. We compromised that I would ride till midday, and then after lunch continue on foot.

I wanted to sing to lighten the mood of the day, but I knew that if enemies were near, my singing would lead them right to me. We talked little and kept grave watch atop Windstar's broad back. At one point, I leaned into Toby more fully than usual, resting my cheek briefly against the back of his neck. I hoped that he felt the depth of caring that I sought to communicate with that gentle touch.

As the hours passed, the landscape changed subtly: fewer boulders, fewer steam vents, and even a few fields of flowers here and there. In the distance, I began to perceive a narrowing of the way as the valley led back up into the forest. I knew that Toby saw it too. We stopped for lunch in the shadow of a great boulder and conferred in hushed tones.

"I am confident of it now, Brie. When I looked ahead, I recognized the trees. However, I cannot figure out how it is that they don't harm you first, if you are on foot. You would be more vulnerable than I, yet I'm sure that in the dream, I was on Windstar, and you were not."

I took a deep breath, thinking of Anna and Isabella. "Are you sure that I am not harmed, Toby?"

He shook his head determinedly. "In the dream, I saw you running away. You had your pack, you did not look back, and no one followed you."

"Which way did I run?"

"You ran toward the tallest tree, the one with the broken top. Do you see it there, far on the horizon?"

"Yes, I see it." I looked toward the tree and felt a terrible constriction in my chest, as though I could not breathe, as though my heart were being shredded with grief. "How can I leave you if you are in harm's way, Toby?"

"You need to promise me." For the first time since that sweet night at the Bartons' house, Toby grabbed me by the shoulders and stared into my eyes. "Promise me, Brie. If you try to help, we may both die. If you run, perhaps we will both live. I don't know why I know these things, but please trust me. Please."

I fumbled for the cross in my pocket, and to my great surprise, a deep sense of peace stole over me, such as I had not felt since leaving Henry and Lily and Lily Mae. "I promise, Toby." He nodded, kissed my forehead with a gentleness that took my breath away, and then released me.

"We need to go," he said then, as though the weight of doom had settled upon him. "You should keep within sight of Windstar and me, but at least fifty yards back. Take shelter as you can from rock and shrub—or whatever else may be out there. We will not have much warning when they come."

I nodded. We said a brief prayer, asking the Lord's protection and guidance, beseeching him that we might be wrong and all would be well. I prayed that God's holy angels might keep watch over Toby and Windstar, protecting them even in the most unexpected ways. Toby prayed that whether together or apart, we would find our way to Nybron and to Anna, ultimately in safety and in hope. And then we set out.

17

*I*t is so hard for me to relate what transpired in the next half-hour. It plays again and again in my mind's eye, vivid and horrifying. I want to trust to hope, that Toby's instincts and his dream protected us both, yet I do not see how that is possible.

We set out with all our senses attuned, Toby and Windstar well in advance of me, never looking back. For about a quarter of an hour, all I could hear was the loud pounding of my own heart against the background of a whining, thin, and whistling wind. I hurried from boulder to shrub, from outcropping to rock, praying that it would be enough. My instincts felt the danger, but not the direction in which it lay. I looked ahead of me and saw Toby pass by a giant rock that seemed my next best hiding place. I took a deep breath, stood quickly to dash toward it from my cover of bristle bushes, and tripped on a jutting root. I fell so hard, it knocked the wind from me, and I lost consciousness for a brief moment. When I came to, I heard Windstar cry out in a high-pitched, frightened tone, and I knew. Toby's dream was coming to pass. As soon as I could rise, I peered around the edges of the bush.

The ambush had come from behind the very rock I had planned to seek as my next shelter. One man lay on the ground already, unconscious or dead, I could not tell. I wondered if Windstar had trampled him. Another was clashing with Toby as he wielded Georgina's sword. A third was creeping toward him from the other side of Windstar, out of Toby's view.

Had I not known of the dream, I would have shouted or screamed, would have rushed forward with my dagger at the stealthy man, seeking to save Toby. But I remembered the certainty in Toby's eyes that to rush to his aid would mean my death. Having tripped on the root had hidden me away from the eyes of the men. Their attention bored in now on Toby and Windstar; a small window of time offered itself to me to flee to the shelter of the woods by the broken-topped tree. In my taut anxiety I had not realized how close we had drawn to it. I took a deep breath, whispered, "O, Lord Jesus, help and save," and sprinted as though with winged feet. For whatever reason, as I ran I saw again the flight of the albatross as it took off from the cliffs, and in that seeing gained strength and hope.

I did not look back. I ached to do so; I had heard cries of anger, of fear, and one sound—which I thought to be in Toby's voice, though I could not be sure—that seemed a deep groan of pain. How could I not run to him? My eyes strained for the edge of the woods, just twenty yards ahead. I heard a horrifying snap of twigs and was tempted to turn back. Would other men be hiding there, waiting to capture me? Was I abandoning Toby to death only to run toward my own?

Yet my feet continued on, almost of their own accord, fueled by fear and yet also by a deeper knowing that this path had been ordained for me and must be followed no matter how dark appearances seemed. I reached the forest and its merciful cover from the men attacking Toby and Windstar. As I rushed in, I saw a flash to my right, and I turned in self-defense, drawing my dagger at the ready.

To my astonishment, an angry ram dodged around me and went careening down the hillside, straight toward the great boulder that obscured the men from my view. We had seen no animals but Windstar in days. In a moment, a second ram, angrier and larger than the first, broke out of the forest and slammed down the hill in its wake, eyes afire. I worried for Windstar; despite all their strength, horses' limbs are so vulnerable. One blow from these rams' horns, and he could be lame.

Yet the vision of the albatross came again, as though in urgency and summons: keep going, keep moving, do not linger. I held my dagger in my right hand, my cross in my left, and rushed ahead among fallen branches and undergrowth that tore at my skirts and slowed my passage more than I had hoped. I lost my sense of time; for long minutes I pressed on, my heart in my throat, ears attuned for any sound. It may have been a half-hour or more before I realized that tears streamed down my face, that prayers had been tumbling from my lips as I ran. Some greater force propelled me, giving speed to my steps, leading me forward and away.

How long did I run through the pathless forest, my back screaming with the weight of my pack, my eyes burning from the tears, my heart torn in two, not knowing if Toby and Windstar had met their end? I do not know. I saw no other animals, and mercifully, wondrously, no human beings. The snapped twigs had proved the harbinger only of the rams and not of attack. As my feet slowed from sheer fatigue as evening drew near, I wondered at their appearance in this trackless wilderness with no wildlife. It made no sense. Were they trained by the men, like giant fierce hounds, to come rushing in at first sign of distress? But as I pondered, the story of Abraham rose to mind: the ram in the thicket whom God had provided in exchange for Isaac. Had the Lord sent these rams as provision for Toby? It seemed fantastic.

Soon the light sank low, as sunset came to mark the end of this dark, dire day. In its last rays, I pored over the map, aware that in my frantic scramble for safety, I had not sought any landmarks, not even the direction of the sun. I noted it now, grateful that its position helped to orient me. I took a stick and traced a compass in the dirt, aware that I would want to set out before the full rising of the sun in the morning, in the diffused, directionless light of pre-dawn.

I knew that I would find no shacks, no caves, and no welcoming inn. I had no energy left, and in the heaviness of my heart I feared the worst for Toby. Yet my tears were spent, and I knew that his encouragement to me, could I hear him, would be to eat, drink, and rest for the night. I glanced around for a good spot not far from my makeshift compass and ended up crawling in under the low-hanging branches of a twiggy, hulking bush in full flower. I ate gratefully of the last of the wheat loaf from Georgina and drank deeply of the water from the cave source. A few nuts satisfied my cravings before sleep took me and all was darkness.

* * * * *

I awoke shivering and with a deep sense of loss. If Toby had survived the attack, wouldn't he have come after me? And then I realized that Windstar could not have safely made his way along the trajectory I had taken. Besides, my helter-skelter flight would only be discernable by the most skilled of trackers or the best of hounds. Even if Toby lived, he could not find me. Fresh tears filled my eyes and slowly slid their way down my cheeks. Oh, Toby, may those rams have been the instruments of God for your protection, though how I cannot know.

I breakfasted briefly as the blackness eased to gray. Emerging from my hiding place, I searched for my compass of the day before. I could just barely make out the letters I had scratched in the ground. Remembering the map, I knew that I needed to head southwestward if I were ever to reach Nybron, and so I began to make my way.

The day weighed heavily upon me, mirroring the weight of my pack and my fear-filled sense of loss. My one comfort came from stray birdsong, the first I had heard since just beyond Georgina's inn. I did not see them, but imagining their cozy nests and their flitting wings brought me my only consolation that painful morning.

Around midday, I heard the sound of a brook and followed it until I came to the tumbling water. I refilled my containers and splashed my face as I leaned over the brook. I perceived a partial, broken reflection of myself in the waters, could see my unruly hair framing deeply worried eyes, a grim mouth. I recalled Georgina's admonishment to hide my hair and tucked it up carefully under my hood.

Just beyond the brook I came upon a clearing, with evidence that not too long before, travelers had made camp there for a night. Beyond the clearing wound a wide trail, the first I had seen. I drew back from it quickly, hiding myself behind a grove of trees and consulting the map. After some scrutiny, I found the place where waterway, clearing, and path came together. Unlike the cave with its cross, this spot bore a scrawled pencil mark, faint but legible: "Linger not." I knew I needed to hurry on my way, but should I take to the road or keep to the trees? Travel by road was easier, faster, but I no longer had Toby's companionship or Windstar's strength and size to increase my safety. I decided that I would keep to the trees, but stay as close to the road as I dared to help me find my way. With good fortune and the Lord's protection, I hoped to reach Nybron by nightfall.

My sense of dread increased as I continued along the way, catching glimpses of the path at intervals, but seeking cover and the protection of bushes and trees. I fingered the pewter cross, uncertain, agitated, far more aware of being alone than I had been on the earlier portions of my journey. My heart told me that both Toby and Windstar were in grave danger, if not already injured or killed. Had there been more men than the three I saw? Could Toby have outrun them if Windstar had been maimed? If Toby had been captured or killed, would they have seen the beauty and strength of Toby's horse and spared him? Even so, they did not seem men who would be kind to their mounts.

I thought once again of Anna's climb up the winding stair, of the way her song had given the group perseverance and hope. To sing in this place would mean revealing my presence. Nevertheless, the first stanza of Anna's hymn circled and banked in my head, like an albatross on the wing, returning, reassuring:

> *"Father mine, my way winds long,*
> *Father mine, the risk grows grave;*
> *Father mine, my fear flows strong,*
> *Yet you shall shield and save."*

I wanted to believe it, yet I felt most attuned to my own fear, flowing strongly and turbulently in my spirit. I thought of stopping for lunch, but recalled the scrawled warning—*Linger not*—and opted instead for a few berries gathered as I hurried along and the last of the nuts Georgina had pressed upon us before we left her inn.

Suddenly I heard gruff voices not far ahead, and I froze where I was, mercifully behind a stand of trees with wide trunks.

"How many more days are we to keep watch, Jer?"

"Griffin will tell us if we are released from duty."

"What danger could two travelers on horseback be to Griffin, especially a young woman of little strength?"

"You know Griffin . . . him and his dreams. He's convinced that he was warned about these two, that they could be his undoing. It seems crazy to me: if it was an army, okay, even a gang of bandits, I get it, especially if they knew about the tunnels under the Praying Oaks. But how could they know? No one knows but Griffin and his closest company."

"Yeah, even you and I miss the entrance half the time! One big boulder looks the same as another, except when the sun is shining just right and that eye-shaped marking twinkles out. I used to think it was winking at me. Now I just feel it watching me, and I hate to go in that way. Too dark, too smelly!"

"Yeah, but sometimes it's good to get to Griffin without his scouts reporting well in advance. You and I both know that the scout out there drinks too much and spends most of his watch snoozing . . . Anyway, we need to guard this road until they come, or until Griffin sends word that the other scouts found them. I'm thinking that Rory and his team would have seen them from far off and surprised them, so we'll hear before too long. You know how exposed the Valley of Crags is. Surely they caught them!"

"I still don't see why he asked us not to kill them. Two quick flicks of the blade on flesh, and we could take whatever it is they have that he wants. Does he even know? Or is it more of that barmy dream-talk? What could these young folks possibly possess that Griffin doesn't have two or three of already? You've seen some of those underground vaults, all of the treasures that he's taken. I say, what good is treasure if you can't spend it and no one knows about it?"

"Griffin is superstitious to a fault. He thinks that he can finally win Anna's love when he fulfills the prophecy:

'Three treasures to hand, two treasures by land,
And one that is born of the sea.
Each has its grace, in time and in space,
But united their power's set free.
None shall say nay to their wielder; pray,
How may this strength come to me?'

"He's convinced that once he has found the right three treasures, everyone will have to bend to his will. Right. Folks have been scouring Nybron and its coast for the treasures for more than a century. At core, he's a fool for power, like all the rest of us. But since he's the most powerful man around—and the most dangerous—I'd rather be on his side than against him."

"Maybe he wants these travelers alive because he thinks they know the secret of the treasure!"

"You're as crazy a fool as he is, Vance. There is no such treasure. It's just the ravings of some old monk, and somehow it's spread and spread. People believe what they want to. When life is hard, they'll dream of magic that will make things easier. There's no easy road, not even for those who rule. You live, you work hard, you struggle, you die. Even if the treasures do exist, Griffin remains vulnerable like any man. I say, a mug of ale and a fine meal's about the best anyone ever gets in this life."

"And a good wench?"

"You're young yet, Vance. Taking a wife means taking on a burden, a big spender, and a nag. Going alone is the best way, take it from me."

At this point Vance murmured something I could not make out, but clearly Jer did. It must have been an insult of some kind, because a scuffle commenced between the two guards that began to escalate into fisticuffs. Seeing my chance, I moved as quickly and quietly as I knew how, away from the road, away from the watch. The forest was very dense at this spot, which was helpful for cover, yet very dangerous for sound. Hurrying past a large cluster of thick shrubs, I startled a deer and fawn, who went crashing toward the men who had been sent to capture me. Everything in me wanted to run, but I knew that keeping to a steady pace made me less visible; for a short time, the men would attribute all noise to the deer. I held tight to my cross in one hand and my dagger in the other and kept moving.

Every moment I expected to hear a shout, followed by the heavy tread of booted feet crashing after me. No pursuit came. Perhaps the men pursued the deer in hope of fresh meat; perhaps they wore one another out in their contending. But as the minutes passed, my sense of imminent threat waned a bit, though I remained on guard. No longer wild with anxiety, I began to replay the watchers' conversation in my mind. My heart clung to hope for Toby: they had been told to spare our lives! The name Anna also stood out starkly to me; I wanted desperately to believe her to be the Anna I sought. At odd intervals over the weeks, I had wondered why, if she yet lived, she had not communicated with her mother and favorite cousin? But if she were a prisoner, particularly a prisoner in an underground warren of tunnels and thieves, how could she get word to anyone? I tried to imagine what it might be like to be trapped in a dark, dank place for as long as Anna had been away, and I shuddered. Not to see the sun, to feel the wind on one's face . . . and yet I knew from her letters that Anna's strength of spirit had overcome several hardships before meeting the bandits above the Nybron cliffs.

In late afternoon, footsore yet hopeful, I decided to stop for shelter within a tight evergreen grove. Even in my flight from Vance and Jer, I had tried to keep moving in the direction of the road and imagined that Nybron lay only a few miles away. Initially I had thought of entering the town as quickly as I could, believing my safety lay in the city, in the hospitality of an inn. But as I reflected over all I had heard, my heart told me that Griffin would have many watchers, both within the city and without. He might have bribed the nearest innkeepers to report my arrival. I knew no one in Nybron, had not thought to concoct a story of why I was there for those who might question my presence or wish me ill. To walk into the town on foot at twilight, alone and without a plan, seemed tantamount to my undoing. What was I to do?

My hiding place proved bristly but dry and snug. Before I forgot, I traced another compass in the dirt. I found that I had just room enough to spread out the map and seek for some inspiration, some sense of a plan. I ran my finger over the road that Toby, Windstar, and I had taken, feeling the tears trace down my face as my finger lingered over the Valley of Crags . . . for I knew that Jer had referred to the place of our ambush. My one comfort had come in hearing that the scouts had been instructed not to kill us; though I hated to think of Windstar and Toby imprisoned in the tunnels under the Praying Oaks, it strengthened my hope that they yet lived. I reviewed the path of my own frantic flight, estimating my current position to be in an unmarked area just a few miles from the gates to the city.

For the first time, I looked in detail at the city of Nybron itself, unfolding a portion of the map that had seemed unimportant when I had focused solely on reaching my destination in safety. I felt astonished as I considered the vast network of streets, recognizing a city far larger than any I had yet seen, perhaps grander than fifty Lanfords set side by side. In my anxiety over the sheer size of the town, I fingered the cross in my pocket and was reminded of the cross that had marked the cave in which Toby, Windstar, and I had safely passed the night. Would there be crosses marking safe places in Nybron itself? I strained my eyes in the fading light to see if Frank had noted any place I might risk as a place of refuge within the city. I scanned street upon street . . . nothing. Perhaps he had not thought that anyone would be foolhardy enough to travel to Nybron without a specific destination clearly in mind.

Another thought occurred to me. Where were the Praying Oaks? Where were the Old Lovers? Had Frank cared for legends and old trees? The streets of Nybron appeared tight and winding, with little room for stands of trees, so my eyes strayed to the outskirts of the city. If I thought of Nybron as a clock face, my hiding place lay at about two o'clock, north and east of city center. The notorious cliffs of Nybron seemed to run all along the southwestern edge, from four thirty to eight or so. From eight to midnight, I interpreted Frank's angular squiggles to be the foothills of mountains to the north and west. So what lay just south of me? The map was smudged and frayed at that very spot, as though someone had written something once and then rubbed it out. My eyes struggled to make out the old marks, obscured and incomplete. I wanted to believe that I discerned the letters "oa" and "ov," but perhaps it was just wishful thinking. Even if the tunnels that might lead me to Anna—or even to Windstar and Toby—lay within a half-day's journey, what would I do when I arrived there? I had water for a day, provisions for less, and I was a woman alone.

Once again, I picked up the cross, fingering it gently, hoping a vision might come. I sensed only the dense forest around me, as well as the isolation and danger in which I found myself. Suddenly I remembered my dream at the Green Boar, with the woman running at full speed beneath the Praying Oaks, terrified, without provision. Had I seen myself? My stomach tightened. It made no sense to walk right into a trap, to find myself in an underground cell, just like I imagined Anna to be. What was I to do? And who might aid me? I began to cry silently, overwhelmed by my circumstances, by the outcome of the many choices that I had made along the way. I could have stayed with Susannah, or with Henry, Lily, and Lily Mae. Yet all along I had felt pushed forward and onward, as though the Holy Spirit sent me daily on the wings of a mighty, rushing wind, destined to travel, to risk, to trust.

Yes, to trust. I raised my hands in prayer. "Please, Jesus, You know well how alone I am. You know what dangers lie before me, around me, even within me. I do not know which way to go or what to do. All along the many roads since I left my family's farm, you have provided. How could I have imagined that my journey would bring me so far, would lead me to friends . . . to Toby? Please, dear Jesus, protect him and Windstar, wherever they are. Please spare them! And please help me to know what I am to do next. Please guide me, and show me your way forward. Amen."

I looked once more at the map. To my joy, a tiny cross I had not seen winked out near the edge of the city, just at three o'clock. I wondered why I had not noticed it the first time, and I realized it was a thin but distinctive "T" in the middle of the words, "Shelton Street." Shelton! Hadn't that been Andrew's last name, carved with care on the base of the king in the chess set? Clinging to hope and with a sense of direction for morning, I lay my head on the pine duff and fell quickly asleep.

* * * * *

Locating the outskirts of Nybron on the morrow proved an easier task than I had hoped. It turned out that my pine sanctuary lay just on the crest of the valley's sloping side. As I emerged from the pines in the morning, just an eighth of a mile onward I was afforded an extraordinary view as I peered through obscuring branches. What I beheld took my breath away. Mountains! The sun glinted and danced on the snow at their peaks, and the sense of majesty and grace put me in mind of an old priest I had met as a young child, venerable, knowing, self-contained. I recalled the way he had set his hand lightly on my head and uttered raspy words of blessing. Just looking upon the mountain range conferred a quiet sense of benediction that echoed those long-forgotten words: *The Lord bless you and keep you, child, even when the way seems darkest.*

And then I looked down, down into the valley of Nybron, down on a sprawling city that stole my breath in a different way: fear, anxiety, a constriction of spirit. Nybron exuded a sense of mystery, of nasty secrets just under a surface of productivity, of energy, of commerce. I did not want to go. Even with the many trees along the sloping valley side, at many points in my descent I would be exposed to Griffin's watchers, or so I imagined. How would I recognize Shelton Street among the labyrinth of roads? And what would befall me there? My twilight hopes dimmed as I faced the shadowy dawn. Both Anna and Shelton were such common names in our land; I was trusting to coincidence, grasping at straws. No. My trust still lay in Christ, and he had not led me astray over the weeks leading to this moment.

I took my first step down toward the valley of Nybron and the unknown.

18

Though I noticed trails on my descent, I avoided them, still keeping to the cover of bushes and tree trunks. By now Griffin and those in league with him would know that only the man and his horse had been found, with the woman unaccounted for. Not all of his spies would be drunkards or distracted by scuffles and forest creatures. I could take no risks. About halfway down the valley, I found a ledge with scraggly bushes that would hide me from all eyes below but allowed a clear view to the south. In the distance, I perceived what must be the Nybron cliffs, rocky and grim, without the thriving woods that grew on this slope or the subtler beauty of the mountain foothills across the way. Then my gaze shifted closer, and I discovered the oaks; the grove extended for many acres, its leaves a glorious canopy. The trees themselves held a grace, a strength, a calmness, born of their endurance and long life. During our time together, Lily Mae had confided in me one day that some of the trees were over four hundred years of age. "They must be mag-ni-fi-cent to gaze upon!" she had gushed, that star-bright smile of hers breaking upon my day with a sweet interweaving of tenderness and joy. My heart ached with the missing of her, knowing how she would jump up and down to be in view of the oaks of Nybron. Oh, Lily Mae!

I ate the last of my dried jerky and gave thanks for a few berries that grew on the ledge. I dared not stop again between here and the city; though hurry would draw attention, so would lingering. I closed my eyes and asked the Lord for direction. As I looked once more upon the city, I spied a steeple near the three o'clock edge, crowned with a cross. Of course! Before I could consider further the dangers ahead, I set my sights on the church, wondering if it stood on Shelton Street.

In my spirit I heard echoes of Anna's song on the steps, *"Father mine, my way winds long . . ."* Once again I longed to sing to lift my spirits but knew it was too risky. I was grateful that my hair had been hidden away under my hood, and I tried to shape my gait to look heavier, more masculine. If Lily Mae could see me now, how she would laugh aloud! Thinking of her face, I nearly giggled myself, choking back the sound just in time as I considered how far it would travel to anyone who might be hidden, watching, attentive. Again I hurried from cover to cover, from tree trunk to scrub to boulder, praying that none would see me. It was early yet; perhaps I would be safe for now.

As Nybron grew close, my every sense was taut, attuned, cognizant of threat. It could all end here and now if one of Griffin's sentries found me before I found help. I continued moving forward, keeping my eyes on the steeple, praying that I had not misread Frank's notations, that I was not wrong to assume the church would be a place of sanctuary. Half a mile lay between the church and my current location, and even at this hour, I perceived a few folks out and about on the winding streets, perhaps making deliveries or hurrying to a place of work that required early hours. In some ways I was glad for their presence; I would not be so visible among others. And yet how I could tell neutral passersby from those who sought me for capture?

I hurried from the shade of a shed to the side of a fence as stunted trees gave way to small outbuildings and homes. I had entered Nybron. I kept my steps heavy, my back bent a bit to hide my feminine shape. It was foolish perhaps, since I wore a skirt, not leggings, but the long cape obscured others' first view of my clothing. I fingered my cross, praying; as I prayed, I saw in my mind's eyes Andrew's beautiful cross, left safe at Henry and Lily's home, and his chess set, left behind for his beloved friend Tom. I thought again of the names etched into the bottoms of the rooks: Nybron, Barrow, Conway, Graceside. Henry, Toby, and I had hunted and hunted for the last three names on the maps in his collection, but had found none of them.

The church lay just two blocks distant. At the corner, a street sign confirmed my hope: Shelton Street. I smiled. My feet seemed to fly of their own accord in the direction of the church, daring to believe that aid awaited me within. I reached the next crossing, distracted by my eagerness, and tripped on the verge. A passing man reached out a hand to steady me, and my heart stopped even as I took it. Did he mean me ill? But as I righted myself, he walked on; it had been only the kindness of a stranger. Taking a deep breath, I made ready to cross the street toward the church. I bent down to brush some dirt off my skirts, and as I raised my head, I looked back toward the buildings on the near side of the street. What I saw made my heart stop: a wooden sign swung from a pole, bearing the proud lettering: Graceside Bakery, Brian and Betsy Jenkins, proprietors. Graceside . . . Betsy . . . Could it be?

I had been so sure that the cross on the map indicated the church. I turned my head to look at the steep steps up to the church door. Only a beggar sat at the entrance, his head bare, his eyes watchful. And then I looked closer: the beggar held a dagger at his side, and upon his feet were near-new leather shoes. Likely, his upraised cup hid his real purpose, a carefully placed spy in plain sight. I shuddered. Had I not stumbled, I would have run directly into a trap!

I considered Graceside Bakery. It also stood on Shelton Street, near the cross mark on the map. If I had a funny feeling after entering, I could simply buy a loaf or two of bread—the Lord knew well how hungry I was for fresh food, after all—and then discern a new plan. I offered a short prayer for protection and entered the door.

The woman behind the counter moved busily from place to place, bringing in fresh stock from her ovens in back. I watched her and felt no nervousness. She called a cheerful greeting and encouraged me to look around, to make myself at home. It would be a few minutes before she would have the case fully stocked for me to choose. My heart told me that, at the very least, she offered welcome and respect for her customers; here was no spy or false front for some other purpose. She looked to be in her early 30's, with more gray hair than one would expect in one so young, yet also with kind eyes and a warm timbre to her voice. I eyed the breads and rolls and buns, and my mouth watered. Everything had been made with care, baked to a crisp crust. She continued to hurry from back of shop to counter and back again, offering me a gentle smile each time. During her last longer stint in the back, I turned to look at a framed print on the wall between two windows, and my heart stopped. It was a pencil sketch of a lazy, contented cat sprawled in a sunbeam, clearly drawn by someone who loved the furry creatures. I remembered Anna's letter, read so long ago in the comfort of Susannah's home. She had shared that Katherine's sister had drawn pencil sketches on her letters to her, including a sketch of a kitten.

The woman behind the counter addressed me again. "Welcome to Graceside! I'm ready now; thanks for letting me put all my stock out first. Few people come for bread quite as early as this, but I like to be ready!" She smiled, and I felt a sense of peace wash over me.

"Did you draw this?" I asked.

"Oh, that . . . that's Jasper, my favorite cat. He's such a beautiful creature that the picture nearly draws itself! Do you like it?"

"Yes, it reminds me of Ebenezer, a cat belonging to a friend of mine."

"Ebenezer! What a great name for cat! Though a bit long to call out, should he go wandering . . ."

She looked at me appraisingly, curious and open. "I don't remember seeing you here before."

"No. I'm very glad to have found you, though. And your bread smells wonderful!"

"Thank you. Brian and I have been up for several hours, getting it all ready. He's catching his nap upstairs now, since he covers the counter in the afternoons. Our daughter, Katie, will aid me mid-morning, after her chores are done."

I smiled, a big smile that reached from my anxious heart through to my eyes. I spoke gently but with focused clarity, "She is named for her Aunt Katherine, isn't she?"

Betsy's jaw dropped. She came out from behind the counter.

"Do you have news of my sister? Are you a friend of hers? My heart tells me that she is dead, yet I have long hoped that I've been wrong. Please, tell me."

She looked into my eyes and saw their sadness, my brows drawn down in concern and care. Betsy covered her own eyes for a moment, took a deep, shuddering breath. "Yes, my heart was right, wasn't it? But I see that you know things, may have a story or two for me. I'll call Katie to stand at the counter, and you and I will have a long talk in the back. While I go fetch her, you choose yourself some breakfast; it looks as though you haven't eaten well in a while."

She hurried up the back stairs, skirts swishing, flour-dusted hands fluttering. I reached for a pair of hot cross buns, smiling in gratitude for the Lord having led me here, for Betsy's kindness. The buns tasted even better than they looked, and both were gone before Katie Jenkins appeared with her mother. She too had warm eyes and grace of movement, with a more slender form than her mother's generous measures. She smiled at me, unspoken questions crowding her eyes, as her mother handed me a thin loaf and a breakfast scone as she bustled me toward a back parlor beyond the kitchen.

"Stories are better told over good food!" she assured me, as she pulled forward a comfortable chair and set about to brew some tea. Jasper eyed me from his perch atop a bookshelf, and I swore that he smiled knowingly. My body recognized a haven of love for the first time since Sitton, and I fell asleep sitting up in the chair.

19

I t was early afternoon before I awoke, with the midday sun slanting through a window across the way. Jasper snuggled on my lap, looking quite pleased with himself.

I heard a man's voice interacting with customers at the front of the shop, but Betsy and Katie were not in sight. I reached for the thin loaf that still sat on the table beside the chair. Though it was no longer warm, I welcomed its nourishment and quality. Crumbs feel on Jasper's head, and he tossed his ears to rid them of their bits of bread. The bell on his collar sang out as he moved, and Katie quickly appeared in the doorway.

"You're awake! I'll go tell mother."

Betsy returned with her daughter, and the two sat side by side across from me once Betsy had set another kettle on to brew. She eyed me with open curiosity and compassion. "You have had a long journey, I imagine. I've never seen anyone fall asleep so fast, and certainly not with a pack still at her back! You are younger than I first thought, though your eyes speak of a grief and worry I would not wish on one of your age. Please tell us what you know of Katherine, and if there is a way that we can be of help to you."

I relayed the story as best I knew it, the journey of the girls, the misfortune of Katherine's fall, the fact that Anna had sat with her reading Scripture as she died. I left out some of the less flattering elements of Anna's narration, wondering if perhaps Katherine's personality had soured with her travels or with some disappointment not associated with her family.

Katie and her mother cried openly, grieved by the details and yet also relieved to know the truth and to learn that all that could have been done had been offered with care and love. As the teakettle sang, Betsy sent Katie to help her father in the shop and shut the door behind her.

"I suspect that you tidied up the story as you know it just a bit. My sister had a prickly spirit that often pushed others away, but I loved her all the same. I hold up her strengths to Katie, since she is her namesake, and I am pleased to say that Katie does not show her aunt's anger or judgment. Perhaps Katherine would be proud of her."

As she filled my cup with sweet-smelling tea, with a rich hint of citrus, she looked at me with a directness that startled me. "You are in trouble of some kind, aren't you? Have you tangled with Griffin somehow?"

"You know about Griffin?"

"All of Nybron knows about Griffin. He is the unnamed presence in the room at all gatherings; most people fear him but few dare speak of him. People who risk speaking out are known to disappear. You are safe to talk with me, but I don't want Katie to know of it; she can honestly say you once knew her aunt and had stopped here on your travels to share what you knew."

"I believe that Griffin holds two friends of mine captive in the tunnels beneath the Praying Oaks."

"Tunnels beneath the Praying Oaks?! How in the world do you know that?"

I described the conversation that I had overheard. She sipped her tea but her eyes never left my face, a vital light rising in them. "The people of Nybron have been trying for years to ferret out his hiding places. Some whisper that he has a network of tunnels under the city—and perhaps he does—but those whisperers often disappear or turn up dead. You may hold a key to a weakness in Griffin's stronghold. Who are these friends of yours?"

I told her a brief version of what I knew of Anna. Knowing that she had been the one to comfort her sister on her deathbed, Betsy's interest in my story strengthened. I relayed what had happened to Toby, Windstar, and me, and her eyes grew dark with worry. "You needn't be concerned about the horse, Brie. Griffin loves his horses, and the one time in all these years that he was nearly caught came about because a horse of his was lamed, and he couldn't bring himself to abandon or kill it. He finally left it to save his own hide. The happy outcome is that one of our wisest farmers restored the horse to health over several months of care—and was able to return it to the original owner from whom it had been stolen."

"As for Toby . . . my dear, do not trust to hope. If he was beset by Rory and his henchmen . . ." Her voice faltered, and she looked away. My heart twisted inside me, and I longed to ask for more, but knew that it would not help. All I could do was to continue to hold Toby in my prayers and try to find a way to his aid, or at least to the aid of any held captive in the tunnels.

"I can't figure out why Griffin thinks that you and Toby would have anything related to the prophecy. And even if you did, how would he know about it?"

"Tell me more about the prophecy. Why is it so important to Griffin?"

"Long ago, two friars from far abroad sought shelter in Nybron. They had come to bring the Good News of Jesus, and at first many were receptive. The church just across the street dates from that time period. They stayed many months, helping our local printers to produce copies of the Gospels, which they then distributed for free to any who wished to be blessed by them. They asked so little of our people: shelter each night, a bit of breakfast upon awaking, a small noon meal. In return they brought us the light of Christ, their vibrant, laughing spirits, their obvious love and compassion. One of the friars possessed the gift of prophecy. He exercised it only rarely, when he felt that a word of admonition or a word of encouragement might stave off an unfortunate outcome. Almost everyone followed his advice carefully, believing that his foreknowledge helped the people of our town to avoid several calamities.

"However, Griffin's grandfather Craggin, like Griffin himself, shaped his choices through greed and selfish gain, not through any concern for others. When Friar John Mark shared a vision he had received that Griffin's grandmother's life was in peril, due to Craggin's choices, he simply ignored any of John Mark's admonishments and continued his reckless course. Within ten days, the unfortunate woman was killed when one of Craggin's enemies sent a warning arrow through an open window of their home. Craggin refused to see his own complicity in placing his wife in danger, and that night he and his cronies set upon the friars and killed them in cold blood. Never has our town experienced such a terrifying storm as swept up in the wee hours of that night, knocking off roofs, scarring the oaks, creating a turbulent mess at the marketplace. In the preternatural calm that followed, our town learned of four deaths: of Craggin's wife and his subsequent rage, of the loss of the friars, who were mourned for weeks thereafter, and of Craggin's own death, felled by a heavy oak branch that ripped free as he crept home in the cover of night from his murderous acts.

None mourned his passing. Some even hoped that by his death our town would be set on a course toward greater peace, freed of his plotting, his greed, his thoughtless attacks.

"But his son—and his grandson in his footsteps—did not see how Craggin had wrought his own downfall, did not see the hand of God in his death. Both have channeled their grief, anger, and greed into ongoing acts of terror upon our town and upon our visitors. Somehow in their twisted hearts, they believe that Nybron itself has done them wrong and its citizens must pay. It makes no sense, but there it is."

"You've said nothing about the prophecy to which Griffin clings."

"Yes, Brian reproaches me often for wandering off the mark." She smiled fondly toward the front of the store. "I have been lucky in love as Katherine was not . . . but that tale is not for this day.

"Friar John Mark rarely shared his prophecies unless he believed that by so doing he could help the hearer to avoid danger or amend his life. The one exception came on Christmas morning, about halfway through the friars' time in Nybron. Just at the close of the morning service, which had drawn many new converts, John Mark raised his hand to bless the assembled gathering. But instead of offering the regular benediction that he uttered weekly, he formed the shape of the cross over the congregation and paused, a strange look on his face.

"'You are entering a season of great peril. The few will enslave the many. Those who reject counsel will take power. For many years, you will only have your faith to see you through the dark days. Trust to God's mercy and to the power of prayer.

"'One day, however, travelers will bear treasures to Nybron that will decide its fate. In wise hands, they will redeem the lost times; in the hands of the proud, they could bring your downfall.' His face changed, and his voice intoned,

> 'Three treasures to hand, two treasures by land,
> And one that is born of the sea.
> Each has its grace, in time and in space,
> But united their power's set free.
> None shall say nay to their wielder; pray,
> How may this strength come to me?'

"Those who assembled that Christmas morning felt frightened and puzzled. What were they to do? Craggin, who heard of the prophecy at third hand, vowed to beset any travelers who came to Nybron, to strip them of any treasures and use them for his own ends. The rest of the town came at the prophecy from the opposite direction: to welcome travelers with open arms and gracious hospitality, believing that at some point the prophesied treasures would come to us to redeem our lost times. Hence our much divided reputation: a town of both great danger and great hospitality.

"After John Mark was killed, the young couple whom he had been training to lead our community once he and his companion heard the call to travel elsewhere carefully reviewed his few possessions. He had a Bible, a small cross, a modest collection of shells from his travels to cities along the shore, and a sheaf of papers. All the papers but one bore Scripture references, prayer concerns, and notes to encourage him in his work of ministry. However, one page stood out among the others. No one had ever seen him draw, and he had been overheard to joke, at first discussion of the church's design, that anything sketched by his hand would surely collapse before it was complete. And yet this page clearly bore his signature at the bottom. He had sketched three extraordinary items: a sword that portrayed the battle of David and Goliath, a dagger with inlaid stones, and a beautiful pearl. It came to be rumored that these were the items of the prophecy, and one who wielded both sword and dagger could not be overcome by any foe."

I stared at her, wordless and afraid. It was very possible that two of those three items were right now upon my person. And the third had been in Toby's hand as the marauders attacked. What did it mean? What was I to do? What should I tell Betsy? My head swam with questions, and my heart beat fast. It seemed incredible that I had been led on a journey to gather these items and bring them to Nybron. And which pearl might it be: the one left me by the albatross or the one from Andrew's field? Surely Andrew's made the most sense; he had been in Nybron after all. But then I remembered Lily Mae's parting words—the albatross will not lead you astray—and I wondered. It occurred to me that the snoring man at Georgina's must have been a sentinel of Griffin's, and that false snores covered his spying. Perhaps he caught sight of Toby practicing his swordsmanship in his room, or perhaps they had known all along that Georgina possessed the sword but felt they must wait for travelers to bring it to Nybron for the prophecy to work.

And did I believe in prophecy at all? The greatest strength I had known was in God's work in the world, accomplished through the power of prayer or the touch of human hands. I was no warrior; how could I face the strength of Griffin's numbers even if I held all three treasures, which I did not? My head hurt with the wondering.

Betsy looked at me intently. "You know more that you have not yet shared, I can see that," she stated simply. "But you have traveled far, and these last days in fear. Why don't you help Katie and me to prepare our evening meal, and we can talk again later?"

I felt grateful once again for her kindness. I had been so blessed on my journeying by hospitable strangers, by others who knew the grace of Jesus but did not know me—and yet chose to treat me with his love. I had not believed such a welcome would be possible, remembering the fears and ostracism in my home town. But then, rarely did I show my giftings. Especially now, I had the sense of larger forces at work, pulling me forward. As I worked beside Betsy in her messy, comfortable kitchen, I let myself relax into the embrace of yet another kind family.

As she prepared our meal, stopping now and again to ask for my assistance, Betsy began to sing in a rich soprano voice:

So she runs, her feet fleet, and wind-winged by grace,
So she runs, with the Lord's light abright on her face,
So she runs, but in running one must have a goal . . .
Does she see that while running, she cannot be whole?
Come home, gifted sister, come home.
Come home, grieving sister, come home.
Come home to your Father's grace; come home, find your rightful place.
Come home, wind-borne sister, come home.

Just when I thought the song had come to its end, as it had in other contexts, she continued:

You bear the gifts, you bear the truth,
Come home to Nybron, come home.

I stared at her, dropping the knife I had been using with a clatter. Betsy stared at me. "What is it, Brie? You look as though you had seen a ghost."

"I have heard that song sung a number of times on my travels, yet never with that couplet at the end. Do you know the origin of the song?"

Betsy looked thoughtful. "The people of Nybron believe that it is one of John Mark's compositions. He and his colleague wrote many hymns, most of them attributed to Timotheus. But there were a few songs that felt more like folk songs, and those closest to the monks believed those compositions to be John Mark's work. *Wind-Borne Sister* is a treasured favorite here in Nybron. I've been singing that tune since I was a little girl."

"Do you think that there is a chance that the song could also be a prophecy?"

"I never thought of it like that. I suppose that it could be."

Dinner proved a laughter-filled, sustaining time; this family clearly found joy in one another and had enjoyed prosperity for a number of years. They were not wealthy like Henry and Lily, yet they had more than enough and felt glad of the chance to share with me. Brian and Katie kept up a warm banter through much of the meal that did my heart good.

By early evening, I became mindful that I was among a family of bakers, who kept of necessity very early hours. Betsy showed me a small but cozy guest room and told me that I was welcome to stay with them for as long as I needed. I offered her money, and she just laughed, "We have more than we need. Pass on the gift to others when you are able."

That night my dreams were dark and troubled. I thought I caught a glimpse of a bloodied, limping Toby, arms bound, eyes blindfolded, being led into a tunnel. Along the passage that he and his captors followed, I sensed the presence of others in pain, locked behind closed doors, dwelling in near darkness. As he passed one door, a voice called out to him, "You bring light with you. You bring hope with you. Be not dismayed." I looked as he could not, and I saw beyond the door the face of a woman in her early 30's, her hair wild, her skin smudged with dirt and grime, and yet with eyes of peace, of strength. Was this Anna? And then the scene changed.

I saw a much larger underground chamber, lit with many torches and augmented with intricate, clever contraptions fashioned with mirrors that made the room seem brighter and vaster than it was. A man with an angry, intense presence stood on the far side of the room, calling out commands. Though his appearance was trim and groomed, his eyes lacked any of the peace that characterized the woman in the cell. He carried a hunted, restless look, as though he sought something that forever eluded him. He looked across the room and spied one of Toby's captors. Toby was no longer with him.

"So, Rory, what news?"

"For once you may be pleased with me, Griffin."

"I'll be the judge of that."

Rory lifted the sheath of the sword off his shoulder and presented it to Griffin. Griffin raised one eyebrow in questioning and slowly slid the sword out of its casing and into the glittering, mirrored light. He gasped. "It is the sword of the prophecy."

"That's what I thought, too," Rory agreed. "The workmanship is extraordinary. I've never seen anything like it."

"Did you find the other treasures?"

"No, the man who wielded this carried a dagger, but it is not the one we seek. We searched him and his saddlebags—nothing else of interest, except the horse of course. He's a beauty."

"What of the woman?"

"We saw no woman."

"But Sark specifically reported a young man and a young woman. You let her get past you?"

"They must have traveled separately."

"They did no such thing. No young woman travels alone on the road to Nybron, no matter how careful or seasoned a traveler she may be. You did not keep your eyes sufficiently open. She is far more important than he is. I saw her in my dream. I can't believe you let her get away!"

"But you have the first treasure, Griffin. Perhaps it will bring you good fortune."

"You know nothing. The treasures have power together, not separately."

The light from the torches seemed to intensify, just as the anger rose in Griffin's eyes. It was as though fire flamed around me on all sides, and I heard Toby crying out in the distance. I could see my hands in front of me, the dagger in my left hand, the sword in my right. Where was the pearl? And then I saw it. The pearl fit into the hilt of the sword, to sit in the curve of David's sling, just before he sent it flying to slay Goliath. Which pearl was it? I could not tell.

20

$\mathcal{A}$s I became aware of morning light filtering through the curtains, I felt a warm weight on my chest. Jasper had found his way into my room. I stroked him gently, thinking of Ebenezer and of Susannah and of how far my journey had brought me. I recognized that I was at a point of decision: should I bring Betsy, and perhaps Brian and Katie as well, into my confidence about the dagger and pearl? Should I try to find Griffin's underground hideaway on my own, or was it best to ask for someone else to journey with me? I did not want to place this family in harm's way. I lay there for many minutes, turning different alternatives over and over in my mind. Up until now, it had felt as though an unseen hand had guided me clearly, intently. I believed that I was meant to come here to the bakery, to bring Katherine's story home to her family. Yet I could not shake the sense that just as I had left Lily Mae far behind out of love for her, so I could not ask these new friends to come with me.

I could feel my own fatigue still weighing on me, heavier and more cumbersome than Jasper's sleeping form. I knew that I needed time to regain strength, to seek clarity. I felt certain that Griffin's watchmen remained vigilant in the town. Perhaps the Lord had led me here as a haven of rest and protection before the last challenging chapter of this journey. I thought of the couplet that Betsy had added to the song and felt the hair rise on the back of my neck. I needed to stand strong.

Toby surged into my thoughts. Had my dreams been visions of what had come to pass in the tunnels under the Praying Oaks? Was he really alive but captive? Or had it been my own wishful thinking? I saw again the face of the woman I imagined to be Anna and felt hope spring anew. By God's grace, I prayed that somehow, some way, I would find a way to free them both. But how?

Katie came in then with breakfast on a tray, the crescent rolls still warm, the tea just right. She sat at my bedside and her smile stretched to her eyes. "I'm glad that you're here, Brie," she told me, "You bring light with you." I felt startled by her words, a direct echo of Anna's from last night's dream. I thanked her for the food and her compliment.

"Mama said to remind you that you are to stay as long as you like. We love to have guests with us, though we seldom enjoy that blessing. Your eyes show how tired you are, how long your journey has been. Make yourself at home, Brie. Let this be a haven for you."

Her words resonated with confirmation of my own first thoughts of the day. She left then to allow me to enjoy my breakfast. Jasper finagled his way to a few small bits of bacon, and then sat up to clean his face with a furry grace. It felt strange to have the freedom to sit and watch him, instead of tensing at every sound, as I had done for so many days on the journey since Georgina's inn.

I spent the next week resting and gaining strength, savoring the Jenkins' hospitality and yet struggling inwardly over what to do. I had no dreams, no visions. I did not leave the bakery, believing that staying hidden would be wisest. On the few occasions when I glanced out the side windows toward the church, I always saw a bedraggled yet watchful man on the steps. The Jenkins loved hearing tales of my journey, and I willingly shared stories of Susannah and Lily Mae. I even found the courage to talk of my mother and Anna, of the early days of my life and its sweetness. They did not push for more, though I often caught Betsy's thoughtful glance upon me. Brian and Katie saw me only as a welcome guest and left it at that.

Late in the evenings, after the family had turned in, I would sit by the fire with Jasper, seeking God's guidance in prayer. I wanted clear answers to so many questions. Should I ask Brian to accompany me? Should I leave the dagger and pearl here at the bakery, rather than risk my capture and their coming into evil hands? Which pearl was it anyway? Was I to gather a group of people to go with me into the tunnels? Would I be using the dagger to attack, to kill? I couldn't imagine it. In recent years the Lord had used my hands and my presence for healing. Even to consider taking a life horrified me. And how was I to get the sword back? If Griffin had it and knew its importance, he would not let it go at any price, likely not even at threat to his own life. But did he have it? Was my vision of that night just a fear-borne dream, not a view into reality? My head would ache as I cried out to Jesus with question after question, hearing no answers.

Most nights, just as I would feel ready to give up and climb into bed, I would receive a word of sweet assurance: "I love you, Brie. I am with you. I will not leave you or forsake you. Trust that Toby and Windstar and Anna will be all right. Yes, they are in danger, but they are all right." My questions would redouble: What am I to do, Lord? And then the silence would resume, a quiet peace at its center, yet with no direction, no clarity, no details or hints of my next steps.

Eight days after I arrived at the bakery, Betsy came into my room in the early evening, just after dinner, and shut the door behind her. We sat together before the fire, where I had passed so many nights. For several minutes she kept silent vigil beside me, mostly watching the fire, but occasionally glancing up to assess my expression. Finally she spoke.

"Brie, I believe that you are the sister of the prophecy. I can see that you are convinced of it also. You seem to be trying to make up your mind about something, and I have wanted to give you room to reflect, to heal, to regain your strength after what the last part of your journey must have been like for you. However, I do not think that you should tarry here much longer. I have heard reports that Griffin's men have begun searching from house to house in the northern streets of the city, and it won't be long before they come here. I have no secret closets or cellars in which to hide you, and I sense that they would not believe even the best of stories that we could concoct. It is clear to me that you need to go in search of Toby and Windstar. I fear for your life if you go alone, but none of us has the kind of bravery it would take to accompany you."

"You have been very brave to show me hospitality for this long, knowing so little about me."

"Perhaps. Nevertheless, I could not let Katie go, and you would not ask that of me, knowing what you do about Katherine. Brian is a wonderful husband, and he loves the work of our bakery, yet he is one of the most fearful men I have ever met when it comes to risk or conflict—and he has a tremendous fear of the dark. He is the last man that you would want in a tunnel with you! And I? I'm afraid my weight would make me a poor choice. I cannot move quickly, and when I do run, I pant like a dog on a midsummer day!" She chuckled in warm self-deprecation. "But you need someone with you, of this I feel sure."

"The Lord will go with me."

"Yes. It is clear that he and his angels have watched over you many times on your long journey, keeping you from harm, bringing you to safe havens, and granting you access to information it would have been so unlikely for you to know. This is what I think, Brie: you and I need to pray together, and Christ will give us an answer."

She reached for my hand. Jasper jumped up on her lap, as though making it known that he too would bring his agreement to whatever petitions we raised. A deep sense of gratitude flowed through me, and I took Betsy's hand in my own.

She began the prayer with words of thanksgiving, for her own family, for their prosperity, for the gift of knowing at last what had become of her sister. I echoed with my own words of thanksgiving for the many faithful, loving people who had come alongside me in ways both small and great as the days had unfolded over the past months. And then Betsy prayed boldly: "We need clarity, Lord. Show us what Brie is to do. Help our hearts and minds to be open to know your invitation and calling for this next part of her journey. She has been so faithful, but she is at a loss. Show us your will."

We sat together in wordless waiting, our only accompaniment the crackling of the fire and Jasper's contented purrs. I expected a vision; I saw nothing. I hoped for a word, even one word of direction; I heard nothing. I gazed at the fire, and tears began to roll down my cheeks. Why did he not answer?

Suddenly I heard Betsy draw in her breath. Her hand in mine was clammy but she held it more tightly than before. Her eyes remained closed, yet a strange light played over her face, as though she saw something not visible to my own eyes. I said nothing, only redoubled my silent prayers for clarity, for instructions, for a way forward.

The minutes stretched on. I wanted so much to ask what she perceived, but I held back, waiting, praying, wondering. Finally a log collapsed in the fireplace with a loud snap. Betsy sat up abruptly, and then whispered, "Thank you, Jesus. Amen," and was still once more.

I turned to her. Her eyes sparkled brightly in the firelight, moistened with tears. "You are to go alone, Brie. I imagine you do not want to hear that, but I heard a voice clearly in my prayer. You go alone. If others come with you, you will draw more attention to yourself. You are to take everything with you that you brought with you to this house, along with new provisions for your journey. You are to leave before dawn. I also saw an albatross; I don't know why. Does that mean something to you? The last word I heard is that you are not to be afraid. The Lord will fight beside you. Your gifts will show forth, and you will not come to harm."

Tears streamed down my face. Go alone into an underground maze filled with armed men, for which I had no map? Go alone bringing the dagger and pearl of the prophecy, not knowing what I was meant to do? Go alone to try to save Anna and Toby and Windstar, when I wasn't even sure if all three were in the tunnels in the first place? Yet I clung to Betsy's mention of the albatross. How could she have known? I had not mentioned anything about that encounter. Surely this was a word from God for me. I took a deep breath.

"Thank you, Betsy. I have been up late praying every night but the first, trying to hear, wanting to see, straining to know. All the questions I have been asking were answered in what you just told me."

Setting Jasper gently on the floor, Betsy rose and enfolded me in a wonderful, warm, sustaining hug. "I believe that you will be all right, Brie. We will be praying for you here, every hour of every day until we hear word of your safety. If things go ill, you are welcome to seek refuge here again, though I do not think it will be safe very long. I will go now and gather the best breads for travel and other cheese and fruit for the journey before you. Trust that the Lord goes before you to prepare the way. You are the woman of the prophecy; he will not let harm come to you."

I wished that I shared Betsy's confidence. I felt no assurance that I was the woman of the prophecy. So often the prophets of Scripture had come to ill ends. Even if my life was to be protected, she had not shared any word that Toby, Anna, and Windstar would live. What lay on the other side of the days to come? As never before, I was being summoned to step out in faith, to surrender in unseeing trust and to fall into the Lord's outstretched arms. Had I the strength? Please, Lord Jesus, lead me, and grant me the grace to follow, whatever comes.

21

I slept very fitfully that night, knowing how important restful sleep would be and yet unable to lay aside my deep doubts and concerns. I trusted what Betsy had told me, but I saw no way forward to success. A lump grew in my stomach and settled there like a ragged stone.

Katie awoke me in the early hours, her gentle face a comforting view. "We will be praying for you, Brie. May all go well with you." She left me then, hurrying below to help her parents with the early-morning baking. I had packed all my things the night before, and so my preparations were completed quickly in the darkness of pre-dawn. Jasper stirred on the bed and mewed plaintively; he did not wish me to go. As I stroked him and listened to his welcome purrs, I wondered briefly if I would live to see him and this family again. I shook my head to clear the doubts; I knew they would only make it harder for me to be aware and alert for all that lay ahead.

Betsy met me at the foot of the stairs. She had assembled a generous but tightly packed set of provisions for me and invited me to sit briefly with her for a quick breakfast and sending prayer. Her signature crescent roll seemed dry and tasteless in my mouth, flavored as it was by anxiety. Betsy caught my eye and spoke reassuringly, "Just pray your way there and back, Brie. Pray your way. I know that the Lord goes before you." She raised her hands then and asked for Christ's vigilant protection over me as I entered upon an unknown and intensely dangerous part of my journey. I raised my hands with her, longing for a feeling of peace, yet feeling only a sense of resolve.

After the prayer, I drank the last of the juice and stood. "I must leave before it gets much lighter, or I worry that Griffin's spies will catch me before I even get to the oaks." She nodded. As we rose from the table, she gestured for me to accompany her into her bedroom, a part of the home I had not entered before. I set down my pack and provisions and looked at her with curiosity. "I have two last things to give you," she stated simply. "That red cloak of yours, though warmer and better-made than my long black one here, makes you far more visible. Let's trade for now, and you can have the red one back when you return." I felt grateful for her confidence as I fingered the cloth under my hand. "This cloak belonged to my great-aunt Betsy—(*Betsy? Andrew's wife Betsy?* I wondered)—who swore that it kept her nearly invisible in dark places. Though why she was abroad on dark nights, I still don't know! I have had little cause to wear it, but feel strongly it will be a help to you. Though perhaps not so helpful as my second gift."

She paused and took a deep breath. "I misled you, Brie, and I hid the truth from you. I told you that I had no cellars in which to hide you. In a way that's true: I haven't a cellar, but my home holds its own secret. She moved a large cabinet to the side, revealing a trap door in the floor below. I gasped. "This opening leads to a tunnel that heads eastward, toward the Praying Oaks. I last explored it when I was Katie's age, when my curiosity overcame my parents' dire warnings. I remember walking for what seemed over an hour before I came to a strange rock outcropping that I first believed to be a dead end. But by way of a narrow zigzag passage among the rock formations, I found myself at a V in the tunnel. I went left; praise the Lord, I went left! I quickly found myself above ground, beneath the Praying Oaks. The sun smiled down through the leaves, and I felt so proud and courageous. And then a man shouted at me, "You there! What are you doing here?" and I ran. I ran faster and harder than I knew I could. Thankfully, I came quickly upon a group of schoolchildren out on a picnic with their teacher. I moved to sit near them, and my pursuer went away.

"Brie, with what I now know, it is my contention that our passageway is part of Griffin's maze, a forgotten branch, given the rock formation. My expectation is that if you take the right-hand way, it will lead you further in the maze of tunnels, toward Griffin and your friends. I remember seeing torches lighting the way on that side, whereas natural light drew me left. You will only need a candle until you reach the outcropping; then you will need whatever cloak of secrecy that this garment, your own stealth, and the Lord's overseeing watch may provide you. I did not tell you all of this before now, as I feared that you would think us compatriots of Griffin—we are not! I also thought it best that you not know until you needed it. Neither Katie nor Brian knows this is here. When you return—provided you come by this exit, for there are many, I would wager—knock loudly on the floor four times, and I will move away the cabinet to let you in."

She continued, "I feel strongly that your chances of getting to Griffin's stronghold are best this way. He may have guards stationed along the twists and turns once you pass the outcropping, but none before. On the other hand, if you risk leaving by the outskirts of the city, you may need to pass as many as a half-dozen scouts and guards. Go with God, Brie, my friend, our hope." Betsy raised the trapdoor and gestured to a lit candle on the table behind her. "This is a special candle, scentless except for when it is extinguished. Be sure to thrust it into the ground to put it out, or the acrid smoke may give you away before your journey has brought you very far."

Once again, through a friend, the Lord had given me the tools and knowledge I needed for the next stretch of my journey. I felt amazed to know that she had held vital answers all along, yet waited for the fullness of time to share them. She kissed my cheek as I put on my pack of belongings and provisions, threw on the dark, black cloak over all, and then lifted the candle. I had worried that I would need to descend a ladder while holding the taper, but the way down was a wide staircase, carefully hewn from the natural rock. As I set foot on sod at the base of the stair, Betsy closed the trap door. I heard the scraping of the cabinet as she slid it back overhead. I held my candle to look up and gaped: the bottom of the trap door was not visible. Some mechanism must slide a heavy second door, one made of rock, into place upon closure of the door above. If Griffin's men had come this way, they would have believed that the steps led nowhere. I took a deep breath, turned away from the stairs, and began to walk toward destiny.

22

I crept along the passage, all senses alert. I took Betsy's advice and prayed my way along the dark tunnel, lifting up petitions for Betsy, Brian, and Katie; for Georgina; for Susannah and Allan; for sweet Lily Mae and her two families; and then, with a catch in my throat, for Toby and Windstar and Anna. Finally, to my surprise, I felt led to pray for Griffin and his men, that God would change their hearts, that the Lord would lead them to amend their ways. Even as I prayed the words, my head doubted any chance of such transformation. But I trusted the Holy Spirit's leading and prayed on.

Long before I felt ready to see it, I came upon the outcropping. Once I put out my candle and slid my way between, I would be in unknown territory. I had no map; I had no instructions. I knew only that these tunnels belonged to Griffin and that he ruled here. As I paused, I felt startled to hear voices not far from me. I shoved my candle abruptly in the dirt and crouched down, far against the wall on my side of the rocks. I listened attentively, praying not to be discovered.

"Jamie, I need your help."

"You always need my help, Rufus."

"I can never remember the sequence of turns to the prisoners, and it's my job to bring them their food today. If I end up on Griffin's doorstep, carrying these bowls of gruel for the third time in a month, he told me he would make me a prisoner myself. I know he means it. Is it right, right, left, left, right? Or is it right, right, left, right, right?"

Jamie made a sound of deep disgust, an ugly blend of spitting, sneering, and scoffing. "Neither, Rufe-doof. That first sequence gets you to the horses. The second takes you right to Griffin. You never remember. Why should I tell you?"

"Because you owe me money. I'll forgive the debt if you tell me."

"Fair enough. For the prisoners, you want right, left, right, right, left. Now give me one of those bowls of gruel, and I'll go back up to my watching post above. Griffin has most of our guards in the city, looking for that mythical woman he is so certain is out there. What woman? I think he's cracked."

I heard the sound of footsteps receding in both directions. Had I emerged only seconds sooner, I would have been discovered. Had I come through only minutes later, I would have missed this critical information. I wished for a piece of paper on which to scrawl the sequences, but instead repeated them over and over. Getting to the horses—and hopefully, Windstar!—proved an easy pattern: it sounded like hoofbeats in rapid succession to me. And to find Griffin, one just made an adjustment to the fourth choice in the sequence. Don't go *forth* to Griffin, I thought. The prisoners' pattern felt different altogether, but I held tight to it, knowing that needed to be my first destination. But what would I do about Rufus? If I went that way directly, I would run into him on the return route, if he were not still engaged in offering food to the captives. Yet I didn't know if he would pass back this way, go visit the horses, or head somewhere else among the winding tunnels. I needed a plan.

I would keep to the darkest spots in the tunnel, moving swiftly, under the cover of the dark cloak that Betsy had leant me. I would not speak unless spoken to, and if addressed, try to keep my voice guttural and broken and low. I would walk with longer strides than normal, hoping not to be perceived as a woman alone. Clearly Griffin's men came roughhewn and aggressive, or he would not have chosen them. I hesitated over whether to leave anything behind here, in this last protected spot. I opted to set aside a small portion of bread and my smallest flagon of water (Betsy had given me three, believing that my friends might be severely dehydrated) but trusted to Betsy's injunction that I carry with me all that I had brought to Nybron. I tucked my hair securely toward the back of my head, pulled the dark hood tight around my face, and took a deep breath. *Lord Jesus, guide my way.*

I slid through the tight opening, barely fitting with the encumbrance of my gear behind and beside me. I stood in the larger tunnel on the other side, trying not to make the slightest sound. To the left, I could see natural light filtering through and longed to move toward the sunshine. Yet I knew that my destiny lay off to the right, into these darker tunnels of uncertainty and challenge. At a distance of every thirty yards or so, a small sconce had been set into the wall and gave off a ring of light. Between the sconces, the passages offered abundant shadows in which to hide. I needed to be attentive to two things, it seemed: staying hidden and perceiving the passage openings. I nearly missed the first right turning, as it lay in a dark, shadowy bend in the wall. I wondered briefly if it were the correct route but felt comforted to discern a small dollop of gruel on the dirt floor ahead of me: Rufus had just passed this way.

The first three turnings passed without incident, though my whole spirit remained on alert. At each turn that I passed, I traced a small arrow in the dirt, pointing back the way that I had come. I did not trust myself to remember the shadowed sequencing in reverse. As I discovered the third right turn, I heard a voice coming toward me, muttering and fussing. It sounded like the voice of an old man, and it certainly wasn't Rufus. I cowered in the darkest shadow, squeezing myself into a large cleft in the side of the passageway, covering all but my eyes with the hood. The gray-haired man passed by, his gait slowed with a painful limp. Not even pausing to think of the risk to myself, I raised my hand beneath my cloak and held it toward his leg, intent on healing. He stopped short, and I nearly gasped. Surely he would see me now! But instead he rubbed his hip, a wondering look on his face. He passed on, no longer muttering.

I stayed in the cleft for several minutes, engaged in internal conflict. Was I to reach for healing here in these tunnels, even at great risk to myself? Did these gifts that God poured out through me at times trump my sense of mission to free Toby and Windstar and Anna? I could not see my way to a clear answer. I knew that others could block the receipt of the gifts if they did not want them; could I also block them by an act of will? And if I did, would I be preventing the very work of God that I felt called to share? Before long it occurred to me that I was wasting valuable time. Soon Rufus would be on his way back, and his young eyes would likely perceive me, even though the old man had not noticed me in the shadowed edges of his view. I needed to trust that the Lord would help me to know at which times to manifest the gift, even if the context were at peril to my friends and myself.

I came to the final left turning. Up ahead, I could hear Rufus moving about, opening slots and shoving bowls in with a grunt or a quick-said greeting, as though against his wishes. I cowered in the shadows just beyond a cavernous opening, with cells lining each side, eight in all. As I peered beneath a ragged outcropping, I perceived Rufus at the far end of the cave. I could also discern large padlocks on every iron door. Where were the keys? Rufus moved one cell closer to my hiding place, and I heard the jingling at his waist. I watched as he unlocked a smaller padlock at the top of a door, allowing him to open the pass-through for food. Other keys, larger and rusty, hung alongside. I needed to obtain the keys from Rufus but not allow him to alert others to my presence. I didn't have the strength to overcome him. My sense of integrity forbade me to slay him; he had done me no harm, was in fact bringing the very food that would keep my friends alive if I did not succeed. Did I have the courage to outwit him?

He moved on to the next cell. I needed to act quickly. Hardly believing the surge of boldness that rose up in me, I stepped into the light. As Rufus locked the top door fast after having passed in the bowl of gruel, he turned and saw me. He took a step back, looking startled and worried.

"Did Griffin send you?"

I nodded, not wanting to use my voice unless I had to do so.

"Is he angry with me?"

I shook my head, and he relaxed a bit.

"Do you have a message?"

Again I nodded.

"Well, tell me then. You're a man of few words."

Praying that I could make my voice convincingly low and gravelly, I coughed twice and then spoke tersely.

"I am to finish the work here. You are needed on the far west side of town. They have found the woman and they need your help."

"Why should I believe you? What is the password?"

I should have panicked and run. Instead I managed a sound much like a scoffing sneer. "You always forget the password anyway, Rufe-doof."

He hung his head. "You're right."

I chanced one more communication. "Go quickly. I've heard there's a hefty reward for the one who ensnares her."

Rufus set down his heavy tray, placed the keys on the dirt floor, and hurried away through the bleak tunnels, dust rising in his wake. I could hardly believe that I had succeeded. I reminded myself that other men faithful to Griffin might appear at any time and hurried toward the keys. As I passed by the first of the cells on the right-hand side, I saw Toby's face through the bars and nearly cried out. He was alive! But I focused on silence and speed, reaching for both the keys and the tray. If someone saw me carrying the gruel, they might assume my identity and not question. I came to Toby's cell once more. His face appeared deeply lined and haggard, far thinner than I remembered him. I wondered also if he suffered from fever, for his eyes shone strangely bright in the darkness.

Instead of reaching for a small key to the pass-through door, I tried several large keys before discovering the one that fit the padlock that held him prisoner. It occurred to me that he might set upon me as I entered, mistaking me for a foe and seeing his chance, so as I entered, I spoke his name, "Toby, I've come."

I set down the tray, trying hard not to look at the filth that surrounded him. I tugged back the hood a few inches, just enough to show my face to him, and then pulled it back down tightly.

"Brie!" Toby's voice, cracked and calloused, troubled me deeply. I worried that he did not have the health or the strength to leave on his own power. He sank to his knees, whether in weakness or thanksgiving, I could not tell.

"You will need the strength of that gruel for all that lies ahead," I told him simply. As he began to eat, I laid my hands upon his forehead and felt the raging fever. Words I did not know cascaded from my mouth and warmth seeped out of my hands, pouring over Toby, bringing God's strength, God's touch, God's healing. I saw that his right arm lay helpless in a sling, and I moved my hands to that side, passing them slowly over his wrist and lower arm. Again, I felt power flow through me, manifesting in strange tongues and a jolt of warmth reaching out to Toby's broken bones.

Suddenly I felt certain that I could not stay any longer in the cell. Someone could come along and close me in, even if they had no keys. "I must free the others," I told him and made my way out, even as I longed to hold him, to ask how he had survived the attack in the Valley of Crags. Glancing across the way, I noticed that the first and second cells on the left-hand side were empty of light or movement. That left five cells to open. Which was Anna's? To my surprise, I heard singing coming from the last cell on the far side. I went straight to the door and matched the key to the lock on the first try, as though guided by unseen hands. As I entered, the woman turned her face my way in surprise, yet without fear.

"You are not one of them," she stated simply. "Like the young man, you bring light."

"My name is Brie, and I have come to free you, Anna."

She heard her name and smiled. "You know me. Clearly the Lord is with you. Have you freed the others?"

I shook my head and gestured at the keys.

"We must hurry," she explained. "They check on the prisoners at least once each hour, and Rufus came late today. We have less than a half-hour before Owen comes, and he is the meanest of the guards."

She rushed out of the cell and over to Toby's. I did not realize why at first, but then turned and saw how he hobbled, each step painful. I could tell that his fever had left him, and he propped himself on the door jamb with the strength of both hands, but his legs offered him no hope of journeying far. As I watched, Anna helped him to a seated position and began to pray aloud, nearly echoing the prayers I had said just minutes before. While she labored, I passed on to the next cell. To my shock, I discovered that it held a little girl, hardly older than Lily Mae. As I entered, she raised her head with a pained, resigned expression.

"Have you come to kill me at last?"

"No, I have come to set you free. You must be very quiet and follow any instructions you are given."

She did not appear to be hurt, only deeply lost in depression and trauma. She nodded and followed me out of the cell, her eyes not yet daring to show any hope. She came with me as I passed to the other side. The first cell on the right also proved empty. Each of the two cells next to Toby's imprisoned a woman, both slightly older than I, one in fairly good health, as though she had not been there very long, the other weaker even than Toby had been. The first woman helped me to pull the second from her cell and lay her gently upon the ground. Anna left Toby's side and drew near.

"Oh, Grace, how you have suffered." As she bent to pray over Grace, I drew out the cross from my pocket and held it toward her. Anna looked up, shocked. "My father's cross! How did you come by it?" She reached out a shaking hand toward me and then stopped. "Do you also have the gift?" I nodded, and she gestured in a way that indicated we should join in agreement in praying over Grace. We spent several precious minutes, laying our healing, warmth-infused hands over the woman's prone body. The little girl and the other woman held hands, puzzled, uncertain, waiting. Before too long, Grace sat up, rubbing her eyes. "I feel light in my veins. I feel different."

Suddenly from behind me, I felt hands embracing me and heard a familiar voice in my ear. "Brie, we need to hurry. We need to get away." It was Toby, and he had moved under his own power. For the first time since entering the tunnels, I felt myself smile. We were not yet safe, but my hope ran high in that moment.

"The women should leave the caves with the little one," I told them.

The girl spoke shyly, but clearly, "My name is Wendy."

"Wendy, you should go as fast and as quietly as you can with Grace and Anna and. . ." "Sarah," she offered.

"Go with them out and away. I have traced arrows in the dirt of the tunnels to show the way out. There is a man guarding the entrance to the tunnel; do not exit toward the natural light. Just as you see the way out, look for a large outcropping of rock. Once you squeeze by it, the tunnel will take you to the home of a friend. You will see steps at the end, but no door. Knock loudly four times in succession, and she will grant you safe shelter. Tell her that Brie sent you."

"Aren't you coming with us?" Wendy dared to ask.

"We need to free the horses," I told her, "Toby and I need to free the horses."

Her eyes grew big. "But the horses are very well guarded, more so than the people, everyone knows that."

I looked at Sarah for confirmation, and she nodded. "Griffin has always valued horses more than people. He never leaves the horses without at least one guard, usually from among the strongest bullies he knows. You should come with us."

I glanced at Anna. For one who had been in prison so long, she held surprising strength. "Brie is right. It is time to set all prisoners free, both human and animal. Sarah, you are in good health; take Grace and Wendy and follow Brie's arrows to safety. I will help Toby and Brie. It will take more than two to face Griffin's guards with any success."

I pulled a loaf of bread and some water from my pocket and saw the hungry look in Wendy's eyes. "Let these give you more strength for the journey, but do not linger long. The sooner you get to the tunnel that leads to my friend, the better. I know that there are fewer guards today than normal, but haste is your best hope. Keep to the shadows. Do not follow the three of us; after the first three turnings, we are headed to the horses, a different way. We will go first; if you hear trouble, wait in the darkest turnings of the tunnel until all is silent ahead. I am convinced that we will be safer in two small groups. If for any reason you are caught, remember not to fight, and say nothing of how you escaped."

I looked again at Wendy, saw her full-moon eyes so full of anxiety, and pulled her close for a quick hug. "God will watch over you, Wendy," I assured her.

"Yes, but will he also watch over you? Horses make so much noise, and they can't keep to the shadows like a little girl." I felt the truth of her words but knew that Toby would not leave without trying to save Windstar. Deeper still, I discerned the weight of the prophecy upon Toby, Anna, and me; we still had far to go.

* * * * *

While the women and Wendy savored the fresh fare I had provided them, Toby, Anna, and I gathered for a hurried conference toward the back of the cavern, not wanting our voices to travel to the others. The less they knew, the better for them if captured. I shared with the other two that I knew the route to find the horses and that many of the regular guards had been dispatched into the city this morning. Yet I also acknowledged our extreme vulnerability against armed men, and the near-impossibility of escaping with a horse of Windstar's size and beauty in our company. One could not ride him out through these tunnels.

Anna interrupted me. "There are many ways out of this warren of Griffin's, especially near where the horses are kept. Griffin knows that horses do better with light and air, space and freedom. They are exercised often outside the caverns, as well as used in raids and attacks. I don't have a map, but I would bet the horses know the way out if given the chance to seek it!" She smiled then. "God's creatures often know their way better than we humans do."

"We need a plan." Toby spoke for the first time in many minutes. "Otherwise we will find ourselves imprisoned again, and this time without a friend to come to our aid." He looked at me with eyes full of gratitude—and something more.

Anna continued, "I imagine that we will find three, perhaps four, guards with the horses. We will be outnumbered, and they will be armed. Do you carry any weapons, Brie? I pulled the dagger from the folds of my cloak and held it out to her. She stared at it, stunned. "That dagger belonged to my family."

"Yes, your mother gave it to me."

"My mother. . ." But all of us knew time to be of the essence; any story-telling needed to be saved for later, much later.

"I have also found this cloak to be very effective in hiding me from others' eyes in the tunnels." They looked surprised, but given my safe arrival in order to free them, they took my words at face value. In the meantime, Toby had been glancing around the cavern. He picked up the discarded metal tray that had held the bowls of gruel. "This could serve as a shield of sorts," he murmured, grasping it by the handles at both ends and turning it upside-down toward us. Anna gestured at the keys that I had nearly forgotten. "Though not nearly as good as daggers, old rusty keys can hurt if directed in vulnerable places." We managed to pry off two of the keys, so that Brie and Toby each had one. Toby kept the tray, for it proved heavy and unwieldy.

I sought to convince Anna to take both the dagger and the cloak; she had been weakened by her years in this dungeon-like place and needed all the protection that she could find. Yet she rejected my offer. "If Griffin and his men discover me, I will not be harmed if I do not fight. He loves me, you see, and I recognize how the Lord has used me as a source of light in a dark life. I am far safer than either of you; they will not hesitate to kill you both." She went and fetched a thin, black blanket from her cell and secured it around Toby's shoulders. "Your white shirt will be too easily seen; darkness offers one of our few advantages."

"But what will we do when we get to the horses?" I hadn't realized that my worry had been spoken aloud until Toby's eyes came once again to my face.

Anna spoke once more, and her voice held a strange singsong quality, as though she were speaking out of a dream or a deep memory. "We will go first to Griffin. If Griffin is not defeated or captured, neither humans nor horses will ever be free in Nybron."

"What?!" Toby gazed on her in disbelief. "We came here to free you, Anna, and we have. If we can just get to my horse, we can ride to safety and away."

"No. Getting into Griffin's caverns presents one set of challenges; getting out doubles both the risks and the likelihood of failure. Even if we manage to free Windstar and some or all of the other horses, Griffin will be after us from all directions. On the rare chance that we were to succeed in escaping, others in town would be killed in our stead. I do not choose that outcome; I will not go with you if escape is your only objective."

I dared to ask Anna then if she knew anything of the Nybron prophecy. She shared that Griffin had occasionally spoken of it, expressing a strange fascination for highly decorated weapons. I told them what I believed about Georgina's sword and the dagger that Susannah had given me, and then I described to them the pearls that I carried. As she listened, Anna nodded. "I feel convinced, then. Our fate calls us to confront Griffin and to reclaim the sword that he has stolen."

"But have you ever been in Griffin's chambers?" I inquired.

Anna smiled then, a broken, sad smile. "When he is deeply lonely, he sometimes invites me to come and sit with him of an evening. Most often I listen or sing ballads from this region. At times I recite portions of Scripture, though he does not know them to be such. Yes, I know his chambers. A pair of guards stands watch at each of the two entrances. And he usually chooses to keep a bodyguard near him, though occasionally he would dismiss him when we were alone." Her eyes clouded over, but she said no more.

Toby suggested, "If Brie's cloak is as much of a protection as she claims, perhaps she can get past the guards, sneak in, and steal back the sword. If all three items of prophecy are in our possession, surely that will give us an advantage?"

"We already have an advantage, for the Lord is on our side," Anna insisted. "Evil's only advantage lies in physical strength and numbers, not in hope or blessing or spiritual might."

"Have you seen where the sword has been kept in recent days?" I asked then. She nodded. "Griffin carries it at his side, even when he sleeps, if my guess is correct. He will not leave it lying unattended for you to snatch it up and run."

I groaned inwardly. I felt no hope of obtaining the sword from Griffin; more likely, he would capture me, and both the dagger and the pearl would come into his possession. I spoke my worries aloud.

"Perhaps we should let him take them," Anna observed.

"You can't mean that!" I nearly shouted in my shock and horror.

"The prophecy came by means of a man of God, and so I believe that only a believer will be able to embody the strength described. I have heard Griffin recite the words, and it has struck me many a time that they include, *"Pray, how may this strength come to me?"* I feel certain that means the wielder must pray for the Lord's help, or no help will come. Griffin is not a believer; he will not understand this."

Sarah approached us then, expressing concern that someone would come by to check on us all too soon. Recognizing the truth of her words, we made ready, enwrapping each person in a careworn cell blanket. As we hurried toward the exit, I realized that we still had not decided on a plan. I would have to trust to God's provision, just as he had provided for me each step of the way until now.

Yet never before had I felt so profoundly afraid.

23

*T*oby, Anna, and I slunk our way through the shadows of the tunnels, following the arrows until the second turning I had taken. Instead of bearing right, heading back toward Betsy's home and the chance of freedom, we crossed over the way and found ourselves in a part of the caverns unknown to me but familiar to Anna. She began to lead us, stepping with a near-eagerness that unsettled me. Had her long years underground upset her mind? We turned left, then right, and my anxiety mounted. Surely we could not just walk into Griffin's compound!

About fifty yards back from the next intersection, Anna stopped suddenly and motioned for us to draw aside into a deep opening in the side of the tunnel wall. At the same moment, I could hear voices heading our way. Toby followed Anna, and I drew in last, turning my back to the passage behind. Would my cloak grant us protection yet again? The pace of the footsteps outside in the tunnel proved hurried, flustered. I heard a gruff voice mutter, "Griffin is a fool to send us out after this non-existent woman with an even more mythical dagger. Hasn't he sent enough men already?" They rushed past us, three or four men it seemed, from the echoes of their footfalls.

After waiting a good length of time, Anna whispered, "I knew that voice. That was Griffin's personal bodyguard. He may not have as many men with him as we feared." Some of the tension in her eyes waned a bit, though Toby's brows remained furrowed with anxiety. His eyes still held great pain, and I wondered what he had experienced while in the cell. Had they hurt him in their efforts to gain news of me?

Anna spoke again, "Let me enter first. Griffin will be startled to see me free without escort, but he knows that I have never tried to escape during my time with him. If there are yet guards, they will not stop me. Wait in the shadows for a chance to intervene somehow."

My stomach churned. I wanted to know what to do, and when to do it, to be assured that we would succeed. What if Griffin demanded that she be returned and locked up more securely than before? Then whoever accompanied her would sound the alarm that all the prisoners had escaped. It made no sense. Yet I felt more than willing to postpone my meeting with Griffin, even if just for a few short moments. As we made ready to leave the cleft of the rock, I experienced a strange flashback to my meeting with the albatross. I stood on the cliff top, gazing at his grace and strength. However, this time, he took up the pearl in his beak and nodded vigorously at me. Feeling foolish but trusting the vision, I took that pearl from my pocket and tucked it in my cheek. I prayed that I would not swallow it.

Anna hurried down the passage. Toby found my hand in the darkness and squeezed once, twice, then caressed the back of my hand with his thumb. His tender touch gave me a welcome bit of courage in the midst of a clamoring fear. He released my hand, and we crept toward the cavern's opening, step by cautious step.

Griffin's voice carried easily to our ears, "Anna! What in the world?!"

"Oh, you know Rufus . . . he doesn't always remember to lock things back up. I thought I would come bring you a little surprise." Anna astonished me with how successfully she made her voice light, even playful.

"What surprise did you bring me?"

"Why myself, of course. You have been so preoccupied of late, I thought you might want a little comforting." She even managed a suggestive laugh. Did she love him, despite his evil doings? I couldn't let myself think on that now.

"May I look at the sword?" she asked him then. "You have raved about how beautiful it us but haven't let me admire it. Surely you trust me after all these years!"

"I don't trust anyone, Anna. You know that. This sword is the key to lasting power. If only I could find the dagger and pearl. Somehow I feel certain that woman has them both. I can't believe that she has eluded my search parties for over a week! I am tempted to search for her myself."

"Perhaps she will come to you, Griffin," Anna said then. I stiffened. What was she doing? "You captured the young man with the sword, and you seemed certain that they were traveling together. Do you think that she would abandon him?"

"We all look out for ourselves first, Anna. Only a very foolish woman would come looking for anyone here. My guess is that she has been in hiding and is looking for just the right moment to leave Nybron for good. That's why I have set up guards on all the paths out of town, even the lesser-used routes. She won't go far."

"You told me that the hilt shows David and Goliath. I would really like to see that part, but you always have your hand wrapped so tightly around it. Couldn't you just set it on the table and let me look for a minute?" Her voice dropped coyly, and I wondered what she might be doing.

Griffin muttered something under his breath, but we heard the thump of something heavy strike the tabletop. Anna gasped and began to exclaim over the detail in the design. "What do you like best about it, Griffin?" she asked then.

"That it's mine. That I'm one step closer to the prophecy's promise of power. What else should I like about it?"

To my surprise, Toby hurried forward at that moment, picked up an apple-sized stone that lay on the tunnel floor, and hurled it into the room. I prayed it would not hit Anna, but knew he had directed it away from either voice as a distraction.

Griffin barked, "What the—?" and I heard his footsteps moving toward the stone. Then everything began to happen at once. Anna drew the sword and held it in both hands before her. I knew how heavy it was from watching Georgina lug it downstairs, so it clearly took all Anna's weakened strength to keep it up. Toby rushed into the room, the tray in front of his chest, and lunged at Griffin, slamming the tray down over his head as hard as he could in Griffin's moment of distraction while staring at the stone. I followed, eyes wide, watching, sure that at any moment guards would come rushing in from either of the two entrances to the chamber. Had he sent every last one to search for me?

Would that the smashing tray had knocked Griffin unconscious, but it hadn't. He stood up, bleeding just above his ear, and pulled out a dagger. I knew that Toby had nothing but the tray and an old rusty key, nothing to protect him against Griffin's attack. Not thinking, but moving as though watching someone else, I pulled out the dagger and went rushing to separate the two men. I heard Anna cry behind me, "In the name of Jesus, we rebuke you! Pray, how may this strength come to me?" And she too rushed forward.

Griffin stared at the dagger as though transfixed. "It is the dagger of prophecy," he whispered, amazed. And contrary to any of my expectations, he took his free hand and grabbed the dagger by its blade, extracting it from my hand. I knew that he must have cut himself badly, but the only sound he uttered seemed one of triumph. "I am stronger than the three of you know, and we are not alone."

He cried out sharply, three piercing shouts, and two guards rushed in from an adjoining chamber. To my amazement, Anna swung the sword, slicing the leg of the nearest guard so deeply that he fell to the ground, moaning. Toby lunged at the second guard, and this time the tray found its mark on the first try: the man fell to the ground, unconscious. Griffin looked surprised but undeterred. "You are fast and clever, but you do not have the advantage that I do. I do not value life. I savor death. You are too loyal to one another to win this fight."

And suddenly I found myself held tight to his chest, one of the daggers at my heart, the other at my throat. Toby dropped the tray with a clatter, horror on his face. Anna stepped forward slowly, very slowly, turning the sword so that the hilt faced Griffin and the blade was in her own hands. In order to claim the sword, Griffin needed to drop his own dagger from his right hand. His left hand, which held the dagger of prophecy, bled profusely from the cuts he had sustained in grabbing it out of my grip. Not believing my own audacity, I waited for the moment at which he dropped his eyes to sheath his own dagger. My left hand encircled his, pointing the dagger away from my heart, and my right hand reached and took the sword hilt. I nearly fell under the weight of the latter, but as my fingers made contact with the silverwork, a surge of energy and hope flowed through my whole body. Gritting my teeth to keep the pearl in place in my mouth, I cried through clenched jaws, "Pray, how may this strength come to me?" A flash of light arced between the tips of the dagger and the sword.

Griffin still held the dagger, but my grip had been so strengthened by the power that came unsuspected upon me that I was crushing his fingers. He tried vainly with his right hand to wrest the sword from my grip, but my hand moved with a grace and dexterity not my own, outmaneuvering him.

Then Griffin did something none of us expected. He pried his fingers out from under mine and grabbed my throat with both hands. Though I felt as strong as two men, I could not break that terrible iron grip. I knew that I could not drop the weapons; if I did, he would surely kill us all. But if I held them much longer, I would die. Unable to bear the pain, I screamed out raggedly, "Jesus, save us!" and unwittingly spat the pearl across the room. Anna rushed for it, and Griffin lessened the pressure on my throat as he recognized the third of his long-sought objects.

Throughout this time, Toby had been silent, still. Now he picked up the sword of one of the fallen guards and rushed at Griffin.

"Let her go, and we will give you your treasures!"

"Put down that sword, young man. Unless you drop it, I will finish my work on this girl right now. She eluded me for too long, and I hate her for it. It would bring me great pleasure to kill her in front of her friends."

Anna stepped forward then, the albatross's pearl cradled gently in her cupped right hand. "I will give you the pearl after you release your hold on her throat."

"Why should I trust you now, Anna? You have betrayed me."

"I will heal you." She put out her left hand toward the open wound on the side of his head, and the bleeding subsided. She reached again toward his hand, and I could tell from his surprised grunt that the pain also receded from there.

"You remember how I helped you before, how I saved your life after your compatriots betrayed you that day. For some reason, you asked them to spare my friend Isabella—perhaps you wanted her for your own, I don't know—and they mocked you and stabbed her to death as she fought. In a rage, you rushed them without thinking, and your two strongest, most clever leaders saw their chance. They set upon you, they would have killed you, and I threw a rock that knocked one out. Do you remember? I would ask that you spare my friend's life, as I once intervened to save yours."

Griffin was no longer pressing deeply into my flesh but instead staring at Anna and at the pearl she held. For a moment, I thought that he would relent, would let her previous act of defense be a reason for bargaining now. Anna raised the pearl closer to his reach, and he snatched it with his now-healed left hand. I stumbled forward, gasping, as his right hand left my throat. I knew that his next goal would be to wrest the weapons from me, and with the last of the strength I held, I turned to face him, raising the sword and dagger to his chin as I cried one last time, "Pray, how may this strength come to me?" Once again, the light arced from one weapon to the other, striking Griffin's face full on as he lunged at me. His face contorted horribly, and he fell, slumping to the floor in a heap.

Anna rushed from the room then, and I wondered if she were hiding tears. But her errand had been practical in nature: she returned from Griffin's bedchamber bearing fancy corded ropes that must have adorned the curtains around his bed. She handed two to Toby and kept two for herself, using one to secure Griffin's feet, the other Griffin's hands. Toby made sure the two guards were rendered immobile as well. I noticed Anna's hands, stretched toward Griffin's face; even now, she was working her healing ministry, even on this man who would have killed the three of us without a second thought. Then she gasped aloud and felt for his pulse. "He is dead," she said wonderingly, brokenly. "Griffin who has worked such death and destruction on the town of Nybron is dead from his own greed for power."

She touched his hand then, uncurling the fingers and lifting the pearl toward me. "But how were you able to wield the power of the weapons without the third item?"

I reached into my apron pocket and pulled out Andrew's pearl, which glowed with an intense, pulsing light. The albatross's pearl had been the decoy that saved my life. Andrew's pearl had been the pearl of the prophecy all along. I took it and set it within the hollow of the hilt that I had seen in the dream. It fit perfectly, with a tiny inner working of silver that released prongs to hold it securely in place, once the pearl's weight met its resting place. For a moment, the three of us gazed in wonder at the sword and the dagger, not believing what they had brought about.

Toby recovered first. "What do we do next, Anna? Griffin's many followers will not wish to relinquish the privileged positions that they have held. Won't another rise up to take Griffin's place?"

Anna gestured at me. "Brie carries the weapons of the prophecy. Because of her faith and her sense of call to this place, she has defeated Griffin. The prophecy declares that she can overcome any foe. It does not matter who wishes to wield power in this place; Brie, by the power of the Lord and the grace of these strange weapons, can overcome him."

I still felt afraid. I did not wish to kill other men. Seeing the contortions in Griffin's face as he fell had horrified me. "Anna, Toby, if either of you wishes to wield these, I gladly surrender them to you."

"Wind-borne sister," Anna spoke with a measured, intense cadence that caught and held my full attention. "You have come home. These gifts came to you. Wield them for peace, and peace will come to this land. Give them up to those not meant to have them, and strife will return. Step fully into your calling. She sang then,

'You bear the gifts, you bear the truth,
Come home to Nybron, come home.'

I broke down and cried.

24

I lost my sense of time. I do not know how long I cried. I do remember the strident, unexpected shout from the tunnel entrance as one of Griffin's men arrived to offer his daily report. He stared in shock and amazement at his former leader's prone form and the bound hands and feet of his guards.

He turned first to Toby, raising his voice but not his weapons. "Did you do this?" Toby shook his head and gestured toward me. I stood tall, bearing the sword in my right hand and the dagger in my left. Once again the blue energy pulsed from one blade to the other. The man's jaw dropped in response. "So it was true all along," he marveled.

Then he seemed to marshal his wits about him. "There are dozens of those loyal to Griffin and only three of you. If I call for aid, you will all be dead within the hour."

Anna stepped toward the man with measured, careful footsteps. "I know you," she stated simply. "You are the one who offered me water and some bread when Griffin brought me here after raping me on the road those many years ago. Under your bluff anger, you are still a man of kindness. You need not live out of your anger any longer. Join with us in convincing your compatriots that peace can return to Nybron."

"I don't know what you are talking about."

Anna shut her eyes and stretched her right hand toward his heart. She spoke as though watching a play unfold before her. "Your mother abandoned you when you were less than two years old, and you never knew your father. Your grandmother raised you after that and taught you the ways of kindness and care for others. You loved her dearly. One day, Griffin's father's men attacked your small holding. You defended your grandmother with love and strength, but you were only eleven. They killed her and then took you hostage. You are not one of them. Honor your grandmother now and stand with the truth."

As Anna spoke, my eyes remained riveted to the man's face. As she related his life story, an inner light began to break over his face, and some of the severity of feature seemed to drain away as though soothed by a ministering hand. Looking closely, I could see that the beginnings of tears had started in his eyes.

He gestured toward me. "She may be the bearer of the prophetic weapons, but you are more truly the prophetess. How can you know these things?"

"I listen with my heart, and at times, God tells me. I have also paid close attention during my many years here in the underground cells."

"Ah . . . so you are Anna. Griffin spoke of you sometimes when he had taken too much drink. None of us could understand why he didn't just kill you, the way he so often took the lives of others on a moment's whim. But he would always answer in the same way, 'She brings light to this dark place. She brings a listening love where others brought only fear.' It made no sense to us that a man so powerful, so angry, and so vengeful would care for any of that, but somehow he did. I begin to see what he meant."

Anna nodded her head. "What is your name?"

"They call me Nick."

"Will you join with us, Nick?"

"Yes. What do you need me to do?"

And so our planning began. Nick had grown to be a trusted leader within Griffin's band, both due to his brute strength and to the focused sense of self he had not lost, despite being raised among the tunnels and dark ways of Griffin's men.

In an odd combination of ministrations, Anna worked to stop the bleeding on the one man's leg while Toby gagged him and his companion. Then the two guards were secured within an inner wardrobe. Others who came to the scene would be puzzled by their leader's absence but not discover immediately what had occurred. Nick proposed to take Toby with him to the horse caverns and tell the few remaining guards that Griffin had called for all of the mounts to be taken to the grove below the Praying Oaks. In so doing, they would oversee the freeing of the horses. I suggested that Anna and I make our way back to Betsy's tunnel, then on to her home and the town. Surely Betsy would know which town leaders were trustworthy to help us round up Griffin's rabble.

But Nick shook his head with vigor. "Over one hundred men are loyal to Griffin, and they do not know that he is dead. Should you meet up with a group in the tunnels, even with your weapons and the weight of prophecy on your side, I do not trust the outcome. You must also come with Toby and me, but keep to the shadows. In the confusion of releasing the horses, make your way out of the tunnels on the far side. Then choose a mount and make your way to the city together."

"But they will be watching for me at every turn! I will be even more visible on horseback. I want to avoid combat whenever possible. Not everyone will stand with us as you have chosen to do, Nick."

"That is true. What do you say, Anna?"

Anna closed her eyes again, listening deeply. To my dismay, tears traced down her cheeks, and she bent to her knees upon the ground, as though a heavy burden had overwhelmed her. "A dead leader does not mean victory when hearts remain full of evil and greed. The storehouse of treasures within these tunnels will motivate many to attack and kill unthinkingly. Horses will obey their masters, even if their masters have cruel hearts. Within hours of the horses' release, we would find ourselves beset by mounted brigands intent on loyalty to a man they do not know is dead and protection of a treasure they hope one day to share."

Toby spoke for the first time since Nick had found us. "But if Brie is indeed the woman of the prophecy, a way forward will be found." I felt startled by the conviction with which he spoke, and the expression on Anna's face showed that she had heard it also. "The Lord has been faithful to us throughout many dangers. He will guide us even now."

"What are we to do, Toby?" I appealed to him.

"I do not wish to leave Windstar, yet I trust that he is in no danger. I think that the four of us should make our way to Betsy's home and set our plan from there. With Nick accompanying us, no one will question our presence if they pass us in the tunnels."

Nick spoke up then. "If that is our choice, we ought not to leave Griffin's body here. It will be discovered before long by its odor alone, even if they don't search his rooms right away. And once they are found, the guards will tell what they have seen."

Toby replied, "One was unconscious when Griffin fell. The other was in such a fog of pain from his injured leg, I doubt that he knows what occurred."

"That is helpful. Even so, I think we should take the body with us. If the townspeople see that Griffin is dead, it will give them hope."

Anna spoke again, "Death is never a sign of hope, Nick. Death is a sign of violence and loss. The townspeople will gain more hope from Brie's faith and your own changed heart than they will from this empty shell of a death-dealing man. Yet I agree; we are wiser to take him with us than to leave him to ignite his followers' anger and greed upon discovering their loss."

Griffin had been a large man, with broad chest and a heavy frame. At first we despaired of how to transport him. His face could not show, or the secret of his death would spread. I finally thought of the cloak that I wore, and of how well it had protected me from prying eyes. We wrapped Griffin in it, with the hood facing backward. Toby and Nick lifted him between them, and it surprised me how difficult it became to distinguish what burden they held. Each took up a weapon from those we had stripped from the guards. Anna grabbed a torch from the wall sconce and took up the tray that had served Toby so well. She smiled a wry smile through her fatigue and murmured, "You never know . . ."

25

e were fortunate to travel through the underground passageways to Betsy's tunnel without seeing anyone. In fact, the tunnels were eerily quiet, and I felt a deep sense of foreboding. I
looked at Toby, trudging ahead of me, carrying Griffin's body with Nick's
help, and tried to reclaim a measure of hope. However, Nick's comment
about all those loyal to Griffin kept spinning through my mind. I did not
want more violence, either by them or against them. What were we to do?

As we passed the entrance, I picked up my discarded water and bread,
passing the latter to Anna, who took it gratefully and consumed it swiftly.
I wondered how often the prisoners had been fed; likely they had not had
anything as fresh and satisfying as Betsy's bread at any time. I felt amazed
at her strength, given the long-term physical privations that she must have
sustained. Perhaps Griffin had shared some of his stores with her during
her visits?

The end of the tunnel came much sooner than I had expected; the
distance had stretched long and threatening when I had ventured through
it alone earlier in the day, but it passed quickly now. We knocked fervently
four times, and as the trap door pulled back, Betsy's earnest face appeared,
relief flooding over her as she saw that I was present and unharmed. I sent
Anna up first and followed after, with Toby and Nick bringing up the rear.
When Betsy saw Nick, she picked up a candlestick beside her and lifted it
toward him, gasping, "This man is . . ." Then as his body was lifted over the
threshold, the hood fell back from Griffin's face, and she saw that he was
dead.

"How is this possible?" She looked from Toby to Nick and back again. Neither answered, busy as they were in removing the cloak and laying Griffin's body in the dark shadows beside the bed. "Does this mean that we are free?"

Nick replied, "Freedom is not won in the death of one man. Freedom is won by changed hearts, like my own. Freedom comes when individuals like these women act boldly in faith. We have much work left to do, for those loyal to Griffin remain intent on doing harm and appeasing their selfish desires."

Betsy's jaw dropped. I wondered if she had met Nick before or seen him in his own acts of doing harm or behaving through selfish motives. Yet she held her tongue.

Toby spoke next, "We need to devise a plan."

I interrupted him, "Did our friends come here safely: Grace, Sarah, and Wendy?"

Betsy nodded, "They are upstairs, staying out of sight. When I heard your knock, Wendy smiled her first smile as she settled in a big tub of warm water. She and Sarah will be fine; I do not know about Grace. She lay down on one of the beds and collapsed; I imagine that she will sleep for days, if allowed to do so."

Toby persisted, "I am glad that they made the journey safely, and we need to be bold to plan what to do next. Nybron is still under threat, as are those of us who escaped from the tunnels. He looked to Betsy then, "And you as our protector have put yourself in grave danger as well." Betsy nodded once and then began a very matter-of-fact review of circumstances.

"All of our window coverings have been pulled down and all windows and doors secured, except the business entry. We must continue to run the bakery, or we will draw more attention to ourselves. Brian has stayed busy there all day, offering the excuse that Katie has caught a fever, and I am nursing her, to the kind folks who inquire. We have food aplenty for all of you. We have extra blankets to keep you warm and enough room above stairs if we are respectful of one another."

Betsy took a deep breath then. "I have prepared bodies for burial before. I suggest that we bury him in the tunnel, for we cannot risk taking him outside. The next time I go out for water from our well, I will bring in our shovel from the shed."

"And if someone sees you?" queried the ever-vigilant Nick.

"I will explain that I need it for cleaning the cinders out of our baking oven."

I smiled. Betsy's cleverness and industry offered great help to us at such a time as this.

Anna spoke then, "I will help Betsy with the body." Her voice quavered a bit, though she did not cry. Betsy gazed at her face; her eyebrows lifted only slightly, but she said nothing.

Finally I spoke. "We have so much to tell you, Betsy, but we cannot spare the time at present. As you may have guessed, this is my friend, Toby; Anna, the woman we had sought; and Nick, who has chosen to help us. And these are the weapons of the prophecy." As I spoke, I drew them out from the folds of my skirts, and Betsy stared in wonder. "I do not know how exactly, but it is by the power of these weapons, and the protection of God, that Griffin came to his end."

"And Brie's willingness to stand firm in faith," Anna added.

Betsy jumped to the same conclusion we had taken at first, "Well then, you need only to wield these weapons against other enemies, and you will triumph. Doesn't the prophecy say so?"

"Death offers an empty answer." Anna's voice held a rough grief, as well as a determined truth. "Though perhaps with the unexpected power of these weapons, Brie could deal more death upon Griffin's followers, I do not think that will serve Nybron or its people well. Death breeds more death and violence tempts more violence. We need a plan that leads to life and freedom without aggression and threats."

At that moment, the door to the bakery opened. After securing the lock, Brian came through from the adjoining room and cried out in surprise upon seeing all of us huddled in intense conversation. He took one look at Nick and stammered, "You . . . "

"I stand with you now," Nick stated simply. "My former leader is dead," he continued, gesturing at the lifeless body on the floor, "And I see now that following him only led to destruction, not to life."

Anna turned to Brian, "Your bread smells and tastes like heaven." The opening and closing of the door had wafted rich scents of cinnamon, nutmeg, butter, and other rich aromas to our noses. After the dankness of the caves, who could resist it?

"The bread of heaven!" I said suddenly. "The bread of heaven!"

My friends' faces held quizzical looks, and Nick cocked his head to one side, wondering just what in the world I meant.

"Nick, how many of Griffin's followers are Christians?"

He laughed, and the sound held an edgy, wry pain. "Perhaps a dozen of us, Brie. And even we have strayed far from what Jesus would have had us do."

"How many of them have tasted fresh bread regularly?"

This time his face held a grim expression, hard with experience. "Only those who stole it. Griffin kept his treasures and his tasty meals to himself. His men were offered the blessing of good horses, if they took good care of them, and the protection of life in a gang—the false safety of their own violence. Every now and then, someone would be promoted to horse wrangler or personal guard, and then some extra benefits came his way . . . but only if Griffin's whims turned in that direction that day. Most of his followers are loners and orphans who had no one or who, like me, had their loved ones killed before their eyes. They have been loyal to Griffin because they don't know another way."

"Then we should feed them," I declared, hope rising within me.

"Feed them! Brie, I know you are a generous-hearted woman, but how will that save Nybron?" Even Toby looked at me as though I had sprouted wings.

I drew them together into a close huddle and explained just what I had in mind.

26

Griffin was interred in the tunnel, about fifty yards from the open space beneath Betsy's house. "I was willing to prepare the body, but I can't abide the idea of him being buried on my property," she apologized. As it turned out, the rock surfaces nearest to her home would have been impenetrable anyway. Toby and Nick discovered softer soil in an alcove further down the tunnel and buried him there, taking care to remove his jewelry and his dagger, which would be recognizable to his followers.

Nick went out under cover of darkness to an apothecary's shop, awoke the stunned proprietor, a close friend of Betsy's, and obtained what he sought. Upon his return, Betsy, Katie, and Brian worked at a feverish pace all that night, mixing and stirring, baking and bundling. Sarah and I were set to sewing sacks from old sheets in which to carry all the bread that we would need, as well as sewing dark cloaks from old tablecloths. Only Grace, Wendy, and Jasper slept well that night.

By early morning, Nick was dispatched to send word to Griffin's followers to gather beneath the Praying Oaks at noon. They had no reason not to trust him; I hoped to the good Lord that we could. Betsy and Brian, who had been awake for over twenty-four hours already, made their way into town, knocking on the doors of trusted friends and whispering requests and plans. Katie kept to the counter, reassuring customers that her fever had left, thanks to her mother's attentions. Patrons attributed her tired face to her illness and asked no more questions. Toby, Anna, Sarah, and I spent time in earnest prayer, recognizing the risks that we would be taking. Though unsure whether my inspiration held any merit, we trusted the Lord who had provided for us so generously and graciously thus far.

By the time the town clock tolled ten, we knew we needed to begin. Toby and Sarah, who fortunately was a gifted horsewoman, would ride Betsy's and Brian's horses, their saddlebags filled with bread, their own backs slung with additional sacks. Cloaks that Sarah and I had fashioned in the night covered their heads, and they kept close the daggers that we had taken up from Griffin's guards. By contrast, Anna and I would return through the tunnels. We knew that Sarah would be at risk for being mistaken for me, but she rode fastest and best. And by now, surely the prisoners' escape had been discovered, as well as Griffin's disappearance, so none of us was safe to be seen.

Anna and I would also carry bread with us, cumbersome as it was. I re-clad myself in the black cloak, shuddering a bit to recall who had worn it last, and I took up the dagger and sword of prophecy. I prayed that I would not need them, but no one could be sure. Anna took up Griffin's dagger, and in her pockets she carried her father's cross, the albatross's pearl, and Griffin's jeweled ring and arm cuff. Katie would stay in the house, checking by intervals on Wendy and Grace, who slept a deep sleep in the rooms upstairs.

Anna continued to astonish me with her vigor and her sense of purpose. I knew that she grieved Griffin, despite the harm he had done her (on repeated occasions, I imagined), and I recognized that she had offered to help prepare the body as her way of making peace with his death. She, like Sarah, would have been justified in asking to stay behind, to sleep out this weighty, risky day beneath Betsy's beautifully stitched coverlets. And yet they had both come, Anna without the greater safety of a horse's hooves and a horse's speed beneath her.

As we hurried down the tunnel, Anna risked speaking to me just once, long before we would reach the juncture with Griffin's passageways. "You wonder why I would do this, why I would risk my life instead of choosing safety. Surely you know better than most of us, Brie, that the way of faithfulness is never a safe road. It means a dangerous and daily trust that asks of us our all. I hated the confinement of the cell at first; I believed that it meant that I had nothing to give in God's service. However, over time I realized that I could offer the greatest gift of all: full surrender in prayer and in trust. I could do nothing for myself, entirely dependent upon my captors and above all upon the Lord for everything. In prayer, I asked earnestly that the Lord would change the hearts of those who imprisoned me, that he would find a way to set Nybron free once more. At last I see the fruit of those prayers coming to pass, through you and Toby, even through Nick. How could I say nay to being an integral part of the outworking of Christ's will?"

I felt humbled by her depth of faith. To a lesser degree, I had experienced the same dynamics on my long journey. However, I had chosen the risks, and Anna's captivity had been forced upon her. Yet I saw that we stood united in this summons to accept putting ourselves in harm's way in the hope of a greater good.

We continued our swift-footed journey along the underground corridors. I wanted to feel hopeful, to trust that all would turn out for good, yet I had a niggling sensation that I had overlooked several important considerations in my late-night plans with the others. As Anna and I reached the stones that obscured the junction with Griffin's tunnels, we heard the clash of swords in the distance, and I gasped. Were our friends already being attacked? What had gone wrong?

We crept forward, listening with every sense attuned. Anna held out the cross her father had fashioned those many years ago, and I reached out to touch it, uncertain of her intent. In that moment my mind's eye focused upon the open space under the Praying Oaks. "Toby and Sarah have not yet arrived," I told her. "The troops are bored, and they pass the time in edgy swordplay." Anna nodded and replied, "I sense that as well. However, we cannot risk traveling out by that tunnel as we had planned, given these conditions. We will need to find our way through to the horse cavern and back that way."

"It will take much longer!" I countered in dismay. "It will place Toby and Sarah at greater risk."

"Yes, but then we also can be mounted. Perhaps the good Lord knew that we would need that extra protection."

Our journey through the tunnels to the horse cavern proved mercifully uneventful. Clearly Nick had succeeded in marshaling Griffin's troops together. With no prisoners to guard and their leader mysteriously absent, the men gravitated toward Nick's leadership as they sought direction. As we began to hear soft whickering in the distance, Anna stopped. "No matter how persuasive Nick has been, I am certain that we will find three or four well-trained guards still with the horses. I pray that we can find a way to restrain them without violence, but that may not be the case. Be ready."

I took a deep breath. I felt grateful for her focused sense of what needed to be done. I prayed a brief request for safety and that violence would not be necessary, and then we slunk into the cavern by way of the shadows on its far side. I nearly gasped to see the sheer number and beauty of the horses. I had expected to see perhaps two dozen, but the cavern arched majestically overhead and outward, providing ample space for securing over forty mounts. Many of them stood as tall as Windstar, and I struggled to locate him in the semi-darkness. Anna, on the other hand, sought out the guards. She grabbed my arm and pointed across the cave. By some great blessing, they were playing a makeshift round of cards in an alcove off to the side, jeering a bit with one another in their gaming. At first I thought that we could just secure two of the nearest horses and sneak out, but Anna forestalled my shortsighted thoughts.

She whispered, "The hoofbeats of horses leaving the cavern will carry far. We would find ourselves quickly pursued by four strong men on horseback, and it would rouse those gathered above to alarm. We cannot risk it. Our best chance is to surprise them and restrain them." My eyes grew wide. How could two women restrain four men? Anna reached out then to trace the sign of the cross on my forehead and murmured, "Remember the One who goes before us."

Suddenly off to my right, I heard a familiar whinny. Windstar had picked up my scent and sought my attention. Anna accompanied me as we moved carefully among the horses and their dung. I wanted to verify that he remained unharmed. I knew that Griffin's men deeply valued horses, but I also remembered the rams and Toby's fears and wondered how Windstar had fared. Emerging around a jagged outcropping, I smiled to see him standing, head high and turned in my direction. Yet his eyes showed pain, and I knew that something must be wrong. As quietly as possible, we made our way to his far side, and I nearly gasped aloud to see the gash in his flank. The men had tried to clean it, but they were not gifted in animal husbandry, and I saw telltale signs of swelling and discoloration. As one, Anna and I reached out, laying our hands upon the troubling wound. I felt a deep shudder travel through Windstar, and he snorted loudly. Thankfully, in a cavern full of horses, a chorus of whickers, snorts, and rustlings surrounded us, so the men heard nothing amiss.

Anna lifted her hands. Her half of the gash seemed less angry, and the discoloration had subsided. I found that I did not want to lift my hands. I remembered Michael, the little boy of Lanford, and his talk of "sunshine" in my hands. I prayed once more, led by my love for Windstar, led by my hope for God's healing, and this time I felt the warmth surging through, outward and upward in a rush of surprising strength. It was Anna who lifted my hands from Windstar's side, and for a moment I could see nothing through the tears that clouded my vision. This time, Anna gasped. Where my hands had lain, we could not distinguish a scar at all. I fell to my knees in praise and astonishment. How could this be?

In hushed tones, Anna shared a new idea with me. Not having any inspiration of my own, I welcomed her plan, and we set about to carry it out.

27

I crept up to the huddled men, attentive to remain just beyond the circle of light from the single torch that burned brightly to one side of them. Anna and I had tied our sacks of bread to Windstar's back with the help of the saddles and tack that were stacked generously around the cave. Having unburdened ourselves allowed us to move more swiftly and sure-footedly in the semi-darkness that offered our protection.

Anna in her turn crept up from the opposite side. I could not see her, could only trust in her presence as she trusted in mine. As we drew closer, I saw that only two of the men carried weapons; the other two had set their swords aside against the wall of the alcove. It would be only a matter of moments for them to take them up again, however. I could hear the men's muttered comments, occasional oaths, and frustrated grunts at unwelcome cards as I drew nearer, though the pounding of my heart began to drown out all sound as we came within yards of our objective.

Suddenly it happened. The nearest horse startled and bucked. The two armed men rushed forward, hoping to restrain it. But in the cover of darkness, Anna had removed all tack and ties from this horse; there was no conventional way to calm or soothe it. One of the men swore, and the horse in its startlement and confusion kicked out. The man took a direct blow to the chest and was knocked to the ground. His partner, in a moment of unthinking compassion, rushed toward his friend and was struck a similar blow to the back. He sprawled in the straw, struggling to breathe. The two men who had lingered in the alcove stared in horror at what had taken place, distracted from all but the sight of the bucking horse. In the midst of this diversion, I ran forward and tossed a heavy horse blanket over both of them from behind.

Meanwhile, I heard Anna's murmurings in the distance. I knew that she struggled to soothe the agitated horse, but I could not help her. As quickly as I could, I grabbed the length of rope that I had carried over my shoulder and bound it around the two men as they sought to throw off the blanket. One of them struck out and punched me severely in the side. The other managed to throw a wild punch that struck his compatriot instead, which won me enough time to bind the knot tight. I took hold of a second rope and wrapped it around their legs, pulling them off their feet. They were very angry now, launching epithets, but they were physically helpless and prone on the ground.

And then I heard it: a muffled scream. I looked up just in time to see that one of the fallen guardsmen had regained enough breath to raise his sword arm toward Anna. I did not think, but only acted. I pulled the sword from its scabbard and lifted the dagger in my other hand. Once again the arcing blue light appeared, but this time, it shot forward and struck the menacing man in his side. He screamed and fell unconscious. To my dismay, this only upset the horse more, and nearby animals were stamping and whinnying in discomfort as well. He reared once more, and I saw with horror that Anna stood directly in his path. I had no time.

Not understanding why I did what I did, I raised both weapons directly overhead, in a gesture that mirrored raising my hands in a prayer of beseeching appeal. Terrified, I sank to my knees, hands still upraised. And then I heard it: a singing tone rang from the sword and dagger, a soothing music of steel and gilt. The horse heard it too, and it shifted its head toward the sound, shying away just enough to miss Anna by the wingspan of a lark. To this day, I don't know how she did it, weak as she was from malnourishment and little sleep. But in that moment of sheer grace, as the weapons sang and the guardsmen moaned, she put her arms around the horse's neck, found purchase on an overturned bucket, and swung herself up. The stallion calmed, and I whispered a broken, "Thank you, Jesus."

I hurried forward to the two men who had been struck by the horse's hooves. The first still lay unconscious. I bound his hands and feet, even as I muttered prayers for his healing. And then I turned to the man who had threatened Anna. I feared that he would be dead, for the blue arcing light had sent Griffin to his grave. But he moaned loudly, an evident sign of life. His clothing had been seared clear away where the blue light had struck, and the flesh showed evidence of a terrible burn. After securing him as I had done the others, I placed my hands on his side.

"What are you doing?" he screamed. "It burns, it burns!" I sought to focus all my strength upon compassion, upon forgiveness. After all, he had not succeeded in harming my friend. His voice changed, grew softer. "Do you have some salve on your hands? Are you a doctor?" I lifted my hands. The wound remained as ugly to view as ever, but I looked to his face. He had lain back and closed his eyes, and the tightness of pain no longer hovered about his brow.

Anna called to me, "We must hurry!" I ran to Windstar across the caverns, using the stool that we had placed there in order to mount to his saddle.

"Are you sure you want to keep that horse?" I asked in amazement, realizing that Anna did not move to transfer herself to the other horse that we had saddled and readied near Windstar. "He saved our lives, didn't he?" she called, and we rode together toward the mouth of the cave and our destiny.

28

ick had drawn a rough map for us the night before, on the off chance that we would need to come out by way of the horse caverns. I blessed him silently, remembering how I had assured him that we would not need that information. He had explained how the cave opened onto a fairly narrow pathway along the cliffs, which then wound back to join up with the field of Praying Oaks to the southwest. Anna rode ahead of me, far more confident on horseback than I. I had never ridden Windstar alone without someone else to guide his head. However, I could feel his joy in being outside again, of being freed of the pain that had bedeviled his body. He stepped with confidence along the narrow path, following Anna and the stallion.

We had to slow our pace at several points, for overhanging rocks on one side and steep cliffs on the other invited careful negotiation. The wind was picking up, and I sensed a storm brewing as I sniffed the sea air. Clearly the other horse had traveled this stretch before and anticipated some of the challenges. Windstar held back at times, needing to be urged ahead. At one particularly perilous spot, I recalled the horrific image of a cliff-side fall that had come to me at Georgina's many long days ago, and I shook my head to clear it away. I did not believe that we would be waylaid by misfortune or accident so close to our goal.

After nearly a quarter-hour on the narrow pathway, Anna stopped the stallion. She turned toward me and held a hand to her ear. I strained to hear and distinguished in the distance the same clash of weapons that we had heard from the tunnels. Did they never tire of their swordplay? And then I smiled: perhaps Nick had chosen to run them in drills for the express purpose of tiring them. They would be worn out and hungry when we arrived with the bread. Yes.

Anna gestured for me to come forward and speak with her. Thankfully, Windstar had stopped alongside a rocky outcropping that allowed me to dismount without much fuss. I hurried forward, puzzled. The heightened wind whipped at my concealing cloak.

"We need to pray," she told me then. "I trust that the Lord is with us, but we need to pray. I know we are late, and yet we cannot fail to ask his aid." She took the hands that I raised to her own and led us in a brief prayer of thanksgiving and trust, as well as an earnest request for protection and success. As we prayed, I saw as on a canvas an image of Anna riding into the circle of armed men, her horse laden with the bread. I shook my head. Windstar and I had the bread. But the vision would not leave me: it was so clear that she was on the gray horse.

As the prayer ended, I told her what I had seen. "That makes sense," she agreed. "The men know me. If I tell them that Griffin has sent me, they may believe, at least for a little while. By contrast, some of them will recognize you as Griffin's target; even more will recognize Windstar. Let's transfer the tack and the bags to this horse. I'll go first into the clearing; you wait in the shadows of the pathway. See how it goes with me before you put yourself in harm's way."

We worked quickly, and thankfully the horses were compliant. I worried about riding Windstar bareback, especially with the cumbersome weight of my weapons. But Anna reassured me, "He knows you. He trusts you. The only risk is that he may be startled or surprised by something. Be mindful of that. In that case, holding him back would be difficult without reins."

Her deeply resonant calm amazed me. My stomach ached with anxiety and the anticipation of trouble. Yet she gave one last tug to fasten the load securely and then remounted her horse as though out for a Sunday ride. We continued carefully forward for another three hundred yards or so, and then she motioned for me to stop. Up ahead, I could see a brighter patch of light, denoting that the clearing was not far off. I saw Anna take a deep breath and raise one hand in the air as though in a final beseeching of God's guidance. Then she rode at a gallop out from the cover of the rocks and scraggly pines and into the very center of danger.

I could not see her, but I heard her voice as she called out in carrying, ringing tones, "Men of Nybron! I come from Griffin with bread to strengthen you for your journey! He knows that many of you have been on watch for long days, and so he conscripted a baker in town for this purpose. He released those of us in prison in order to help with the baking and the transport." At that moment I heard hoofbeats from across the clearing: Toby and Sarah were riding out as well, released finally from their anxious, desperate waiting.

And then I heard Nick's voice, with an angry growl in it that frightened me. "You expect us to believe this? Griffin is missing, but he sends us bread? That makes no sense, woman. Why should I believe you?"

A short pause ensued, during which I heard the questioning mutterings of the men in the crowd, mixed in with the angry rustling of wind through the oak trees on the far side. I did notice that the clashing of weaponry had subsided, which provided some comfort. Then Anna's voice rang out louder still. "He sent his armband as proof of this errand." I imagined her holding it up high, praying that she would not be questioned.

"And where is he now?" a different voice snarled. "Why should we believe this escaped prisoner? This could just as easily be a trap!"

Then Nick's voice came again, "Rory, only you would doubt the goodness of fresh-baked bread. Give me some of that, woman!" As per our plan, I knew that he took the small loaf held out to him (one made from a different recipe), broke it, and handed pieces also to Rory and to Anna. I imagined him smiling broadly as he tasted Betsy's best-baked bread. I knew that Toby and Sarah would see that as their cue to begin handing out loaves to the hungry men around them. All eyes would be on Nick and Anna, as stomachs grumbled and longed for the goodness of the loaves. We knew that getting the bread into the men's hands would make it harder for them to resist. The silence in the clearing stretched eerily. Once more I heard Nick's shout, "This is the finest bread that I've tasted in many a year!"

From my sheltered spot, I heard the hubbub of men clamoring for victuals, hungry men, tired men, men who rarely received anything good and who lived life ever on the alert. I wondered about Rory, though. Clearly he had been Griffin's second-in-command, sent to capture Toby and me. I pictured the gash on Windstar's flank and suspected that he had caused it. We had not considered his doubt—and his influence.

"I will not partake of this supposed gift. Who is to say but that this loaf just shared is free of poison, while the others now in all of your hands are rife with it? I say that you tear off bits of each loaf and stuff the prisoners and their horses full of it, and then wait to see what befalls them!"

I shuddered. Rory was clever, and he had the men's attention. What is more, I could tell that his voice was moving steadily toward my hiding place. Did he suspect that Anna had not come alone? What should I do? I felt paralyzed with uncertainty and longing for direction.

However, decision was wrenched from me in that moment. The newly wild wind grew in intensity, causing the pine branches above and around us to shake and flail. Unexpectedly, a gnarled, dead bough broke free, crashing down just behind us. Windstar, who had held himself as attuned and tense as I, lost his head and bolted. Only because of my hands clenched tight in his mane did I not fly off as he rushed ahead, oblivious of everything but his fear. I ducked my head, just missing being thrown to the ground by an overhanging branch. And then I heard a sickening sound: the gruesome thud and groaning cry of a man being run over by a horse at full speed. I could not see ahead and dared not look back for fear of losing my precarious balance. Windstar galloped onward, slowing his pace only as the wild wind quieted around us.

Once more Nick stepped into the breach. "Who are you, woman? How dare you lead your horse in running down one of our leaders?! Will you run me down too? If you try, I will run your horse clean through!" He held high his sword, and I shuddered to think of it slashing its way through horseflesh. What was I to say? What was I to do?

Anna shouted into the tension, "Like me, she was a prisoner set free to prepare and bring bread. Clearly she has no reins, no way of guiding her horse. The stallion startled from the commotion and storm, and Rory's demise is his own doing. Let's eat this good food that Griffin sends with his compliments!"

Though I kept my head down to hide my face, I could see from the corner of my eye that Toby and Sarah were distributing the last of the loaves. Nick had judged well, and we had made enough. And then he startled me by speaking again, "I trust this bread, but not these prisoners. Dismount, all of you, and bring your horses to me!" Surprised but choosing to trust, the four of us slid off our mounts. Toby had drawn close, and Windstar snuffled Toby's hair. I saw a deeply relieved smile trace my friend's face as he ran his hand over Windstar's healed side. Toby must have known about the injury done to Windstar when they had been set upon in the Valley of Crags and feared that his horse would die of the wound. Nick took the reins of the three bridled horses and reached up with his arm around Windstar's neck.

"You there, tie them up!" he called, and I recognized Rufus as the one summoned to bind our hands. We did not resist, and I thought back to Lily Mae's last admonishments—"Only in surrender could there be life." Is this what had been meant?

"Now eat hearty all! This is fine bread indeed!" He broke off a large piece of a new loaf and chewed noisily. The men followed suit, and I relaxed a bit. Perhaps Nick had only embellished a bit for effect and to gain the men's trust. Would all be well?

Out of the murmur of satisfied eating, almost muffled by the storm winds, another voice arose. I recognized it as the edgy tenor of one of the road guards, Jer. "We still have no proof! Anna could have stolen Griffin's armband. This prisoner is likely a gifted bareback rider who ran down Rory on purpose. Where is Griffin after all? His guards were set upon last evening, and we find no sign of him. In their pain and confusion, they re-member little, but keep speaking of a strange blue light that brought death. I don't trust you, Nick. Perhaps you are a traitor, allied with these prisoners. What say you to that?!"

"Griffin yet lives! I spoke with him just hours ago." I felt impressed by the confidence in Nick's voice. Had I not seen Griffin's corpse myself, I would have believed him also.

"Then where is he, Nick? Why is he not here to partake of this feast?"

"He is on a secret errand. You know of his strange dreams and visions. He told me of a vision of an albatross that came to him just two nights past. He has gone in search of this bird." I gasped. I had said nothing of the albatross to Nick.

Jer laughed aloud. "No albatross has been seen in Nybron for forty years. You lie poorly, my man."

"But it's true!" This time it was Rufus who spoke. I gazed on his pale, rat-like face and wondered that help would come to us from such a quarter. "I overheard him in the corridors the other night. He just kept muttering, 'An albatross, an albatross. Why an albatross in Nybron?'" Jer and Nick both stared at him in open surprise.

"I know it sounds crazy, Jer. But I know what I heard. Griffin gets these odd notions and goes off on them now and then. We all know that. Many a time, it has led to great treasure. Who are we to question?"

The skepticism in Jer's eyes receded. He recognized that there could be no reason for Rufus to lie. He gestured to the gathered company. "Fine. Eat at your own risk. For my part, I will not!"

Betsy's baking worked a holy magic of its own. Who could resist the flaky crust, the soft interior, the redolent accents of her own secret recipe? I watched the men eat and thanked the Lord for her gift of crafting art in bread. Only Jer and a few other men who looked to him as leader avoided the bread. Meanwhile, the storm continued to build around us: gathering clouds overhead, heavy winds, and a dense humidity in the air that promised rain before too long.

I looked toward Anna, and she smiled reassuringly. Jer had begun to pace back and forth, not far from a pile of boulders. Unexpectedly I recognized the distinctive eye shape that Vance had described many days ago, very faint in outline, as storm clouds masked the sun. It occurred to me that Jer and his minions might rush to seek shelter in the tunnels when the rains came in earnest. I did not care about the treasure, but I thought of all the horses, still trapped underground. And thinking of the horses made me mindful of the guards whom we had tied up in the horse cavern; if Jer came upon them, he would spread the alarm all too quickly. What should be done?

One by one, I saw men's lids growing heavy, saw heads nodding a bit, and smiled to myself. So the heavy doses of sleeping medicine that had been baked into the bread were working after all! But Jer, eagle-eyed as he was, noticed as well, and he began barking orders, "Vance, get up! Rufus, what right have you to think of napping when there is work to be done? Cal, open your eyes!" The men, so addressed, struggled to their feet, swaying a bit. I saw a dawning awareness in Jer's eyes, and he strode toward Nick, unsheathing his sword as he went.

"These men look drugged, Nick! And I'll bet it's due to this bread you so generously offered all of us!"

"Nonsense!" Nick replied. "Everyone worked very hard these last hours, practicing their swordsmanship and self-defense. They haven't had good food in months. Between their morning efforts, the satisfaction of full stomachs, and the storm's heaviness in the air, they're just a little sleepy."

"You lie! I kept a particular eye on Brendan; he's a glutton, as we all know, and he took two loaves when you weren't paying attention. And look! He's out cold over there, as though dead to the world. Amos, has he got a pulse at all?"

Amos leaned over Brendan and sleepily searched for a pulse. "Righty-ho, Jer, slow and sure, sleeping like a baby; soon he'll be snoring away, I'll wager."

"Griffin would never have sent drug-filled bread to his men. Not with that motto of his—'Stay alert, stay alive.' You're a traitor!" With those words, Jer swung his blade violently in Nick's direction. Thankfully, Nick was quick, and his blade met Jer's in a resounding crash just as the first raindrops began to fall and thunder rumbled menacingly nearby. Those men not yet asleep looked on with dazed gazes, too tired to brush the rain from upturned faces.

During all of this, I had not been paying any attention to Toby, tied up on the far side of Anna and Sarah. Now I realized to my astonishment that he had freed his hands. Had Rufus tied a faulty knot, or had Nick brought him into his confidence? Either way, I wondered about my own bindings: could I loosen them as Toby had done?

The clash of swords continued as Nick and Jer fought on. The few other men who had not partaken of the bread had gathered round to cheer Jer on, which drew their attention away from us. With my teeth I pulled at the ropes, discovering a loose end not tied off. Anna looked wonderingly at me, and then she began to do the same. Sarah seemed to gaze off into some middle distance; her exertions on horseback clearly had drawn all the strength she had left from her long days underground.

Then a lightning bolt split the sky, striking one of the oaks to my right. Under the ensuing distraction of fire and crackling and the threat of a falling tree, I heard a high-pitched whistle that might have been a birdcall but was not. From their long-held places of secrecy, the townspeople of Nybron rushed into the clearing. The women carried ropes and twine, with which to secure the drowsy men. The men held swords and knives of their own, and they ran toward any of Griffin's band still standing. For just a split second, Jer turned his head in astonished horror, and Nick's blade found its way home.

Toby rushed to Windstar, wanting to calm his horse amid the chaos. The other three horses stamped and tossed their heads, unsettled by the storm and by the many shouts and violent movements encircling them. I saw Anna break free of her bindings and turn to aid the horses. And then a flash of silver flew past my head, straight toward Anna. I turned in the direction from which it had come, and discovered to my horror that Rory had not been killed outright, as we had thought. All this time, he had been out cold or playing dead. Either way, he had risen up on his left elbow—for clearly his legs had been terribly damaged—and heaved his dagger with all his might toward my unsuspecting friend.

A rush of energy filled my body, and I wrenched my hands free of the ropes. Standing up, I pulled the sword and dagger of prophecy from beneath the obscuring folds of my cloak and raised them to the heavens, rain drenching me, the wind sending leaves and small branches in gusts past my face. As I rose, I heard a terrible cry, the cry of a man in tremendous pain, but knew I could not pause. I prayed to the Lord for strength, for wisdom, for freedom for the people of Nybron, and the blue light crackled with heightened intensity, as though it drew greater strength from the electricity in the air all around. Townspeople standing near me fell back, in surprise and awe. Individuals closest to me gasped in surprise, perhaps recognizing the shape and size of the weapons I held as embodiments of old legends they had long stopped believing.

"Pray, how may this strength come to me!" This time, the blue light surged in multiple directions, the brightest arc headed straight for Rory's chest, while others, less distinct but still shockingly intense, arced outward toward other men who threatened the people of Nybron. I heard groans and screams all around me, some dull, others edged with deep fear and pain. I turned my head, scanning left to right, finding only villagers standing, their mouths agape. Finally I turned to behold what I most feared. Had Toby rushed in to save Anna from Rory's blade? Would I be too late to save my beloved friend?

It was indeed a man who lay on the ground at Anna's feet, a knife protruding from his back. But as I rushed forward, my hands outstretched, I recognized Nick's face. His eyes were cloudy and seemed to focus on something far distant from the clearing in which we were gathered. Anna's hands were on him, but as I drew near, she shook her head at me as tears streamed down her cheeks. Nick struggled to speak, and I bent down to make out the fading words.

"So there is . . . an albatross, after all . . . I made that up, you know . . ."

Nick coughed up blood and sputtered painfully. "Don't know why Rufus . . . agreed like that . . . Thought he was half-witted . . . Ask him later . . . when he wakes up . . ." Another heavy fit of coughing shook his whole body as Anna stroked his back helplessly. "Didn't know . . . I'd die so young . . . At least I die free . . . So glad you came . . . Now I go to Jesus without fear . . ." I made the sign of the cross on his forehead, and a half-smile played on his face as the last light went out of Nick's eyes.

Toby came forward then, stammering, "Brie, look!" I turned in the direction of his shaking finger. Atop the boulder, just above the sign of the eye, stood my albatross, wings outstretched. In the half-darkness of storm, I could not see the shell pattern on his head, but I knew it was he. How did I know him? How do we know things like that in any case? We look with our hearts and the truth is made known; in the deepest places of seeing, we find recognition, we find homecoming. In his mysterious ways, the Lord had sent this bird, as messenger, as guide, and now as herald. At last the people of Nybron could claim their freedom and find a new way forward.

Sheathing my weapons, I walked forward carefully across the clearing. The villagers parted to let me pass as I stepped over the snoring forms of Griffin's men. I held up my hands, in praise, in prayer, in welcome, and the albatross swooped down and landed beside me on the ground. I had forgotten how large it was, with a wingspan of nearly twelve feet. I could not have held it on my outstretched arm, much as I longed for that contact. I knelt down beside it and very tentatively, very gently, reached out a hand to stroke the cream-colored feathers.

In that moment, the world receded, and I was back once more on the cliff near Susannah's home. Without thinking, I took a deep breath and began once more to sing that sweet old hymn of the sea. The bird gazed upon me, attentive, proud, at peace. As I gained courage, I sang louder, and soon I realized to my surprise that voices had begun to join with me. This song of longing, of journeying, and of faith had been written on the hearts of the people of Nybron, just as it had been written on my own. And so we joined our voices as one, serenading this strange and beautiful bird, yet more truly praising and glorifying the Lord of all, who had come to set us free.